Scott Hunter was born in Romford, Essex in 1956. He was educated at Douai School in Woolhampton, Berkshire. His writing career began after he won first prize in the Sunday Express short story competition in 1996. He currently combines writing with a parallel career as a semi-professional drummer. He lives in Berkshire with his wife and two youngest children.

2022

CLOSER TO THE DEAD

Scott Hunter

A Myrtle Villa Book

Originally published in Great Britain by Myrtle Villa
Publishing

All rights reserved
Copyright © Scott Hunter, Anno Domini 2022

Acknowledgements

Thanks to Stuart Bache (Books Covered) for the cover design, to my man on the inside (he knows who he is), and to my insightful and excellent editor, Louise Maskill

For RE. RIP.

Still a mystery after so many years…

'The Devil doesn't materialise in red cape and horns. He comes as everything you've ever wished for.' —**Anon**

Author's Note

This is the ninth book in the DCI Brendan Moran series. I try to write each book in the series so that it can be read in isolation from the other books without troubling the reader too much about past events. In the case of *Closer to the Dead*, however, I do think that it would be beneficial for readers to have read the previous two books, *When Stars Grow Dark* and *The Cold Light of Death*. If you haven't, it's not too much of a problem – *Closer to the Dead* will also work on its own – but you might be tempted to backtrack to the earlier books in the series when you've finished!

SH
December 2021

Prologue

Tracey Whittaker was beginning to feel an overwhelming sense of relief. After weeks of training she had almost completed her first international flight. Her uniform was still spotless, her blouse was crisp and clean, and a quick toilet break had reassured her that her make up was holding up well. The aeroplane was ahead of schedule – just eleven hours and eighteen minutes had elapsed since they had taken off from Beijing airport. The passengers were content. Justin, the cabin crew team lead, was happy, and Tracey was looking forward to going off shift and heading back to her apartment in Maidenhead for a well-earned weekend. Her next scheduled flight wasn't until Monday morning, to Cape Town this time, and Tracey couldn't wait to spend twenty-four hours in the sun, relaxing at the hotel with Ailsa, her new work buddy, who had managed to wangle the rota so they were together.

All in all, everything had gone brilliantly. The flight had been uneventful, except for a little turbulence over the Caspian Sea. In spite of the nervous fluttering in her tummy, which she'd been sure every passenger could hear, her pre-flight spiel had also gone smoothly – even the life-jacket demo that had caused her so many problems in training had gone without a hitch. Meals had been a walkover, duty-free the same. Tracey felt that, all in all, she was going to enjoy her career as a stewardess.

She'd made a few new friends on board, too. The nice gentleman in D27 – Chinese, or perhaps Korean, Tracey wasn't sure, had been very appreciative of her service. He'd been nervous, she could tell, and Tracey had gone out of her way to reassure him. He looked to her like a university professor or senior businessman, but even high-ranking passengers got scared, or at least unsettled, by turbulent weather – that was only natural.

The seatbelt signs came on, and the captain announced their imminent arrival at Heathrow. Tracey walked slowly down the aisle, checking that everyone had obeyed the seat belt mandate. She passed her professorial friend and smiled to herself. Her reassurances had obviously worked well. He was fast asleep, belt fastened.

Tracey moved on, nodded politely to the passenger in the row behind, a Korean lady – *Yoon-suh Mook,* Tracey mentally practised the pronunciation. She was a hard-looking character; polite though, although perhaps a little too demanding. Still, she had seemed satisfied with Tracey's service throughout the duration of the flight, and now even offered a smile as Tracey went by.

All seemed to be in order, and presently Tracey took

her seat by the exit along with her fellow cabin crew. The port wing dipped as the pilots brought the airliner around for its final descent.

Tracey braced herself just before the wheels touched the tarmac – this was the bit she didn't much care for. Take-off and landing were the two most hazardous events of the whole flight, the time when things were most likely to go wrong – but of course, they wouldn't. They never did.

The plane touched down and the brakes quickly brought the aircraft to the required taxiing speed. Within a couple of minutes they had reached their allocated arrival space and the captain shut down the engines.

As soon as they came to a halt, the passengers were on their feet, scrabbling for luggage in the overhead lockers. Justin went through the standard *Welcome to Heathrow* routine and thanked them all for flying with the company.

As the passengers filed past, Tracey felt a surge of pride. They were thanking *her* for looking after them.

'Bye,' she said to each in turn.

Her demanding lady came past, and unexpectedly stopped and held out her hand. 'Thank you for a lovely flight. You're very sweet.'

Tracey was slightly taken aback, but managed to articulate a reply. 'Pleasure,' she heard herself say, 'I'm glad you enjoyed the flight.'

'It was just *perfect*,' the woman said. 'I'm sure I'll be flying with you again – very soon.'

'You have a fan,' Justin stage-whispered in her ear.

'Well done. Good job.'

Tracey flushed with pride at the compliment. Justin gave her a nudge. 'Your mate in D27 is still out for the count. Would you mind?'

'Sure.'

Tracey sashayed down the aisle. Mr Tang was certainly relaxed; she'd done her job too well.

'Mr Tang? We've arrived. You're free to continue your journey.' She touched his shoulder gently. Mr Tang's head lolled to one side, and his jacket fell open.

Tracey screamed.

Mr Tang's shirt was soaked in blood, and the tip of some sharp implement was protruding from his breastbone like a nail hammered through a soft piece of wood.

She became aware of someone standing behind her. Her voice sounded small, faint. 'Justin,' she began, 'I think … I think he's dead.'

'Yes, I do believe you're right.'

She turned at the unfamiliar voice. A man with a prominent Adam's apple and protuberant Roman nose was standing in the aisle, two seats away, at D25.

'But I … I don't know what to do,' Tracey told him. It was the truth. The cabin was empty, there was no one else on board, just the two – *three* of them, if you counted Mr Tang – but he was … he …

'Nothing *to* do,' the man said. 'You're all done and dusted. Now, I suggest you toddle off and forget all about it – best not mention it to anyone. I've just told young

Justin the same thing. He got the message – popped off shift, lickety-split.'

Tracey swallowed hard, was about to reply, but something in the man's tone warned her that obedience might be the best option. She nodded, squeezed past him and headed for the exit on wobbly legs.

'Mind how you go,' the man called after her. 'Dangerous things, aeroplanes.'

Chapter One

'*Stay*. Go on.'

'No.'

'Please?

'No.'

'For me?'

'I can't, Charles, you know I can't. I've promised the Wing Co.'

'Oh, stuff the Wing Co. and his lah-de-dah wife. They'll find someone else to babysit. You deserve a night off.' Pilot Officer Charles Summers grinned, poked her playfully in the ribs.

'Ow, that hurt.' Laura Witney grimaced, pulled away. 'Look, I really have to go. He's picking me up in twenty minutes and I need to be ready.'

Someone clanked a coin into the juke box, and Kenny Rogers' gravel-smooth voice filled the bar.

'Oh, Laura, don't take your love to town...' Charles sang along, imploring her with hands joined in supplication.

'Idiot. I'm not going to town. I'm going to Wing Commander Akkerman's house to sit in front of the telly all evening while their little monster snores his head off in his cot. I hope.'

'I'll come with you, then. We can have a cuddle on the sofa.'

'I don't think so, Charles Summers.'

'You'd really leave me all on my own on the squadron's anniversary?'

'I don't think you'll be alone. I think you'll have women throwing themselves at your feet all evening.'

'Now you're taking the mickey.'

'It's a party. Of course you'll have fun. What about Rita?'

'Your buddy? Are you kidding me?'

'Well, why not? She likes you. I've seen the way she looks at you.'

'Ha ha.'

'Well, I have. So you'll manage perfectly well without me. Now I really am going.'

'Wait.' Charles caught her arm. 'What if this is the last squadron anniversary? Or I might get posted ... anything might happen. Why don't we just have one night that's ... special? That we can remember?'

'Charles, I hardly know you. I'm sure we'll be able to have a drink or something, later, when I'm free. But it's the *Wing Co.* I promised him.'

Charles let go. His hand dropped to his side. She looked at him, at his forlorn expression, and felt a mixture of both amusement and attraction. He was a good-looking lad, smart in his pressed uniform, a promising pilot and navigator with a solid career ahead of him. But Laura wasn't ready to think about a serious relationship. She was ambitious and had absolutely no intention of staying in the Catering Division forever. She was aiming for an Air Quartermaster's role – she wanted to fly. So, romance was off the cards, and it was obvious that Charles was a hopeless romantic. It just wouldn't do. She had to let him down, but gently.

'Go and play the field, Charles. That's my advice. We'll still be pals, and of course you can buy me a drink sometime. Now I *really* must–'

'All right, I give up. But make sure the Wing Co. leaves a bottle of wine out for you. I mean, it *is* the squadron's anniversary.'

The disco crew had arrived and were hauling loudspeakers and sundry equipment onto the small stage. Behind the bar, staff in tuxedos scurried about, preparing themselves for a long night. Charles inclined his head towards them. 'One for the road?'

'Bye, Charles. Have fun.'

'I'll walk you to the meet.'

'You don't have to, it's OK.'

'I insist.'

Laura felt a wash of exasperation. 'Come on, then. I'm

late already.'

They left the mess together, Charles wearing a broad smile. People were starting to arrive in ones and twos, even though the official start time wasn't for another forty minutes. They saluted as they walked.

It was a dull evening and the rain was falling steadily from a darkening, grey sky. RAF Brockford always felt more institutional in wet weather, the huddled groups of buildings appearing to Laura to take on the appearance of looming concrete predators, out to devour her.

Their footsteps echoed on the tarmac as she pushed the thought away; it was just her silly imagination. She liked it here. She loved the lifestyle, the friendships, the camaraderie. It suited her outgoing nature. She came from a loving home, but as an only child she had often felt lonely; she had always promised herself that when she finally struck out on her own she would make as many friends as she could.

She felt a warm glow of satisfaction at the thought that she had more than realised that ambition. She had a wonderful group of friends. Julie, Nick the chef, Lynn, Margaret. She glanced to her left; she supposed Charles fitted into the same category, although he clearly had ambitions beyond the platonic.

'Penny for 'em.'

Laura laughed. 'I was just thinking that I like it here.'

'Outside in the wet, when you could be indoors with me, having fun?'

'*Charles*. I mean the whole thing of being here. The

lifestyle.'

'You like slaving away in the kitchens?'

'For now, yes. It's important, catering. It has to be right.' She realised how defensive she sounded. 'The food has to be good, that's all.'

'An airforce flies on its stomach?'

'Yes, it does. And we're good at what we do.'

A car sloshed past, headlights dipping as they were caught in the glare.

'Of course you are. The food is fantastic. It's a million times better than the slop I was expected to eat at school.'

'You were at boarding school, weren't you?' Laura turned her head, intrigued.

'Yep. Eight long years.'

'Poor boy.' She grinned. 'Was it awful?'

'For the first couple of years, yes. But once I'd got used to it, not too bad. Sixth Form was a good time.'

'OK, here were are. Thanks for escorting me.'

They were just outside the WRAF barracks; a tall streetlamp caught them in an orange funnel of rain.

'You'll be soaked.' She reached out and straightened his lapel. 'Go back.'

'So will you if the Wing Co's late.'

'He won't be.'

'We could wait in the porch.'

'Not allowed. You're a bloke.'

'Oh, come on. That wouldn't technically be inside the building.'

'You know what the Dragon's like.'

The Dragon was a familiar nickname for Wing Officer Philippa Franks, overseer of the air base's WRAF accommodation. No man dared set foot inside, for fear of incurring Franks' formidable wrath.

'All right, then. If you're sure.' Charles finally accepted defeat.

'See you tomorrow. Have a good evening.'

'You too.' Charles gave a mock salute, turned on his heels, and trotted off towards the mess.

Laura's raincoat was struggling to resist the downpour and she was already feeling water seeping through the material to the wool of her uniform. She looked at her watch. Eight-thirty. Akkerman would be here shortly.

She stamped her feet and wished she'd worn her winter shoes. A second set of headlights picked out the furrows and imperfections of the service road as a car rounded the corner of the women's barracks and cruised gently towards her.

Laura ransacked her brain for the name of the Wing Co's baby. It was a boy, she remembered, but was it George or John? She couldn't recall. *Damn*. That wasn't good. She wanted to make an impression.

The car slowed, came to a halt. Laura squinted through the glass but the water droplets made it hard to see. She opened the passenger door and in the sudden dim illumination of the car's interior light she recognised the driver.

'Oh! Hello.'

'The Wing Co.'s running late. You've got me instead.

Said I'd do him a favour and collect you.'

Laura hesitated, but only for a moment. She was grateful to get out of the rain.

She got in, shut the door. Darkness enveloped the interior, and the car moved off.

The radio was playing quietly as they drove, The Human League's pleading chorus cutting through the speakers even at low volume... *Don't you want me, baby?* ...

Laura hummed to herself as the driver made a left turn. *Wait...*

The Wing Co.'s accommodation was in Copley, the village on the other side of the air base.

The *other* side.

She moistened her lips. Better not say anything. For all she knew, there was a quicker route. She didn't drive, so she rarely paid much attention to where any provided transport was taking her. But Copley *was* the other way, surely...

The road narrowed. Now they were surrounded by trees, dark shapes flitting past the window. Laura felt the first pang of disquiet. She wanted to speak, but her throat felt constricted. She heard herself ask the question, 'Where are we going?' Her voice sounded strangely distant, as though it belonged to someone else.

The car turned onto a slim lane between sentinel-like trees and rolled to a halt. The engine died. The driver turned and looked at her. She felt a hand rest gently on her knee.

'What are you doing?'

In the faint light emitted from the dashboard she saw the glint of a blade. The hand on her knee made a sudden lunge, caught her arm and held it tight.

Panic rose in Laura's chest. She pulled away. 'Get *off*. What do you think you're–?'

The knife moved in a swift, jabbing motion and a sharp pain in her bicep made her gasp in shock. Her free hand felt for the door handle, but it clicked uselessly back and forth despite her frantic tugging.

Locked.

She had to defend herself, but the attack was so unexpected, so shocking...

Scissors...

She always kept a pair in her tunic pocket in case she needed to trim a nail, or tidy a thread. Her hand went to the pocket, fumbled for and hooked the finger ring. She withdrew it in one motion, struck out, and felt the blades sink into flesh.

Her assailant made no sound. The knife darted again, this time piercing her thigh. Laura screamed, dropped the scissors. The blade made a third cobra-like strike. Laura lifted her arm but the limb felt heavy, sluggish. She whimpered. Surely this was just a nightmare? It couldn't be happening...

The knife made another swift motion and she felt a thump in her lower abdomen, as though she'd been punched. Something warm trickled down her leg. Her vision fogged. Her legs kicked ineffectually.

It's my birthday tomorrow. The thought tumbled in her brain, a final flash of recollection, a last despairing kick.

I can't die. I can't...

The darkness reached a new shade of opaque.

Her life flickered – once, twice...

Then went out.

Chapter Two

Thames Valley. June 2021

DCI Brendan Moran turned on his recently installed – and somewhat functional-looking – office TV. He glanced at his watch. The first of a series of television appeals concerning the brutal murder of an RAF aircraftswoman was about to begin.

Moran settled in his chair as the announcer introduced the bulletin. The newly appointed Major Crime Investigations Manager, John Herbinson, and Thames Valley's media officer, Tim Kennet, appeared onscreen. Kennet began by outlining the events, so far as they were known, of the crime that had taken place on a wet February evening forty years previously.

Having recently met up with Herbinson, Moran already knew the facts. A young woman due to babysit for a senior RAF officer had disappeared on the night in question, having accepted a lift in an unidentified car. She had been discovered the next morning by a local dog walker; her bag, scattered overnight belongings and body were found in a rural location a mile or so from the now defunct air base, RAF Brockford.

Herbinson was explaining that a lack of DNA meant that the perpetrator, even if they were still alive, could not be identified unless close friends or family were prepared to come forward with information that might lead to an arrest.

'Forty years is a long time to keep something like this to yourself,' Herbinson was saying in his still discernible Canadian accent. 'Someone's conscience is bearing a heavy load. Perhaps someone confided in *you*. Perhaps, even now, what you learned is playing on your conscience. I would urge you to come forward, anonymously if you like, and provide such information as will assist us in making an arrest.' He paused. 'Laura Witney's mother and father suffered a tragic loss, and although they are no longer with us, we have an obligation to do all we can to bring the perpetrator to justice. And to achieve that, we need *your* help.'

Moran nodded approvingly. Herbinson had struck just the right tone – simultaneously serious and persuasive. Tim Kennet moved onto another cold case, a series of burglaries in which a pensioner had been viciously assaulted.

Moran turned off the TV, went back to his desk. The buff folder resting there was dog-eared, fat, its contents inconclusive. The cover was annotated with a list of names to whom the files had been referred over a long period of time. Moran's name was the last, scrawled in biro by some hard-pressed admin assistant. The only other name on the folder was written in bold felt tip.

Laura Witney. '81.

Forty years, Moran reflected, was indeed a very long time. The RAF base no longer existed, its personnel redeployed and most, by now, probably retired or deceased. The original investigation had foundered after numerous interviews, a good number of red herrings, and a general dearth of suspects. Blanks had been drawn with potential boyfriends (Laura had no official escorts of the opposite sex, despite having had several male admirers), fellow aircraftswomen, camp visitors, senior officers, and a clutch of local ne'er-do-wells.

Whoever had stabbed Laura Witney to death that wet and dismal evening had no apparent motives relating to sex or thievery. To all intents and purposes, Laura's murder seemed to be an example of the classic worst-case-scenario type of police investigation: a motiveless act of senseless violence.

Moran rested his hand on the folder. A Pandora's box, if ever there was one, and now the finger was pointing in his direction. It was his turn to sift the clues, check the suspects, go over the notes one more time.

Forty years.

He was glad that Herbinson was fronting the appeal, heading up the cold case. It meant that he could get on with the job instead of fretting about PR, being chased by the powers-that-be, or worried at by the press, as was their wont; they tended to harass him like a dog with a penchant for Irish trouser cuffs.

As for Herbinson, he was a straight talker. Canadian by birth, he'd moved to the UK following the early and unexpected death of his wife. His experience in the Canadian police was extensive, and he didn't suffer fools gladly. People fell into one of two categories as far as Herbinson was concerned: clowns and good guys. Moran believed – and hoped – that he fell into the latter category. Herbinson allowed the good guys to get on with the job in hand, and the clowns were unceremoniously cast aside, usually with some observational and less than complimentary Canadian epithet to accompany their departure.

Moran's fingers drummed a slow rhythm on the folder. He was still short-staffed, but those he had available were hard-working, mostly experienced and reliable. Chris Collingworth seemed to have knuckled down after his unfortunate encounter with MI5. Bernice Swinhoe was both thorough and highly motivated, and DC Bola Odunsi was … well, experienced, yes, but tended to go off on tangents, given the opportunity, sometimes with questionable results. The detective constable was personable, but over time this had proved to be both an asset and a liability. Moran had had words, and he hoped that, going forward, Bola would exercise due caution in his dealings with both persons of interest and colleagues alike. Moran was optimistic, but the jury was still out. Bola would have to prove himself.

Moran's one concern was the absence of both Charlie Pepper and George McConnell. Charlie was seconded to a special MIT, assembled specifically to bring Connie – *Zubaida* – Chan to justice, and George was on an extended week's leave with DC Tess Martin, currently convalescing with her parents. Moran was sure there'd still be plenty for George to do on his return; a forty-year-old case wasn't going to be solved overnight.

Neither is it going to be solved by daydreaming, Brendan...

He opened the folder and began to read.

Chapter Three

George was content, more so than he'd felt for a long time. And yet, at the back of his mind, the place where he kept all his little, niggly problems, something was amiss. Tess was quick to pick up on his mood. She gave him a mild dig in the ribs as they walked.

'So, how about you, George McConnell? How've *you* been?'

Her voice was still a little hoarse, hesitant from lack of use, but her strength was improving every day. He'd intended to just spend the weekend with Tess and her parents, but she'd persuaded him to extend his stay for a week. The previous morning she'd brought him a cup of tea in bed, and before he was fully awake had slipped her hand into his. Nothing could have been more natural, more perfect, and yet, more than twenty-four hours later, he still had difficulty believing that his feelings for Tess had finally been reciprocated.

Now, as they walked hand-in-hand along a tree-lined footpath, watery sunshine dappling the contours of the footpath ahead, he wondered why the elation he should be feeling was proving so elusive. What was nagging at his subconscious?

He gave a noncommittal grunt. 'Me? I've been fine. Busy, as always, but all right, in the main.'

'In the main?'

'Yes.'

Tess laughed. 'You're such a *man*, George.'

'Where have I heard that before?'

She nudged him again. 'Probably from your other girlfriend.'

'Ha ha. Like I have time for more than one.'

'You have a point, there.' Tess grinned. 'What with working for the guv, and all.'

'The last one,' George shook his head, 'the Emma Hardy case, wow, it was an emotional ride for sure. It got to all of us.'

'I know. I get that. I'd have been the same. That poor girl, all those years, she never knew about her past?'

George opened the stile gate to allow Tess to go through. They were on the edge of Roegreen Woods, a popular dog-walking spot. The footpath stretched ahead of them between two fields, one freshly ploughed, the other showing signs of new growth – corn or wheat, George wasn't sure. A line of trees directly ahead, punctuated by gaps in the foliage, invited the walker to choose an entry point, any one of which might lead in different directions through the woodland.

'Aye, it was a shock, right enough. But she's a toughie,

Emma Hardy. She'll cope.'

They walked in silence for a bit. Above the treetops, two red kites circled in the up-current.

'You still haven't answered my question.' Tess tilted her head playfully.

'Truthfully? I'm glad on two counts: one, that you're on the mend, and two, this peace and quiet is something I could get used to. I like it here. I can feel myself starting to unwind a little.'

'Good.'

Should he mention his disquiet? No, best not. *Don't spoil the moment, George...*

Besides, there was truth in what he said. He *did* like it here, and he *was* beginning to unwind ... except...

'Ah, we're not alone.' A figure had appeared in one of the gaps. They were still too far away to make out any detail, but George caught a glimpse of black hair, a red top, a flash of denim. Then the figure was gone, swallowed by the woods.

'Oh.' Tess laughed. 'You scared them off, George.'

George responded with a laugh, but it sounded hollow. For a moment his heart had stopped. Up until now he had dismissed his concerns as paranoia, tiredness. Now, he was on full alert, but he daren't share his thoughts with Tess, not now.

'Probably lost their dog. It's a warren in there.' Tess kicked a stone. It went spinning off into the ploughman's furrows.

'Yep, expect so.' George was thinking furiously. Should

they turn back? Take another route? He didn't want to freak Tess out. Or maybe … maybe he *was* just being paranoid. The distant figure could have been anyone, in truth. But there was something about the posture, the attitude.

Since Tess had mentioned Connie Chan during a recent phone conversation, George had begun to wonder. Chan was still at large. Tess had worked on a case involving the Malaysian murderess before, while she was at Southampton. She'd learned enough about Chan to be scared at the prospect of an in-the-flesh encounter.

He'd thought better of calling DI Charlie Pepper before he'd set out from Reading, but now perhaps it might be advisable. Charlie would have the latest, whatever that might involve. Recent sightings, fresh leads … just a quick phone call, to set their – *his* – mind at rest…

'George. Come back.'

'Mm? Sorry. Daydreaming.'

Tess caught him by the shoulder and he stopped, surprised. She took his chin, held it, looked him right in the eye. 'George. One thing I ask, just one thing.'

'What?'

'Don't hold anything back from me. Tell me the truth. Always. Can you promise me that?'

'Yes, of course.'

She held his gaze for a moment, then let him go.

They walked on. George wrestled with himself for a bit, then said. 'My previous … problem. It's all good, these days. I'm doing well.'

'Say the word, George. It helps. Let's address the elephant in the room.'

'In the field, anyway.' He laughed. 'OK, the drinking. I haven't had a drink for over twelve months. I still go to the odd meeting, but I'm OK.'

'I can tell the difference. I'd know if you relapsed.'

'Well, I'm not planning to.'

'Good to hear.' She squeezed his hand. 'OK, so woods or stay in the field?'

They were on the threshold, by the first gap. The trees were packed densely together – it was an old forest, planted way back, probably sometime after the Norman invasion. Tolkien's *Fangorn* came to his mind, and George felt a shiver run down his spine.

'You know what? I feel like staying out in the open today. The air is so clear.'

'Fields it is, then.' Tess grinned happily.

They followed the footpath around the wooded perimeter, and as they turned the next corner, a vista of irregular fields stretched before them like the patches on a pair of jeans George had once worn at University. The ground sloped gently downward, creating the illusion that they were floating high above the earth, a king and queen of all they surveyed.

'Pretty, isn't it?'

'Aye, it is that.'

They walked on, George resisting the urge to glance behind him as the woods receded into the distance.

Just paranoia, George, that's all…

Closer to the Dead

Chapter Four

'OK, so let's look at the facts.' Moran addressed the upturned, attentive faces. The team was small, five in total this week until George's return. Resources were thin on the ground and getting thinner every month, so John Herbinson had done well even to get authorisation for this meagre number of experienced officers. The Crime Investigations Manager was loitering next to the exit, as if expecting a more urgent appointment to whisk him away at any moment. His body language telegraphed his personality; impatient, determined, thorough. Moran approved of all three attributes, and so far their relationship had progressed smoothly, but it was early days and he wondered how things would go if any disagreement reared its head along the line.

He'd had the measure of his ex-boss, DCS Higginson – they went back a long way and had developed an understanding over the years. But the reporting hierarchy had been reshuffled and the winds of change had blown Herbinson his way, so it was a case of back to square one.

It took time to build trust, to get the measure of a man, to understand what made him tick. But then Herbinson probably felt the same; this was new territory for both of them.

Nevertheless, however things panned out, Moran was ready to fight his corner – even though the experience of a manager breathing down his neck was a new and not altogether comfortable prospect.

'Forty years have passed,' Moran began. 'Anyone here remember 1981, apart from myself?' He gave a wry grin. 'No? Thought not.'

Herbinson was smiling too. Moran estimated the CIM's age to be at least fifteen to twenty years younger than himself. It was a fact of life he'd long accepted that at this late stage of his career most of, if not all, of his colleagues' dates of birth fell into the category of, for him at least, recent history.

Deal with it, Brendan...

He turned to the board, where he'd pinned a black-and-white photograph of Laura Witney. She was standing outside her barracks at the defunct RAF base, smiling a little uncertainly at the photographer. Her hair was piled up and she was clutching a small handbag.

'I'll be frank, we don't have much,' he confessed. 'The original investigation fizzled out. No suspects emerged after four months hard at it.'

'The base is closed now, guv, is that right?'

Moran nodded. 'Yes, DC Swinhoe. Which means that we're left with existing evidence only, along with a number of names to reinterview, should we feel that to be necessary. There's one in particular I'd like to speak to, a close friend of Laura's, name of Charles Summers. He was keen on her, but as far as I can make out from the file, they remained friends only. And he was the last person to see her alive.'

'Apart from the killer,' DC Bola Odunsi added.

'Indeed, DC Odunsi, apart from the killer.'

Moran was glad to have Bola on board, but he was keeping a watchful eye. Bola was impulsive, prone to indiscretions, but experience was experience, and for a case as cold as this one Moran would rather have a flawed experienced officer on the team than a rookie.

'The night in question there was a party on, a function to mark a squadron anniversary. Laura was seen in the mess early that evening, around six pm. The record of the interview with Charles Summers confirms this. They had a drink together, he walked her to her barracks where a car was due to collect her and take her to Wing Commander Akkerman's house a mile or so away, to babysit for the family.'

Moran pointed to the board, at a photograph of a young, chisel-jawed man in his early forties wearing the uniform of an RAF Wing Commander. 'Wing Commander Dennis Akkerman. Married – or was at the time – to Jane Akkerman. Two kids. One, again at the time, a daughter, aged nineteen. The other, a son, Christopher. Eighteen months.

'An afterthought,' someone muttered.

'An accident, more like.' Another officer's rejoinder provoked a burst of laughter.

'All right, all right.' Moran held up his hand to quell the noise. 'Let's concentrate on the important stuff.' He turned back to the board. 'The Wing Commander is still alive. The Witney file contains a comprehensive transcription of interviews held at Castle Hill by–' Moran consulted his notes, '–one DI Purcell and DC Raymond. I'm content that at least *some* pertinent questions were asked, and that the answers to those were satisfactory, if inconclusive. I'd like to begin by having a chat with Akkerman – or Air Commodore Akkerman, as I should correctly call him, retired as he is. The officers still like to be addressed according to their rank, even in their dotage.'

He paused. 'The Air Commodore's wife is deceased, but the daughter and son are probably still alive. I'd like to speak to both.'

Bernice Swinhoe frowned. 'The son would have been too young to take much in, guv. Is it worth spending any time on him?'

'He might shed light on family interactions over the years. You never know what might turn up. Point taken, DC Swinhoe, but we'll keep him on the list for now. The other POIs, in my opinion, are Charles Summers, and the daughter – we don't have an address for her yet, but no doubt Akkerman can supply us with one. However, I'm also interested in Laura's colleagues, people who worked directly with her.'

'Laura was in Catering, guv, right?' Bola asked.

'Yes. I have a list of associates we need to work through in addition to Charles Summers. Some we may track down, others – well, let's see how it goes.'

'What about the pickup car, guv?' Bernice Swinhoe wanted to know. 'No one got a look at it?'

Moran drew a deep breath. 'Charles Summers didn't wait for Laura to be collected, so no, no one knows what car picked her up, or indeed *if* any car picked her up, although the distance of the murder site from the air base suggests that a vehicle must have been used at some stage. DC Collingworth?'

Chris Collingworth had his hand raised. 'Public transport, guv? Is it possible she hopped on a bus?'

'Unlikely,' Moran replied. He tapped the board where a rough map of the area had been pinned. 'There *is* a bus stop outside the base, but we'd have to wonder why Laura would have made the decision to use a bus when we know she was due to be collected.'

'Maybe she thought they'd forgotten her?' Bola suggested. 'Or that they'd been held up by some domestic issue? So, she took the initiative?'

'All right, well let's not discount it.' Moran turned back to the board. 'Here's a shortlist of interviewees – colleagues of Laura's: Julie Parker, Nick McBrain – the chef heading up the catering operation – Lynn Stamford, Margaret Gibson, Rita Dempster. They worked closely with Laura. I've read their statements; I suggest you all do the same. It'll help to build a mental picture of the environment she was working in.

'I'd like speak to each in turn. You may need to put in some effort to track them down; we have names and addresses of next of kin and so on if you need to refer. In the meantime, let's hope that the appeal produces some results. There's one other thing I should mention – Laura kept a diary, quite a comprehensive, day-to-day summary, personal thoughts, comments about colleagues, and so on. As reluctant as I am to invade her privacy, I do feel that it's necessary to examine it to see if it might shed any light. It's the closest we'll get to speaking to Laura personally. When I've finished with it, I'll pass it on; one of you might spot something I missed. Any further questions?' Moran surveyed the room. 'No? Off you go, then. We'll have a daily washup at say, five-thirty?'

When the team had dispersed Herbinson left his observation post by the door and came towards Moran with measured, purposeful strides.

'Don't rely on the appeal, Brendan. It's thorough, old-fashioned police graft that's needed here.' Herbinson's eyes bored into his with their usual intensity.

'And here's me thinking I was the old-fashioned one,' Moran replied.

'I'm not teaching granny, Brendan. I just want to make sure that we're all pulling in the same direction, that's all.' Herbinson examined Moran for any sign of reticence. 'The original case investigation was a sloppy affair, and Laura Witney's parents died without answers. That's unacceptable. You know enough about me by now to have figured out that I'm not a loose-ends man. I don't do sloppy. I'm a results man, always have been, and I intend to achieve results – positive results. Another thing; I don't carry people on my team. Anyone not cutting the mustard will be out, pronto. Sound reasonable?'

'I'll make sure the team are aware, John. Thanks for the heads up.'

Moran watched Herbinson walk away. They were OK at present, respectful of each other's positions. But how long would that last?

Chapter Five

Connie Chan was happy – or as close as she could get to happy. She had a clear goal, a focus. And she was working alone, which suited her. She missed Isaiah Marley's quiet presence, but not in any strong emotional sense. He'd been useful, accommodating, that was all. He was dead, but she was very much alive, and very much focused on her new mission.

The first step was an important one; to intercept the Irishman's communications. If she listened in she would learn all she needed to know. DC George McConnell's weekend visit to Chepstow was ideal for two reasons: number one, she was within striking distance of base, and two, the policeman was distracted, focusing on his recuperating girlfriend.

The house was vulnerable, with only an old couple, the woman's parents, in residence for most of the day. McConnell and his girlfriend had so far stuck to a pattern of mornings out and about and afternoons at home with the parents, which was exactly what she wanted. She needed a window of around, say, thirty to forty minutes to do what she needed to do, and this morning presented an ideal opportunity; McConnell and the woman had left the house shortly after nine.

Connie Chan felt a cold thrill of anticipation.

The road was quiet, a backwater. Everyone of working age was at work; just mothers and pensioners at home. She glanced in the mirror. A test smile. All good. She smiled again.

Show time.

'Good morning, Mr Martin. I'm from Haven Lodge – we're in Lower Church Street, near Severn Quay. I understand you're thinking about residential care? I have some *very* helpful details, and maybe you'll have a few questions too? Do you have time for a little chat?'

'Oh. I wasn't expecting–'

'That's all right, Mr Martin. We're a proactive organisation. We come to the customer, we don't wait for the customer to come to us.'

'I see, well, in that case–'

'Who is it, Jim?'

Mr Martin turned his head to answer his wife's question. 'A lady from the new care home.'

'Oh?' Patricia Martin appeared in the hallway, guiding her electric wheelchair between coat stand and hall table with the expertise of long experience. She whirred to a halt just behind her husband. Chan immediately knew that the woman was the one to win over.

'Good morning, Mrs Martin. I was just explaining to your husband–'

'Yes, I heard you. How did you know we were looking? I don't recall contacting you.'

'As I said, we're proactive, Mrs Martin. We have a database of over-seventies kindly supplied by the council. We make a point of personal contact, no obligation.'

Mrs Martin looked her up and down. 'You'd better come in, then.'

Mr Martin stepped aside. 'After you, Miss...?'

Chan smiled sweetly. 'Chandra. Thank you.'

She followed Mrs Martin into the lounge. She'd have to be quick with the preamble.

'Can I offer you tea? Coffee?'

Jim Martin was relaxed, amiable, his wife still suspicious. 'Oh, just water, thank you. I love your blouse, Mrs Martin. Such a pretty colour.'

'Thank you. It was a present – from my daughter.'

'How lovely.'

'She must be around your age, Miss Chandra. And how long have you been at Haven Lodge? I didn't realise it was open – they've only recently finished building it, haven't they?'

'Ah, the company work well in advance.' That sounded plausible. Chan kept the smile going. 'We're very excited about opening – we have an open day next month.'

'Perhaps we'll go,' Patricia Martin said. 'But it's such a bother getting from A to B.'

Chan sensed that the battle was half-won. 'Well, that's

why I'm here. To provide a solution for you that's comfortable, easy, enjoyable, free from all the hassle.'

'It's a big step, giving up your home, Miss Chandra,' Jim Martin said as he reappeared with a tray bearing a water jug, a glass, and two cups of tea.

'I understand.' Chan nodded. 'I really do. But we try to make the transition as smooth as possible.'

'We'll be discussing our options with our daughter, of course,' Mrs Martin said. 'But she's our priority for the moment.'

'She's been ... unwell,' Mr Martin explained. 'We're looking after her while she convalesces. But she's doing much better,' he added. 'And it's probably time we thought about our futures again.' He glanced at his wife for confirmation and Patricia Martin returned a grudging nod.

'It's never too early, in my experience. I'm sure your daughter would agree.' Chan frowned. 'But if you don't want to worry her, then no need to mention my visit. You can keep it as our little secret.' Chan affected a complicit chuckle with which Mr Martin joined in. 'One moment.' She dipped into the bag she'd prepared. It had been straightforward obtaining the promotional material – the library had received a batch of brochures to display, pending the home's opening, so Chan had simply helped herself to one and studied the details. She was confident that she would appear well versed in the layout, facilities and so on.

'Here we are.' She handed the brochure to Mrs Martin

who took it with a curt nod. Jim Martin went to his wife's side and peered over her shoulder.

'Perhaps I could use your...?' Chan gave the couple an apologetic smile. 'While you're having a browse?'

'Of course,' Mr Martin said. 'Up the stairs, first on the left. Mind the stair lift, makes it a bit awkward going up.'

'Thank you.' Chan shouldered her handbag. 'I won't be a moment.'

Now she had to move fast. She took the stairs nimbly, reached the landing. Which room? Ah, there. A door ajar, a glimpse of a male jacket, too young for Mr Martin. She pushed it open. This was it. The guest room – DC McConnell's room. Just a single bed, a bedside table with a closed laptop perched precariously by the lamp. An MS Windows laptop, not a Mac. That was good, easier.

She opened her handbag and withdrew a small device. It looked innocent enough – similar to a standard external drive – and inserted it into the laptop. She opened the lid, booted the machine. She didn't need a password; the spyware she'd purchased – at considerable expense – bypassed the usual login protocols. It was designed for optimum speed. The guy had estimated an installation time of around forty-five seconds for Windows 7, a minute for Windows 10, and ninety seconds for a Mac OS.

This was state-of-the-art spyware built, according to her technical salesman, from a bootleg piece of Russian kit. But Chan didn't care about its provenance, so long as it did the job. She'd been impressed by the demo – it was undetectable once installed, and she'd be able to monitor every activity on the target laptop – email, web searches, WhatsApp messaging, Skype calls, you name it.

She glanced into the street. No sign of McConnell or the daughter; she'd timed it perfectly, but she didn't want to push her luck.

The amber indicator turned green. All done. She withdrew the device, switched off the laptop, found the bathroom, flushed the toilet, and went downstairs where she could hear the Martins' voices raised in earnest discussion.

'Aye, we like it very much,' Mr Martin said, glancing up as she entered the room. 'I think we may well pop along to your open day.'

This was going even better than Chan had expected; they were unlikely to mention her visit to the daughter, and even if they did turn up at the open day and ask for Miss Chandra, it mattered little. Chan's eyes automatically traversed the lounge. There were few items of value on display; this was a couple of modest means. But her visit wasn't about money. Money wasn't an issue right now.

'I'm so glad you like the look of it.' Chan composed an appreciative grin. She sat down and folded her hands in her lap. 'Well then, do you have any questions for me?'

Chapter Six

Feb 2ⁿᵈ 1981

Not in a good mood today. Don't know why. Maybe the weather – so gloomy for May. Rita a pain tonight. What's wrong with her? Told her I'd do the rolls yesterday. She got all huffy ... time of month? Letter from Dad. All good at home. Nick was funny – told R to stop moaning, put her on veg prep!! – that really got to her. So tired now – can't be bothered to read. Goodnight dear diary!

Moran closed the diary, sighed. He felt irrationally uncomfortable reading the words of this long-dead young woman. Maybe it was because it brought Laura Witney back to life, her thoughts and hopes, daily trivia and emotions as fresh and vibrant as the day she wrote them. But it was a temporary resurrection; when he closed the diary, the spell was broken and her ghost withdrew back into the small, neatly inscribed pages.

He sighed. Uncomfortable or not, it had to be done. He

wanted an insight into this doomed girl's life, some clue as to her connections, work, and social life to point him in the right direction.

Moran set the diary down, went through to his kitchen and, with a small flicker of guilt, poured himself a glass of Sangiovese. He'd have to watch the vino – it was getting to be a habit, an easy reach after a hard day. It wouldn't do to get himself into a situation like George's; although he was under control at present, Moran knew it wouldn't take much to drive the Scotsman back to his old habits. Still, a half-glass to stimulate the old synapses wouldn't hurt.

Archie regarded him hopefully from his basket under the table, brown eyes appealing, enquiring. Is it time? Are we heading out? A spot of duck harassing, perhaps? A quick sprint along the water meadow?

'Not yet, boy. Later.' Moran bent and stroked the spaniel's head. 'I have some thinking to do.'

He headed for the lounge, intending to resume his perusal of Laura's diary, but the phone interrupted him on the way.

Damn.

He set his glass down on the hall table, picked up the heavy Bakelite receiver.

'Moran.'

'Brendan? Hello. It's Alice Roper.'

Moran's stomach performed a smart backflip. 'Alice! Hello! Nice to hear your voice.'

'I hope I'm not interrupting anything?'

'Not at all,' Moran lied. 'How are you? How's Peter?'

'Oh, the same as ever, you know.'

'And Emma?' As he asked the question he bit his lip, afraid to hear Alice' reply.

There was a momentary hesitation, then Alice said, 'She's all right, Brendan. Coping, I'd say. She'll need time to process everything. It's been overwhelming for her.'

'Of course.'

Alice's sister, Emma, had disappeared in 1976 while serving as a detective sergeant in Reading. Her memory loss following a head trauma had been so severe that she had forgotten her past entirely, and settled into an alternative life in Carlisle. 'And have they made their decision about relocation?'

'Yes. She and Adam felt it was the right thing to stay in Carlisle. They have a life there, friends.'

'I understand.'

'But she'll visit from time to time, of course – and we're popping up to see them next week, as it happens.'

'I'm glad it's working out.'

'Yes. Well, Peter would like her to live with us, naturally, but I think he's coming round to the idea that Emma lives in a different town these days. As long as she calls him every day, he's happy.'

Moran was aware that Peter, the autistic brother, was a full-time job for Alice, but he was good-natured enough and Moran had warmed to what Alice had called their 'strange little household.' He'd been intending to call her for weeks but had held back, not wanting to appear pushy, but now … now, here she was, taking the initiative. He felt gently encouraged.

'That's good to hear, Alice.'

There was a moment of silence, which Alice broke.

'I was wondering–'

'Yes?'

'I was wondering if you'd like to come over sometime for something to eat. If you have time, that is. I mean, I know you're busy, a policeman, and all that goes with it–'

'I'd love to. Just name the day and time.'

'Oh, good. How about tomorrow evening? – I know it's probably too short notice, but–'

'No, that's fine. I'll be there.'

'Great! Say, sevenish?'

'Seven-thirty too late?'

'No, not at all. Seven-thirty, then. Anything you don't eat?'

'I was brought up to eat what I'm given.'

She laughed. 'Well, that's settled.'

'You're very kind. I'll look forward to it.'

'Me too. Bye for now.'

Moran signed off and stood quietly in the hall, thinking. Part of him was delighted – excited, even. But there was a small issue – a link to a property scam, a money laundering operation – that was a little troubling. He doubted that Alice had anything to do with it or had any knowledge of it, even. According to George it was her stepbrother-in-law, Mark Collier, who was behind it – and

Mark Collier had vanished, quite some time ago. Moran didn't like loose ends, and this was a loose end if ever there was one, a trailing lead from the Emma Hardy case that really should be followed up.

He picked up Laura Witney's diary and continued his interrupted journey to the lounge. He sat down, placed the diary carefully on his lap, and set the glass of wine on the side table.

The truth was, he was afraid to follow any such lead, in case … *admit it, Brendan* … in case it incriminated Alice Roper.

Moran filed the thought away. He needed to concentrate on the here and now; he'd talk to George about the Collier thing on his return. He took a sip of wine, opened the diary. The sound of his neighbour's mower filtered in through the open window. Mr Ainsworth, the constant gardener. The thought amused him. At least his new neighbour was an ordinary fellow, and not a sleeper for the intelligence service, as his predecessor had turned out to be.

Concentrate, Brendan.

He turned to the next entry.

Feb 3rd 1981

Nick got me to do the lasagne today! Finally!!! And I made a damn good job of it, too. Compliments all round at lunchtime service. Guess who wasn't impressed? Got it in 1. Riiiita. Such a pain … I ignored n e way. Charles asked me out for a drink again!!!! The boy is persistent, I'll give him that. I said maybe next week. Couldn't bear to see his disappointment. I like him, but .... I dunno. We'll see. Had to borrow M's razor this morning – cut myself of course – I must have looked a sight with a huge great plaster on my shin. Oh well. Teach me to stock up next time I'm in town. Which is ... tomorrow! Yippee! Day off, at last. V tired now. So .... off to bye byes. Yaaaawn. Goodnight dear d! X

Rita again.

Rita Dempster clearly didn't see eye to eye with Laura. It was surely worth a follow-up. This was the woman who lived locally, or at least had lived locally the last time she'd been questioned.

Start with the obvious, Brendan.

Very well. Tomorrow, he'd have a little chat with Ms Dempster, and see what she had to say for herself.

Chapter Seven

Rita Dempster's last known address was a stone's throw from the old Castle Hill Police station. Moran parked in a side street and crossed the busy road towards the flats on the corner of Castle Hill and Tilehurst Road. He'd been unable to find a telephone number, so he'd decided it was just as easy to pay a personal visit.

He inspected the column of doorbells. Flat five. Beside the grimy button for flat five, a faded label read 'Dempster'. He pressed the button and waited.

Traffic roared by, heading in and out of town. Not the quietest corner to pick, but Moran supposed that you could get used to anything, given enough time. Residents living around Heathrow Airport apparently stopped hearing aircraft after a few months of acclimatisation, or so he'd been told, although this wasn't something he'd ever felt inclined to put to the test; he enjoyed the peace and quiet of Pangbourne, and that's where he intended to stay.

His reverie was broken by an electronic cough and a

voice demanding to know who had rung the bell.

'Ah. It's DCI Brendan Moran, Thames Valley Police. Is that Ms Dempster?'

A pause, then, 'What do you want?'

'I'd like to ask you a few questions regarding Laura Witney, if I may.'

'Oh God. Not again. I thought we were finished with all that.'

'Nothing's finished until we have the person responsible in custody,' Moran countered. 'I'll only want ten minutes of your time.'

A weary sigh. 'Come on up, then. Two flights of stairs, then first on the left.'

'Thank you.'

Moran went in as the lock clicked and made his way up as instructed. He turned left to find the flat door already open and a woman awaiting his arrival with folded arms and a cynical expression. 'I hope this'll be quick. I'm busy.'

She turned around and led him into the flat. He closed the door behind him.

Rita Dempster planted herself in the centre of the living room, arms still folded. 'Well?'

'Well, it's forty years since Laura was murdered. We'd like to think that her friends and colleagues are as keen as we are to find out what happened.'

Rita let her hands fall to her sides. She was a slim, hard-looking woman in her mid-sixties. Her dyed blonde hair was cropped short, a rebellious streak of crimson highlighting proclaiming her personality to the world. A tough cookie, or just a persona to hide behind? Moran intended to find out.

'May I?' He pointed to a nearby armchair.

Rita sighed. 'Why not? Make yourself at home.'

She freed a dining chair from beneath a teak dining table and perched on it. 'It was sad, what happened to Laura,' she began, unprompted, 'but you'll have seen from the interview notes that we weren't exactly buddies.'

'I gathered as much,' Moran said. 'But you worked together for … quite a while. A year or so?'

'Yep. We slaved away in those kitchens for ever. Chef had it in for me. Laura was his favourite.'

'And that still rankles?'

Rita tossed her head and gave a harsh laugh. 'Hah! Not really. It pissed me off at the time, sure. But things move on. Leaving the RAF was the best thing I ever did.'

'You weren't cut out for a military life?'

'I thought I was, at first. When I joined my head was full of glamorous fantasies. You know, seeing the world, maybe even crewing an aeroplane, or at least getting trained up in some specialism. But I ended up working as a bloody skivvy in the kitchens.'

'Laura was ambitious, wasn't she?' Moran wanted to get Rita's perspective.

'She worked hard, I'll give her that. She had her eye on the future, seemed content enough to wait out her term in Catering. Maybe I was too impatient.' A shrug. 'That's my character, I suppose. We're all prisoners of our personalities, aren't we, DCI Moran?'

'That we are,' Moran agreed. 'But tell me, did you have a major falling out? Or was it just that you didn't see eye to eye?'

Rita ran a hand through her crop. 'I used to be a bit of a bitch, I'll admit. I gave her a hard time. She was the goody-two-shoes, I was the one who got all the crap jobs, or at least that's what it felt like. I'm prepared to admit to being a pain in the arse, but that's all. I'd never have hurt her.'

'And what about her friends, other colleagues?'

'I didn't mix a lot with her set, to be honest. She seemed to attract people I found a bit twee. Privileged backgrounds, you know. Me, I was brought up on a local council estate. Not a lot in common with the public school set.'

'Of which Charles Summers was one?'

'Oh, him.' Rita paused to get out a packet of cigarettes. 'You don't mind?'

'Go right ahead.'

She lit her cigarette and blew smoke through her nostrils. 'Charles was a pest. She told me that much. But I got the impression she liked him.'

'Did you get to know him?'

Rita tapped ash into an overflowing ash tray. 'Not really. We crossed paths occasionally, mainly in the mess. He was friendly enough, I suppose, but very plummy. Not my type.'

'You know that he was the last person to see Laura alive?'

'Yes.'

'What do you think happened that evening?'

'I was working. It was the night of a squadron do in the mess – Charles' squadron. The anniversary. Laura was off – but she'd turned down Charles' offer of an invite because she'd agreed to babysit for the Wing Co. You've got all this in your files, surely?'

'I'd like to hear it from you.'

Rita gave a terse shake of her head. 'I saw her in her room around five-thirty. I was about to go on shift. I don't remember talking to her, but I definitely clocked her round about that time.'

'And this was in the female quarters?'

'Yes. I went on shift directly after that. Never saw her after. And then, of course, we heard the news the next day.'

'Did you leave the barracks on a regular basis? I mean, to socialise in town, pubs, clubs, or whatever?'

'Sure. Not every week, but we did go out.'

'And did you meet any of the locals – get to know them socially?'

'Sometimes.' Rita blew a stream of smoke towards the window in deference to her guest. 'You're meaning local lads, right?'

'Yes.'

'There would always be one or two who'd … make a play, you know? But Laura didn't get involved – at least not to my knowledge. I'd be surprised if she had. Anyway, it's not the sort of thing that would have stayed a secret for long.'

'Right. So Laura kept herself to herself, in that sense.'

'I'd say so, yes. I mean, she'd go out with close friends, but she wasn't in any kind of relationship – so far as I know. She was too keen on her career.'

That accorded with what Moran had understood from the case notes: Laura had been hard-working and dedicated. But what about her other friends and colleagues?

'Are you in touch with anyone from those days?'

Rita gave a bitter laugh and shook her head. 'No. When I left Brockford I didn't look back. I haven't seen any of them since.'

'You're working still?'

Rita stubbed her cigarette out, folded her arms. 'Just part-time. Enough to keep the wolf from the door.'

Moran was satisfied, for the time being. 'Thanks for your time. If you do recall anything that might help–'

'I know. I'll give you a call.'

'Thank you – oh, one final thing.' Moran had stood up and Rita did likewise. They faced each other across the room. 'Did you know the Wing Commander?'

'I knew Akkerman, yes. He was all right.'

'What about his family? Did you know them?'

'I met his wife a couple of times. She was plain, I thought. There was a daughter, I can't remember her name, but she'd have been about our age. I only met her once or twice – at mess functions, Christmas and so on. She was a bit spiky. Not that I had anything to do with her.'

'Was she a student, working, or–'

Rita shrugged. 'No idea. She lived with her parents, the Wing Co. and his missus, and the baby.'

'Quite an age gap.'

'Yes.' She shrugged. 'But that was their business.'

They were at the door when Moran asked, 'And you were working that evening? That would be until what time?'

The arms were folded again. 'Until late. Half-ten, or eleven, I can't recall exactly.'

'And you went straight to your room afterwards?'

Rita hesitated. 'I did. But then I thought, what the hell … why should everyone else enjoy the party and not me. So I went to the mess for a while.'

'You had an invite?'

'Not exactly, but I knew the right people. It was late, they'd all had a few, so it wasn't hard. They'd have let anyone in by that stage.'

'And you stayed till?'

'Around one, I guess. I was tired. It'd been a long day.'

'Did you notice anything unusual?'

'Like what?'

'Did anyone leave the mess, and return later, perhaps?'

'God, I wasn't paying that sort of attention to anything or anyone. Why would I?'

'And Charles? Was he there?'

'Yes, he was. Matter of fact I had a couple of dances with him.'

'And how was he?'

A look of exasperation was beginning to cloud Rita's face. 'How did he seem? Merry, having a good time.'

'Not distracted in any way?'

'Chief Inspector, you're asking me to remember how someone was forty-five years ago when I spent all of ten minutes with him.'

'Any small detail might help.'

'He was OK. Normal. There's *nothing*, really.'

Moran held up his hand. 'All right. That's fine. Thanks again for your time, Ms Dempster.'

'No problem.'

Moran made his way down the uncarpeted stairs, his footsteps echoing in the stairwell. Was she concealing something? He couldn't recall anything in the original statement to suggest that Rita had, in fact, been present at the mess party. In fact, he was pretty sure she'd told the investigating officer at the time that she'd gone back to her room and stayed in.

As he reached the front door the building shook as a lorry sped by, vibrating the molecules and atoms of the century-old brickwork from foundations to rooftop.

Moran had a feeling that he might need to shake Rita Dempster a little harder the next time he called by.

Chapter Eight

The hotel was in poor shape. Anyone could see that, even from a good distance. The driveway was overgrown, reclaimed by a generation of weeds, the paintwork was peeling and window frames hung loose, dangling from rusted hinges and weatherworn fitments. It had closed ten years previously and no-one had stepped forward to claim it, either for refurbishment or demolition.

Local kids had found the prospect of exploration exciting to begin with, but rumours of a strange presence had scared them off, especially after one recent incident when two twelve-year-old boys claimed to have witnessed a weird, unexplained light spilling from a downstairs room accompanied by an eerie moaning, as though some tormented soul had taken up residence and was making it clear that it wanted to be left alone.

Which wasn't so very far from the truth. Connie Chan had found the derelict building three weeks after making her escape from the Sussex hospital where she was being treated for a head wound, a nasty gash inflicted by DI

Pepper that had left her suffering from concussion and shock.

She'd needed time and space to heal and think. The hotel, nestled deep in the Wye Valley, had proved to be an excellent choice. The name had come to her attention via the Brodies, the care-home magnates, during her time working in Scotland. The hotel had been on Duncan Brodie's hit list as a possible acquisition, and the information had stuck in her mind, filed away for future reference.

She knew enough about the Brodies' current circumstances to be comfortable that she would remain undisturbed for some time to come; Brodie's wife would shortly be imprisoned for murder, and Brodie himself was apparently too frightened to travel far. And with good reason, because Brodie was unfinished business. After she'd dealt with the Irish inspector and his team, Brodie was next on Chan's list. She was very much looking forward to meeting him again.

She'd chosen a downstairs suite as her preferred space, close enough to the rear entrance and yet deep enough in the interior for her to feel secure – not that anyone was going to be looking for her in this remote spot. Adults weren't interested and the kids hadn't come back, so her isolation was complete.

Power had been an initial problem, but she'd solved that by acquiring a small generator. Compact and efficient, it supplied her with 2000W of power – plenty to cover her requirements for lighting, heating, laptop and, as and when necessary, food.

Although the hotel was damp in parts, the rooms she had chosen were sound, warm and comfortable. For security she'd set up three external cameras, their fields of vision displayed prominently on a large monitor on top of the IKEA dressing table that doubled as her desk and operations centre.

The specialist team that had been convened to track her down had conspicuously failed. The thought pleased her. They had no idea where to begin looking.

Naked, she padded to the tall vanity mirror and inspected her body. It was lean, the muscles honed and sculpted. Her small breasts were firm and round, her stomach flat and hard, like a tabletop. She'd come directly from a cold shower – by some fortuitous oversight the water authorities had yet to cut the water supply – and was now ready for forty minutes of Tai Chi.

First *Neigong*.

Breathe...

She assumed the familiar positions, described the age-old movements, concentrating only on the moment, allowing her mind to empty and release all negativity. The energy flowed through her body, empowering, healing.

And now the fight, *Taolu...*

Her movements were assured, lithe, symmetrical.

She watched the woman in the mirror as though from somewhere beyond the physical world, from some elevated place not subject to a restriction of four dimensions. She liked what she saw; the choreography of the cosmos was, in some indefinable way, encapsulated in the sure, poetic language of the perfect physical body reflected in the glass.

She was the heart of this building, the core. It was her domain; every nook and cranny, every molecule of brick and plaster was a part of her, and she a part of it.

Chan concluded her exercises; now her mind and body were perfectly aligned, perfectly in synch.

She poured herself a mineral water, sat at the dressing table and took a faded photograph from a black attaché case. The photograph showed a man and a woman standing beneath an arch of bougainvillea, dressed for an evening out, arms interlinked. The woman had thick, glossy black hair worn in a casual braid over her breast. The man was handsome, with a thin pencil moustache and piercing eyes, bright and intelligent, full of life.

She examined the image, poring over every pixel of colour, as if simply by concentration she could breathe life into the static image and summon the subjects into her presence. She yearned to feel them, touch them.

A fantasy, of course, but to reach for the impossible was a vital component of her ritual. Impossible today, perhaps, but Chan had no doubt that there would come a time when their souls would be reunited. She *would* see them again, her beloved parents, who had been taken from her the very night the photograph was taken, just a few, short hours later.

What would she have said, had she known at the time? What words would they have exchanged? But her young, ignorant hands had merely held the camera steady, clicked the shutter, frozen the moment; she had waved, wished them a happy evening with friends, and had gone about her own business, the trivia of a teenage girl – magazines, make-up, pop stars, and eventually, the last untroubled sleep she would ever know.

Her eyes watered. She touched first her mother's, then her father's face, her fingers gentle on the celluloid.

What have I become, Abah?

Her face twisted as she strove to control her emotions.

She stroked her mother's forehead.

Oh, Umi ... why? Why did you leave me?

She bent her head, allowed the sorrow to overwhelm her. The daily observance was cathartic, a necessary ritual for her mental wellbeing and, more importantly, her resolve.

Presently she slipped the photograph into its pocket in the attaché case, snapped it shut, and turned her attention to her laptop. It was time to attend to the matter in hand.

He slim fingers danced on the keys. She clicked the target icon, waited.

The screen expanded to show a window within a window, a replication of DC McConnell's desktop. She selected *email*, opened the inbox, and began to read.

Chapter Nine

DI Charlie Pepper was in a pensive mood – preferable, she felt, to the prevailing mood in the room that could be reasonably described as downbeat. Several months had elapsed since Connie Chan's escape from Crawley General Hospital, with very little progress made regarding her movements immediately afterwards, and even less on second-guessing her current whereabouts.

Chan was a ghost; friendless, contactless, rootless. She could have gone literally anywhere. She could even have slipped the borders and left the country, although Charlie's personal feeling was that she wouldn't have done so, not without concluding her business here. And Charlie was pretty sure she know what that business entailed: finishing what she had started concerning Duncan Brodie, the care home millionaire.

The MIT had been allocated a room in central Birmingham, a city that, being a Coventry lass, Charlie was familiar with from her teens. There were four detective constables, a detective sergeant – Ian Luscombe

– and herself, the DI in charge, seconded to the specialist unit.

The press were harassing her, her seniors were harassing her, and the parents of the injured A&E nurse were harassing her – and who could blame them? Jennifer Sobie had survived, but only just. Physically she was healing, but her mental trauma would take a good deal longer to dissipate. People wanted answers. They wanted to know why it was so difficult to bring Chan to justice. She was a single woman, wasn't she? Slight in stature? She was recognisable, surely? How hard could it be to trace her?

But they didn't know Chan. They hadn't faced her, tackled her in the flesh. Charlie's encounter with the Malaysian had left her with a clear impression of Chan's psyche; it was the memory of the look in Chan's eye, the savagery of her assault that regularly woke Charlie at night, shouting, sweating, near hysterical. On one occasion she'd lashed out, struck Ian Luscombe in the eye, given him a shiner that had drawn winks and comments the following day.

Chan was a constant presence in Charlie's mind. Until she'd got the woman under lock and key, she wouldn't be able to relax. Life was on hold, and she wasn't sure how much longer she could exist in this strange bubble. She wasn't beaten, far from it, but she badly needed a lead, something to gee the team up, get things moving.

'Just spoke to Brodie.' A familiar voice broke into her reverie. She turned in her chair; DS Ian Luscombe was half in, half out of her office, his expression noncommittal except for the eyes, which were smiling and looking directly into hers.

'Oh yes. And?'

Luscombe shrugged. 'He just wants to make sure he's well-protected. Last night the duty uniforms mucked up their changeover – left him exposed for a half-hour. The longest half-hour of his life, so he was telling me.'

'She won't be that unsubtle about it,' Charlie ran a hand through her hair. 'When she strikes, we won't have any warning. It'll be a *fait accompli*.'

Luscombe raised an eyebrow. 'We don't even know if she's in Scotland.'

'We don't know *anything*, Ian.' Charlie rapped the desk with her knuckles. 'It's like chasing a ghost. No leads, no clues, no witnesses. Nothing.'

'There's still a chance the Fiat might–'

'We don't even know if she took it or not,' Charlie interrupted. 'It could have been any opportunistic car thief.'

A grey Fiat 500 had been stolen at around the same time that Chan made her escape, but the CCTV cameras trained on the hospital car park had been out of operation, and ANPR had so far failed to track down the missing vehicle.

Luscombe nodded thoughtfully. 'True.'

'We're out of options.' Charlie ticked them off. 'We've spoken to Isaiah Marley's mother, all the care homes Chan's been involved with – or been seen around. She hasn't revisited the Swan in Petworth – why would she, anyway? – she hasn't been back to Brodie's old school – same, no point. So, if she's not holed up waiting for a chink in Brodie's armour to appear, then where the hell is she?' She sighed deeply. 'Chan could be literally *anywhere*, and six of us can't possibly cover "anywhere".'

'Agreed. We need a lead.' Luscombe half-spoke, half-sang his reply, but Charlie wasn't in the mood for levity.

'Any joy from Interpol?'

'Not so far. They're sympathetic, promised to let us know if and when blah, blah, blah.'

'What about that family, the one she au paired for? In the South of France?'

'Nope. They've not set eyes on her since the day they woke up and found her gone. The kids, well, *ils sont toujours tristes*, according to my contact.'

'Ian, just come in and shut the door, would you?'

She waited a second for Luscombe to comply. Now she could safely dispense with formality. '*Toujours tristes*? Wow. Not-bad-looking *and* multi-lingual?' She slipped her tongue firmly against the inside of her cheek.

'*Tch*. Hardly. It's the *auld alliance*, that's all.' Luscombe dismissed the compliment, po-faced. 'My grandmother spoke the language fluently, as did her own mother. I sometimes feel I've let the side down by not keeping it up.'

'That won't do.' Charlie adopted a stern expression. 'I read Balzac for A-level. I could lend you a couple of novels.'

'Bedtime reading?' Luscombe's eyebrows rose fractionally.

Charlie repressed a smile. 'But we digress, DS Luscombe.' She was silent for a moment. 'So, if *we* can't get to Chan, you know what we should try?'

'Vice versa?'

'Yep.'

'Bait? Brodie?'

'Not sure.' Charlie frowned. 'It depends how much she wants him. She might be fishing other waters.'

'I get the impression she's the type that likes to finish a job properly.'

'So do I, Ian. So do I.' Charlie drummed on her desk top. 'OK. Can you assemble the troops? We'll have a brainstorming session, let's see how innovative we can be.'

'Will do.' Luscombe scratched his chin. 'Boss, I think it might be worth having a chat with your guv. He's the fella's had the closest contact with Chan, bar yourself.'

'I might just do that,' Charlie said, glancing at her watch.

'There's another option you might consider, too.'

'Oh, yes?'

'I had a call out of the blue from a psychological profiler, a Mr Savage. He's worked on key cases, with pretty impressive results.'

'Tell me more.'

'Interesting guy. Well qualified – half the alphabet after his name. Turns out he's heard about Chan. He was also very enthusiastic about your ex-guv's past casebook. He's just finished up at Braintree in Essex, and he sounded keen.'

'So we'd have exclusive dibs on him?'

'Well, he enjoys juggling multiple cases, so he told me – usually works on several at a time. I'm not sure what his current workload is, but I don't think it would deter him.'

'Hm. Sounds useful. I might mention him to DCI Moran – George tells me he could use some help right now.'

'My thoughts precisely.' Luscombe cocked his head. 'He mentioned the Laura Witney *Crimewatch* appeal – says he loves a challenging cold case. So ... if we share him, it'll be easier on our budget, right? Catch you at the briefing. Shall we say ten minutes?'

'Sure.'

Charlie sat quietly, lost in thought. It would be good to catch up with Moran, but part of her didn't want to admit how little progress they had made. She didn't want Moran to feel she was relying on him, to think she couldn't sort this on her own.

That's just pride, Charlie ... that's all...

But this profiler guy, he could be useful for both of them, and she'd maybe save a little face – OK, and a little money – by recommending him.

Hello, guv ... I come bearing gifts ...

Chapter Ten

'So, you planning on keeping the POIs up to speed this time around, Bola?' Chris Collingworth was trying to keep a straight face as he waited for the lights to change. 'Make sure they're in the know?'

'If that was a joke, you'd better get a new scriptwriter, my friend.'

Collingworth affected surprise. 'Hey, no offence.' The lights went to amber and he floored the accelerator.

'Take it easy.' Bola gripped his seat belt.

Collingworth turned his head. 'I'm driving ab-so-lutely normally. What's up with you?'

'I'm not talking about the driving,' Bola growled. 'I'm talking about that motor-mouth of yours. Better keep it in neutral while you're with me.'

'Ooh. Touchy.' Collingworth tutted, shook his head.

'Let's just concentrate on what we're doing, OK?'

'Fine by me.' Collingworth overtook a lorry, swung the car into the path of oncoming traffic, swerved back into the left hand lane with a second to spare. A bus swept past, their mirror almost brushing the vehicle's bodywork.

'Do that one more time and I'm out of here,' Bola told him.

'Promises, promises,' Collingworth simpered.

They lapsed into a sullen silence.

Bola simmered as the countryside flashed past the passenger window. He'd drive next outing. Why the heck did George have to be away *now*? They worked well together, had a good understanding. But Chris Collingworth? Well, Collingworth was still Collingworth, despite his much-vaunted reformation. Sure, his mind was more on the job these days – he wanted to make sure he nailed the next sergeant's vacancy, so that was a given – but he still riled the hell out of pretty much everyone in the team.

'Watch out. School ahead.' Bola issued the warning as they approached Bradfield College. 'Right here.'

'You're in the wrong job, my man. Should have been a driving instructor.' Collingworth went through some temporary lights on amber.

'Rich kids' zone,' he muttered as a group of teenagers crossed the road a few metres ahead of them.

'Rich zone, period,' Bola replied. 'All the way from here up to Yattendon and beyond.'

'Nice pub in Yattendon,' Collingworth remarked. 'Bit pricey, but worth half an hour of a lunchtime.' He paused. 'Bet George knows all about it.'

Bola gave Collingworth a weary look. 'Leave George alone. He's all right.'

'You know what they say.' Collingworth nodded sagely. 'Once the demon drink gets hold of you–'

'He's doing *fine*.'

The ensuing silence crackled with tension.

'The Willows, it's called.' Collingworth said. 'Yattendon Road.'

They cruised through the village into a narrow lane, each checking the parade of imposing-looking houses crouched behind tall hedgerows. Some gates clearly stated the house name, others were not so helpful. After ten minutes of fruitless searching, Collingworth turned the car around and headed back into the centre.

As Collingworth brought the car to a halt outside the village stores, Bola clicked his window open and hailed two passers-by. 'Excuse me – any idea where we can find a house called *The Willows*?'

'That's my homestead,' the nearest man said. He was dressed in the traditional garb of the country gent – green Barbour jacket, check cap, Hunter wellingtons. His companion, a ruddy-faced man in his seventies, peered in at them.

'Police, no doubt. What d'you want in this neck of the woods?'

Collingworth ignored the other man's question. 'Air Commodore Akkerman?'

'Yes. And you are?'

Collingworth showed his warrant card. He jerked his thumb to the left. 'And this is my colleague, DC Bola Odunsi. We'd like a word, sir, if that's convenient.'

Akkerman pointed to the row of cars parked outside the village stores. 'Well, you can park there – I'm having lunch at the Royal Oak. Care to join me?'

'We'll only take ten minutes of your time.' Bola leaned across to speak to the Air Commodore. 'But thanks all the same.'

'Very well. I'll meet you in the bar shortly.'

Akkerman and his friend strolled across the road to the pub and Collingworth squeezed the Astra into a tight space next to a Porsche 718 Cayman.

Bola got out, straightened his tie. Air Commodore Akkerman was clearly a man of substance, and he felt uncomfortably underdressed. He glanced at Collingworth for reassurance just in time to catch the possessive look on his colleague's face as his hand briefly caressed the Porsche's bodywork.

'What are you staring at?'

'Nothing. Let's do this.'

Air Commodore Akkerman and his friend were the only occupants of the Royal Oak's bar. Akkerman looked up as Bola and Collingworth came in. Akkerman's friend muttered something inaudible and discreetly went to find a menu from the restaurant area.

'And how can I help you gentlemen?'

Akkerman was a tall, slightly stooped man in his mid to late seventies. His neatly styled hair was full and thick, dense eyebrows overarching grey eyes which, although clear and alert, also seemed tainted with melancholy as if some long-fought internal struggle had left him weary and disappointed. He still wore a tangible air of authority, however, and Bola had to work hard to overcome an irrational sense of inferiority as he opened the conversation.

'It's concerning an unsolved murder, I'm afraid,' he began.

Akkerman's hand shot up to silence him. 'Ah. I knew it. The Witney girl, correct? All happened a very long time ago. I'd have thought that if you people haven't figured out who's responsible by now, you're hardly likely to find success forty-odd years later. Am I right?'

'We've reopened the case, sir,' Collingworth explained. 'As it's the anniversary of the crime, we're appealing for new information. The anniversary of a serious crime very often prompts people to come forward and provide us with exactly that.'

'If you say so.'

'Laura Witney was due to babysit for you on the night in question, is that correct?' Bola cut to the chase. It was clear that he would have to push through Akkerman's reticence to get the answers they needed.

'*Must* we go through all this again? Ah, Ted,' Akkerman called to his friend who had just reappeared, 'this is going to take a while, I'm afraid – d'you mind having a word with James, get him to hold fire on our table for twenty minutes or so? You can have a half in the snug while you're waiting.'

'Right you are. Take your time – I'm in no hurry.' Ted acknowledged the unscheduled delay to his lunch with a casual wave before exiting the bar a second time.

'The Brigadier.' Akkerman smiled sadly. 'Far too easy going, that's his problem. People-pleaser – always has been.'

'I think he's just being polite, sir.' Bola found himself defending Akkerman's departed buddy. 'I'm sorry to hold up your meal. I'll try to keep it short.'

'Not as short as my answers, am I right?' Akkerman jutted his chin.

'So, on the night in question,' Collingworth began, but broke off in mid-sentence as the barman appeared with a cheery greeting.

'What can I get you gentlemen?'

Bola sighed. It was only after they'd placed their order and a half-pint of ale had been placed on the bar in front of Akkerman that the Air Commodore returned his attention to Collingworth.

'On the night in question, my wife and myself were due to attend a squadron party, as previously stated.'

'And Laura was to babysit?'

'Yes.' Akkerman took an irritated sip of ale. 'You know all this.'

'But you were late collecting her,' Bola chipped in. 'And when you got there, she was nowhere to be seen. Did you look for her?'

'I went to the mess, asked if anyone had seen her. Someone told me she'd been there earlier, but had left at around six forty-five.'

'And do you recall, Air Commodore, whom you spoke

to?' Collingworth was putting on his politest accent.

'I spoke to a young pilot by the name of Charles Summers. As previously stated.'

'So, then you went straight home?' Bola prompted. 'Or did you stay for a bit?'

'No, I didn't stay. My wife called an alternative babysitter and arranged for her to come over.'

'I see. And your wife and daughter were at home that afternoon and early evening?'

'Yes, as I recall – until we left for the party.'

'And your daughter stayed at home?'

'No,' Akkerman said patiently, 'she had some arrangement of her own that evening. Otherwise she would have babysat for us.'

'Do you know what that arrangement was?'

'Why don't you consult your earlier paperwork? It's all there, I'm sure.'

'We're just concerned that something might have been missed, Air Commodore.' Bola gave Akkerman a friendly smile. 'Where might we be able to contact your daughter?'

Akkerman inspected his beer. When he looked up again, his eyes were unexpectedly watery. 'Well, there's a question. I wish I had the answer, but sadly, I don't.'

Collingworth frowned. 'You're not in touch?'

Akkerman shook his head. 'Not for a very, very long time.'

'I'm sorry to hear that, sir,' Bola said.

'Didn't enjoy life at home. Wanted to make her own

way.'

'So she … started work elsewhere? Or–'

'Very academic,' Akkerman said. 'Bright spark. Mathematics and the like. Went up to Cambridge.'

'And when would that have been, sir?' Bola wanted to know.

Akkerman screwed his eyes shut – either because the question brought back unwelcome memories, or to summon his own powers of recall, Bola wasn't sure. 'Eighty-two, three. Sometime around then.'

'And after that?'

'Your guess is as good as mine.'

'You haven't seen her since, not been in touch at all?' Collingworth tried to squash a note of incredulity.

Akkerman ran his finger around the rim of his glass. 'I'm afraid not. If you do manage to track her down, I'd be grateful if you'd let me know.'

'Of course.'

'And your son?' Collingworth went on. 'Where might we find him?'

'In the States, I expect.' Akkerman replied. 'That's where he said he was going.'

'You're not in touch with him, either?' Bola was confused. Surely someone wouldn't lose touch with both their children?

'No. He went to America. That's all I can tell you.'

'And when was this, sir?' Collingworth had his notebook out.

'Years ago. I forget.'

Bola was thinking hard. Something wasn't right here. 'Your wife, sir? Surely–'

'She was admitted to a specialist hospital in 1985,' Akkerman said, his tone expressionless. 'Where she died, two years later.'

'I'm so sorry to hear that,' Bola said. He couldn't meet the older man's gaze. Wife dead, two children estranged. That was more than tough; that was disastrous. Now he understood the Air Commodore's haunted look.

Collingworth was scribbling away, his orange juice untouched. He looked up. 'So, your son would be … forty now?'

'Yes.'

'Do you perhaps have a last known address?' Bola asked.

'He was flat-sharing, I believe, somewhere around the turn of the millennium. He never gave me an address.'

'I see. What about your daughter, sir? A last known place of abode?'

'She was friendly with a few of the women at Brockford. You might try one of them. I can't offer any more insight, I'm afraid.'

Ted shuffled back into the bar. 'I say, James just told me they might have to give the table away if you're going to be much longer.'

'I think we're finished, Ted.' Akkerman raised his eyebrows at the two detectives, as though daring them to disagree.

'Yep, we're done.' Bola drained his coke. 'Thanks for

your time, sir.'

'Yes, well good luck to you both.' Akkerman took his barely-touched half of ale and followed Ted out of the bar.

Outside, a note had been left on their windscreen.

Next time you park your car an inch away from mine, kindly leave a can opener so I can get in. Next time I'll have yours towed out of the way.

'Friendly locals, anyhow,' Bola said.

Collingworth screwed the note up and chucked it over his shoulder. 'Bloody Porsche owners. Bunch of tossers, the lot of them.'

Chapter Eleven

Moran drew the blind against the evening sun. It would soon be midsummer's day, but his mind was a long way from summer. He returned to his desk, picked up the diary's narrative from the last entry he'd studied.

Feb 4th 1981

So ... Charles wants me to go to the 43 bash at the end of the month. What to do? I said I'll prob be working but he said go on take the evening off – you can give them plenty of notice. Yikes. No excuse. If I say yes, he'll take that as a come on. If I say no ... ohhhh I don't know what to do!!!! Weather rubbish today. Pouring. On evening shift again. Rita was off – hurray!! Made the main tonight – Lancashire hot pot. Nick very pleased with me. He said best hot pot he's tasted since he last made one! Got to be a compliment, right?

Pub with Lynn and Marg tomorrow night. Keeping it quiet in case R tags along, which she would, just to be a pain. What else? Need to go into Brockford Sat – coming up to curse week and run out of the necessary. Might go to flicks too - depends what's on. Letter from Mum – don't forget Dad's birthday (as if). I thought don't forget mine! Dad's had a cold but is better this week. Mixie caught a mouse in the larder!

Got to go. Eyes closing. I can hear R playing her b record player – sure she does it deliberately. If the Dragon's on her rounds she'll be for it. Oh well, her problem. Good job I can sleep through anything. Night, dear diary xxx

He was developing a soft spot for Laura. When he put the diary aside it was like time-travel, the return to the present almost a physical jolt. He found that he needed a good few seconds to reorientate himself. The minutiae of this lost young life, was beginning to get to him. Cinemas and pub meets, invitations to parties, annotated shopping reminders, letters from home – it all painted a picture of a normal, happy young woman, finding her way in the world, carving out her independence. So far there was not the slightest hint of the evil that was lurking in the background, just out of sight, waiting for the moment to strike.

Moran sat back, glanced at his desk clock. Seven forty-five; time to call it a day. Perhaps a pint on the way home, or a walk by the river, clear his head a little and get his act together for the morning briefing. Maybe he'd give Alice a call after dinner.

Moran's heart lurched.

Dinner.

Alice. Tonight. *Tuesday*.

Oh *no*.

Should he call, or just get himself over there ASAP?

Brendan, you Irish eejit ... how could you forget?

Moran swept his keys from the desk and exited his office at a speed that made several late workers crane their necks above their workstations.

Traffic was easing and he made the crosstown journey in record time. He parked and checked his watch. Ten past eight. Forty-five minutes late. Could be worse...

As he waited for Alice to answer the door he composed himself.

A rueful smile, Brendan, a little shake of the head...

He waited, admired the flower beds in the front garden. Roses still looking fresh, grass mown neatly.

No response. The front curtains were drawn so he couldn't see if there was anybody about. He rang again.

The door opened, just a little. Alice stood in the narrow space.

'Brendan.'

'I'm so sorry I'm late, Alice – I got caught up in–'

'Thursday, we said, I think?'

Moran was nonplussed. They had definitely had an agreement for this evening. 'Ah – I'm pretty sure we said today.'

'Well, I'm sorry. It'll have to be Thursday now.'

'Right. Well, OK, my fault, I'm sure.'

Her face was pinched and anxious.

'Is everything all right? Peter–?'

'Yes, he's fine. We're both fine.'

Moran nodded. Something was up, but she clearly did not want to discuss it. 'Well, I'll leave you to it, then. See you Thursday.'

'Yes, lovely. Bye.'

'Bye.'

The door closed and Moran walked pensively back to his car.

He sat for a moment, wondering what to do. Presently, he put the car in gear and drove a short distance, turned around, came back, found a space on the opposite side of the road with a clear view of Alice's front door.

That pint will have to wait…

Half an hour passed, then another. He was beginning to think he was on a fool's errand when the front door opened and a man stepped out, looked quickly right and left, made his way down the drive and across the road to a parked Ford Transit. Moran watched as the guy indicated and pulled out of the space, accelerated away towards Wokingham.

Right.

Alice answered the door immediately. Her shoulders slumped when she saw him. 'Brendan.'

'I'm too long in the tooth not to recognise when something's wrong, Alice.'

'You'd better come in.'

This time the door was opened wide.

Peter was sitting on the settee, a frown marring his usually carefree expression, but when he realised who it was, the frown cleared immediately. 'Oh. Hello Brendan. I'm glad it's you and not Mr Collier again.'

Collier. The name rang a distinct bell. The stepbrother-in-law, the guy George had mentioned in connection with the late Cyril Duboff's funds.

'Hello Peter.'

'Peter, how about you watch some TV while I talk to the Chief Inspector.' Alice had composed herself, and with her encouragement Peter agreed that was a good idea, as long as Brendan wasn't going to arrest Alice.

'Not at all, Peter. I'm here to help.'

'That's good,' Peter grinned. 'See you later.'

'Sure.'

They went through to the kitchen. 'Can I make you some coffee? Or tea, or maybe something stronger?' Alice clasped her hands. 'I'm sorry about tonight,' she went on without waiting for his response. 'You're quite right, of course, it was tonight we agreed, but then he turned up out of the blue, and...'

Moran could see she was close to tears. 'Let me make the tea. Just sit down and tell me all about it.'

'Oh, well, I–'

'Go *on*.' Moran pulled a stool out from under the breakfast bar. 'Have a seat, and tell me what's up.'

'It's complicated.'

'Try me.'

'The man who was just here–'

'Mark Collier. Your stepbrother-in-law. Yes.'

'You *know* about him? But how–?'

'I'm a policeman, Alice. It's our job to be thorough, to check facts, relationships, alibis, all that stuff. It's our bread and butter.'

'I see. So it was in connection with my sister, when you traced her?'

'Yes. One of my team was investigating a murder victim's financial affairs, and Collier's name popped up. You're not implicated in anything, don't worry, it was just something one of my team felt it was proper to mention.'

At least, I hope you're not implicated...

'Maybe you'll feel differently when I've explained what he wanted.'

'Maybe,' Moran said. 'Now, where do you keep the teabags?'

'Left hand cupboard, by the kettle. That's it.'

Moran fiddled about with mugs, teapot, milk, boiled the kettle, made the tea, presented Alice with a mug. 'OK, so what did this Collier want?'

'There's a company, Collier Holdings Ltd. My husband was a shareholder. It's a property company. I mean, for buying and selling residential property, you know, for business.'

'OK.'

'I didn't have any dealings with it, and my late husband never mentioned it really. I left all that financial stuff to him. But when he died, I received a note from the solicitor after probate informing me that I was a quarter shareholder in the company.'

'The other shareholders being?'

'Mark, a lady called Carol Shanahan, Cyril Duboff – the man who was murdered, but you know all about that – and myself.'

'Let me guess. Mark Collier wants you to sell him your shares?'

'No.' Alice shook her head. 'I recently received yet another communication regarding probate – this time from Cyril Duboff's solicitor. Apparently Duboff had stipulated that in the event of his death, his share of the company should pass to my husband – that is to say, to me.'

'So ... now you're the majority shareholder.'

'Yes, I own fifty percent of the company. But I don't want it, Brendan. I don't want it if Mark Collier is involved.'

Moran nodded. 'What did he ask you to do?'

'He wants me to visit Carol Shanahan in prison, persuade her to sign a formal agreement of sale for a property the company owns. And he wants me to agree and sign as well, of course.'

'He wants to liquidate the asset? Presumably as he needs the money?'

'The place has been on the estate agents' books for a very long time, but Mark received an offer out of the blue, completely unexpectedly.'

'So, what's the problem?' Moran sipped his tea. From the lounge he could hear loud TV commentary – some

Olympic athletic event, one of Peter's favourites, no doubt.

'The problem is that he wants me to sign my shares over to him, to give him control of the company. And he wants to keep *my* share of the sale of the property. He threatened me, Brendan. He told me that if I didn't comply, if I made a fuss, told anyone, he'd–'

The tears came. Moran set his tea down and went to her. 'It's all right. We'll sort this out. It'll be fine.'

'He said he'd hurt Peter,' Alice blurted, then relapsed into sobs.

Moran's stomach knotted. What kind of person would threaten an autistic man? He placed a hand gently on Alice's shoulder. Even this small intimacy felt premature; in terms of physical contact, their relationship had yet to progress beyond formal handshakes. He withdrew his hand as she composed herself, folded her arms.

'That tells me all I need to know about him,' Moran said. 'Did he say when he's coming back?'

'Sometime this weekend – he's visiting the property tomorrow, and in the meantime I'm supposed to be arranging everything he asked for.'

'In which case–' Moran topped up Alice's mug from the pot, '–that gives us a few days to work something out, right?'

Alice forced a smile. 'If you say so, Brendan.'

Peter called from the living room. 'Alice? Are you coming to see the race?'

'Which is it, Peter?' Alice shouted back.

'The 1500 metres. 1984.'

'OK – coming.' She shrugged. 'One of his current favourites – Steve Cram.'

Moran drained his tea. 'I'll leave you to it, if you're all right.'

'I'm all right, yes. And I'm sorry about tonight.'

'Don't be. Can I call you tomorrow?'

'Please do.'

Moran drove home in a whirl of emotions. He was relieved that Alice seemed to be innocent of any wrongdoing concerning the misappropriated funds, but incensed that Collier had considered it legitimate to use Peter as leverage. How low could someone sink? An autistic man, for heaven's sake?

He was too angry to return to Laura's diary entries, so instead he took Archie for a long walk by the river. The tranquility of the water meadow combined with the warm summer evening eventually calmed him enough to ease his mind. He'd deal with Alice's problem according to the law, which, given the alternatives Moran had been considering, could only be a good thing for Mark Collier.

Chapter Twelve

Moran arrived at Atlantic House the next morning to find a visitor waiting for him. DI Charlie Pepper was chatting with Bola and Bernice Swinhoe by the coffee machine. When she caught sight of him her face broke into a wide smile. 'Morning, guv.'

'Good morning yourself, DI Pepper. And what brings you to our leafy suburbs at this bright and ungodly hour?'

Charlie laughed. 'I left at six to miss the traffic.'

'Did you indeed? And can anyone join in, or is this a private coffee break?'

'I'll get you one, guv,' Bola said. 'Cappuccino, no sugar?' He fiddled with the machine, punched buttons. The coffee machine whirred into life.

Moran was pleased to see Charlie. He'd been concerned about her since her close encounter with Chan, which had shaken her badly. But she'd been appointed as the MIT's senior officer as a direct result of that incident, which had been seen by the powers-that-be as a practical feather in her cap, something to command the respect of her subordinates.

'Ah, thanks, Bola.' He accepted the steaming cup. 'Now, I'm sure you two have better things to do than listen to our gossip, eh?'

'We're all caught up, guv. No worries.' Bernice grinned.

'Catch you later.' Bola also shot Charlie a grin as he and Bernice went off to their workstations.

Moran was curious as to why Charlie had made the journey south. 'So, what do you think of our prestigious new offices?'

'Very swish, guv.' Charlie grinned. 'Bola gave me a quick tour.'

'But you're not here to check out our interior design, I suspect.'

'No,' Charlie admitted as Moran ushered her into his office. 'I wanted to talk to you about Chan.'

'Ah.'

Moran invited Charlie to sit at his coffee table, a new innovation provided for senior officers so that VIPs or peers could discuss matters of concern on equal terms without the barrier of a desk between them.

'A bit like a dentist's waiting room, if you ask me,' Moran said half-apologetically. 'But HR have decreed that we all must have these 'chat-stations', as they insist on calling them.'

'All you need now is a selection of *Hello* magazines,' Charlie teased. 'Or maybe a few copies of *Trout Fishing Monthly.*'

Moran chuckled. 'That'd be right.' He sipped his cappuccino. Charlie looked a little pale, a hint of dark semicircles beneath her eyes. He said, 'You look well, Charlie. Birmingham is obviously doing you good.'

Charlie shrugged. 'It's my home turf, pretty much. I know the area.'

'And the investigation?'

Her face clouded. 'Nothing concrete so far. Since she left the hospital, zilch. There was a car stolen at around the same time but we can't trace it. She's gone, guv, and to be honest, I don't know where to look next – it's even possible she's fled the country altogether.'

'I somehow doubt it.' Moran finished his coffee and tapped the empty cup with his forefinger. 'I think she'll stick around. She has a good system going here.'

'Yep, Ian thought that. Do you think she'll have another go at Brodie?'

'She might,' Moran agreed, 'but she's not stupid. She'll know you're watching him.'

'True.' Charlie leaned forward, began to speak faster. 'Guv, we've been digging into her past. We already knew about her parents' car accident, the abuse she suffered from her uncle – but we discovered something else.'

'Go on.'

Charlie ran a hand through her cropped hair. 'Her mother's side of the family – there were problems. There was a sister–'

'Chan's ... aunt, then?'

'Yes. There was something amiss, something serious

enough for the mother to take drastic action. She was put up for adoption.'

'Oho. Given away.'

'Yes. We don't know where, exactly, but we do know the country. She was fostered here, guv, in the UK.'

'The papers don't give any clues?'

'It was all done anonymously, deliberately so. It was hard enough getting the Malaysian officials to tell us anything at all, let alone an address, or a name.'

'I'll bet. But you think that's why Chan ended up here? Because she's looking for her relation?'

'It's a possibility. She must have known something about her own family. Her mother would surely have mentioned her sister in some way or another.'

'Interesting.' Moran scratched his cheek.

'What do you think?'

'Chan's past is characterised by tragedy and abuse, so it makes sense that she'd want to trace a lost family connection, try to make things right, establish contact with her own flesh and blood.'

'I sense a 'but' coming.'

Moran smiled. 'More of a *however* than a *but* … an analysis of her motives doesn't necessarily bring you any closer to finding her.'

'True.'

'Might be worth pushing the Malaysian button again – to find a more helpful official?' Moran's brow furrowed. 'But even then, a name or address doesn't guarantee much of a lead. We're talking, what, 1970, or thereabouts for the adoption?'

'Sixty-nine.'

'Right. So the aunt will be in her … mid-sixties by now? Could be living literally anywhere – and that's assuming she's still alive.'

'But what if Chan had some clue from her mother, or found some paperwork before she ran away?'

'Uh huh. It's possible. She was in Scotland,' Moran pointed out, 'so perhaps that was her starting point. She may have returned north to resume the search. Maybe that's why she temps at nursing homes? As well as being a source of potential income for her, is she looking for the foster parents, or for the aunt herself?'

Charlie sighed. She'd not wanted to appear vulnerable before Moran, but something about him compelled honesty. 'It's all so speculative, guv. I just feel like I'm clutching at straws.'

'Sometimes straws are the only leads we have,' Moran said. 'The cold case we're working on right now, for instance. We've virtually nothing to go on. All we can do is keep clutching at those straws until we eventually pick one that has substance.'

'The straws being the POIs.'

'Exactly.'

'The list for Chan is a short one.'

'There's Duncan Brodie,' Moran reminded her. 'She spent quite some time with him. She might have let something slip. Then there's the staff at the Brodies' care home – I forget the name. She mixed a little with them.

Or Isaiah Marley's mother?'

'Ian's already spoken to her – nothing came of it.'

'Keep chipping away. Something will drop out.'

Charlie was quiet for a moment, studied her nails. Outside Moran's office the noise and chatter of the day's business was in full flow. 'I was thinking, maybe…'

'Yes?'

Charlie looked up. 'Of maybe getting a profiler in.'

Moran made a *comme ci, comme ça* gesture. 'If the budget will cope, why not? It can't do any harm.'

'You don't approve, guv. I can tell.'

'Call me old-fashioned, if you like.' Moran smiled. 'These psychological gobbledygook guys might come up with general theories, but often not much else – and they can be well wide of the mark, too. They might even send you off on a wild goose chase with nothing to show for it at the end.'

'At least I'd be chasing something.'

'Don't let me put you off. If you have someone in mind, try them out.'

'I do, as it happens.'

There was a knock on the door. Hesitant, more like a scuffle on the woodwork.

'That'll be him, now.' Charlie got up and opened the door. Moran's mouth fell open in surprise.

A small man with side-parted, thinning hair, an even thinner face, and tortoiseshell spectacles stood framed in the doorway. 'Hello.' the newcomer's voice was hesitant, nervous. 'DI Pepper?'

'Yes. Good of you to come, Mr Savage.' Charlie extended her hand. 'May I introduce you to DCI Brendan Moran?'

Chapter Thirteen

Moran sent for a coffee for his new guest. Mr Savage was still standing despite Charlie's invitation to join them at the coffee table. He hovered somewhere between the door and the table as though considering whether or not to make a run for it.

'We won't bite, Mr Savage,' Charlie assured him.

'Valentine is better, I think,' Savage replied, pushing his glasses up his nose, which was small and, Moran observed, somewhat inadequate for the task of supporting the tortoiseshell frames.

Savage moistened his lips, took a step closer. 'First name terms always make for better team cohesion. My name is rather androgynous,' Savage allowed, 'but there we are. My parents chose it and I'm stuck with it. It's usually shortened to Val.'

'Val thinks he might be able to help you with your cold case,' Charlie cut to the chase, gesturing encouragingly to Savage. 'Perhaps you can give DCI Moran a brief rundown? What you were telling me the other day?'

'Oh yes, I will. Absolutely.' Savage slid into the chair beside Charlie, keeping a wary eye on Moran. 'I like to work on multiple cases, you see. They tell me that the male psyche is rather lacking in what modern phraseology terms 'multi-tasking', but I find that I'm rather good at it.'

'Are you indeed?' Moran glowered.

'Yes, in fact the more the merrier.' Savage clapped a hand to his head. 'Now why did I say that? I *do* hate the expression, don't you? It implies mirth, whereas these matters are clearly very serious indeed. I must stop using it, but it tends to trip off the tongue.'

'Tell me,' Moran asked, 'what have you been working on recently?'

There was another knock at the door, and, at Moran's response, one of the canteen staff came in with a cafetiére and a plate of biscuits. 'Just here is fine, thanks.' Charlie pointed to the table.

'No Bourbons?' Savage frowned. 'I prefer Bourbons, if you have any?'

'Sorry, sir, we only have digestives at present.' The canteen lady tried to flatten her sarcastic tone and made a poor job of it.

'And this is white sugar, I think?' Savage picked up a sachet and held it up for her inspection.

'Yes, sir. Would you prefer molasses, demerara or–'

'Demerara would be absolutely top billing, thank you.'

Moran and Charlie watched agog as Savage turned his attention to the milk. 'Fresh? I do hope so.'

'UHT, sir.'

'Oh dear. That won't do.'

'Shall I call Harrods for you, sir? I'm sure they'd be happy to fulfil your order.'

'Harrods? Dear me, no. That would represent *far* too much of an imposition on my part.'

'It's all fine, thanks.' Charlie stepped in to end the exchange. The canteen lady departed, muttering, and, with a pout of disappointment, Savage reached out and helped himself to a digestive.

'I like a little chocolate in the morning. It helps me focus. The Incas knew about chocolate,' he said earnestly, 'a short, sharp energy boost. Helped with their hunting.'

Moran's head was spinning. 'Mr Savage, I have a busy morning ahead. Can I suggest that you spend some time familiarising yourself with the Laura Witney case, and then perhaps book appointments to speak with each of my team in turn?'

Savage had poured himself a coffee and was now stirring it suspiciously with the wooden stirrer provided. 'Hm, yes. That would be a sensible, if rather lengthy way of gathering data. I prefer to take a faster route, if at all possible. As you are the man at the top, a reasonable assumption would be that you have all the necessary information stored in your head. One briefing is all that should be necessary, just to see where you are as of...' he glanced at his watch. 'Nine fifty-three, Wednesday the twelfth of June. I'm assuming, naturally, that you keep abreast of hourly developments regarding your team's activities. Interviews, phone calls, POI statements and so on?'

'Of course.' Moran shrugged. 'But I'll need to run this past our Crime Investigations Manager before I share any information.'

'All taken care of.' Savage raised his forefinger. 'We had a lengthy conversation only last evening. Canadian fellow, I believe. We got on rather well.'

'Did you? Did you indeed?'

Charlie was biting her lip in a not-entirely-successful attempt to repress a smile. 'I'll leave you two to have a chat, shall I? I'll be outside, guv. If you need me.'

'I might well.' Moran assumed a look of mock helplessness. 'Just don't leave the building.'

Moran escaped after forty minutes and went to find Charlie.

'Ah. Guv. How was it?' Charlie wore a look Moran interpreted as concerned optimism. 'How was Val, specifically, I mean?'

'Let's take a wee walk, shall we?' Moran guided her away from Bola's workstation towards the lifts. They went down to the ground floor and found a quiet spot in the visitors' reception area.

Moran drew himself a cup of water from the cooler, and they sat down. 'He's bright, no doubt about that. But a little … how can I best put this?'

'Eccentric?'

'Yes, that, for sure. But there's something else too.'

'I know he's a little … unusual, guv, but his track

record is pretty good.'

'He's been telling me all about it. The London strangler. The Canterbury serial, the Braintree insurance fraud.'

'And more besides,' Charlie said. 'His profiles are always accurate. His references are excellent.'

'I'm sure. I just wonder if I can actually work with him without killing him.'

'Give him an office, he'll beaver away on his own. When he has something to share, he can attend briefings. That's how they've managed him before. It seems to work.'

'A 50-50 split of his time between your case and mine?'

'If you're agreeable.'

'Well, you've already tapped up Herbinson.' Moran narrowed his eyes.

'Yes,' Charlie said. 'And, as Val says, he seemed more than amenable to the idea.'

'I see.' Moran nodded. 'So it was just a case of sweet-talking old Brendan round?'

Charlie winced. 'Well, I wouldn't put it *quite* like that, guv…'

'Would you not, DI Pepper?' Moran mock-growled. He took a swig from his cup. 'Well, I suppose I can give him a try.'

'That's great, guv.'

'This wouldn't be anything to do with budget, this job share scheme of yours?'

'Well … I suppose…'

'It's fine, Charlie.' Moran let her off his hook with a grin. 'We could both use a little assistance, for sure. I'll let our Canadian friend worry about the pounds, shillings and pence.'

Chapter Fourteen

Feb 8th

Dear diary ... can't believe I'm actually still writing every day. Bet in a year or so I'll have given up! So ... today. Usual stuff at work. Nick was a bit moody. Think his girlfriend's been giving him a hard time about his hours. Can't blame her I s'pose, but it is his job ...

Pub this eve − the Green Door. Charles arrived with new haircut - he's nearly bald! So had the p taken out of him all evening - not that he minded much − he is Mr thick skin. Rita showed up with Isabel. Both moody cows. Rita was act. OK later, but Isabel still grumpy. Maybe they fell out, who knows with those two? ... Had two Babychams and two Chivas Regal. Last one was a bad idea. V squiffy on way home but C propped me up. Didn't take advantage tho' bless him. Have tkn 2 anadin + drunk a pint of water so will prob pee all night. Bfn...

Isabel. The Wing Co.'s daughter. He glanced at the

clock; it was later than he thought. The phone rang. He heaved himself up from his armchair and answered the call.

'Moran.'

'Guv? Just a quick one.'

'Go on, DC Collingworth.'

'I've tracked down one of Laura's buddies – Charles Summers? He lives out near Maidenhead, place called Waltham-St-Laurence.'

'I know it.'

'Want me to pop over with DC Odunsi tomorrow, guv?'

'I think I'll take this one, if you don't mind, DC Collingworth.'

Collingworth's tone signalled his disappointment. 'Oh. OK, guv.'

'Keep going with the tracing – you're doing a great job. Summers could be a key POI.'

Collingworth brightened. 'Sure thing, guv. Will do.'

Moran replaced the receiver, went through to the lounge. He rarely ended a day with good news, but today was, apparently, a happy exception. Summers had been a close friend of Laura's – although not as close as he would have liked, by the sound of it. Hopefully he would be able to fill in gaps, or, even better, add some hitherto unrecorded snippet of information that might point the investigation in a new, more fruitful, direction.

And then there was Savage. Would he come up with anything useful? Moran doubted it. He smiled as he remembered Charlie's small subterfuge. She was struggling, that much he had gathered, but she was dealing with a clever adversary, and Moran wasn't sure that he'd have been much further forward than she was in the hunt for Chan. Maybe Savage would roll the die in her favour – and, for that matter, his. For all his peculiarities, Moran was content to give the guy a chance.

He went back to the diary, but found his mind wandering. The evening was warm and sultry, his back door open onto his modest wilderness of garden to allow the air to circulate. Somewhere in the distance the buzz of an electric lawn mower rose and fell, disturbing the stillness like an atonal orchestra tuning up in an empty auditorium. The Met Office was predicting higher temperatures over the coming days – the classic summer heatwave. Archie was lying in a shady spot by the door at full stretch, eyes closed, doing his best to keep cool. Moran went into the kitchen, doused a tea towel in cold water and draped it across the slumbering spaniel's body. *There you go, boy. That'll make you feel better.*

He returned to the kitchen to fix himself a drink. Too warm for red wine tonight; he poured himself an apple juice, dropped a few chunks of ice in the glass for good measure. A cold beer later, perhaps. He went back through to the lounge and sat down. Should he call Alice? Or would it be best to wait until she called him? If Collier had returned early, she would have told him, surely? So all was probably well – for now. He was still in two minds as to how to deal with Collier; he could make a few calls, get uniform to keep an eye – or he could deal with it himself.

No ... bad idea. Too personal.

Not that it was *personal,* not yet. But…

Enough. Moran picked up Laura's diary, turned to the next entry.

Feb 9th

Woke up with headache, sore throat. bldy flu bug has finally caught me. Great – NOT. Lunch was busier than usual – some dignitaries in from London. Nick chuffed as he got loads of complements for his lamb-in-hay. Felt pretty rubbish all day. R was in a good mood for a change - quite chatty. Who knows why? Didn't bother to ask, couldn't be a'd. Lynn coming out of herself a bit – she actually spoke to me today. I s'pose after what happened she's every right to be mis. Life is horrible to some people. Think I'm running a temp now so going to sleep with hot water bottle and double paracetamol. I can hear the Dragon bawling someone out – probably R trying to smuggle a bloke in, knowing her.

I hate being ill…

And it's been raining all day.

Nite dear diary. X

'Good night, Laura.' Moran shut the small dog-eared book, laid it gently on the side table. The lawnmower had fallen silent at last, and the atmosphere felt heavy and oppressive. He needed air, a relaxing stroll in the dusk.

He prodded Archie gently with his toe.

'Come on, boy. Let's go and see how the moorhens are coping in the heat. You can join them in the river for a bit.'

Moran knew Waltham-St-Lawrence from years before, when he'd visited a pub called The Bell with a group of colleagues from Thames Valley HQ, back in his early days in Reading. The memory of his fiancée's sudden death at the hands of terrorists had still been raw, a bleeding wound. He'd tried to join in with the jokes, the banter over the beers, but his face must have given him away. A young WPC had watched him carefully, studying his reaction to the ongoing *craic*. Before he knew it she'd taken him aside, led him into the small garden at the rear of the pub, sat him down, and taken his hand in hers. 'Now, Brendan.' She'd looked him steadily in the eye. 'You can't live your life unhappy. You have to look at the years ahead, not what's behind. You have to choose life, not death – don't look back in sorrow, look *ahead*. You'll never forget her, I know, and that's only right. But she wouldn't want to think of you as unhappy, that's for sure.'

He'd never forgotten the young girl's words. He remembered her soft Midlands accent, the sincerity in her manner, the reassuring squeeze of her cool, dry hand. Amanda, that was her name. He smiled at the recollection. She'd moved on shortly after that evening, and he'd heard through the grapevine that she'd left the force, got married, moved to France to start a new life and family.

Moran was no more superstitious than the next Irishman, but he'd occasionally found himself wondering if Amanda had been some kind of angel, sent to rescue him from despondency and propel him into a more hopeful future. In many ways she'd succeeded. Sure, life would never be the same without Janice, but he'd begun to find a way through, immersing himself in work, making new friends, trying to keep positive. He remembered Amanda fondly now as he passed The Bell and turned right into Halls Lane.

Number twenty, number twenty-three … *Ah*, here. Moran brought the car to a stop.

Right, Mr Summers. Let's see what you have to say for yourself.

Chapter Fifteen

The house was a detached new build, the front garden a work-in-progress. Five or six bedrooms, Moran estimated, as he approached the front door. At least. A Mercedes Estate was parked in the drive, alongside a powerful-looking motorcycle, one of the newly-produced Triumphs – a Bonneville, he remembered the model. A classic in its day. *Very nice too, if that's your thing.*

The front door opened before he reached it. A woman in her sixties wearing a patterned Laura Ashley dress and carrying a Waitrose shopping bag started as she saw him.

'I'm sorry if I startled you,' Moran apologised. 'I'm looking for Charles Summers?'

'Charles? He's in the garden. And you are?'

Moran showed his warrant card.

'Oh dear. What *can* he have done?'

Mrs Summers' voice was cool and refined, no doubt a product of some exorbitantly expensive private girls' school.

'It's a routine call, nothing to be alarmed about. I just

need to ask your husband a few questions.'

'By all means. You don't need me, do you? I'm off to the supermarket.'

'Not unless you were around RAF Brockford in 1981, or thereabouts,' Moran said.

Mrs Summers shook her head. She was slim and attractive, wore her highlighted hair just touching her shoulders. The gold bracelets on her wrist jangled as she rummaged in her handbag. 'I wasn't, I'm afraid. Now where *have* I put the car keys?' She looked up. 'I didn't meet Charles until the late eighties, but I think I know why you've come. I saw it on the news. Laura ... what was her name?'

'Witney.'

'Yes, the poor girl who was murdered.' She paused in thought. 'I doubt whether Charles can tell you much. They interviewed him several times back in the day, and everything he knew was taken note of.'

'Yes indeed, but you never know,' Moran said. 'Memories don't always play tricks – sometimes they can be refined by the passing of time.'

'Well, good luck with that. Charles can't remember what happened last week, let alone forty odd years ago.' She waved her hand. 'Just pop through the side gate, there – you'll see him. Now if you'll excuse me?' Mrs Summers fanned her face. 'I simply *must* get the aircon going. I'm expiring standing here.'

Tradesman's entrance, Moran thought, as Mrs Summers unlocked the Mercedes and revved the engine.

Ah well, at least you know your place, Brendan.

The Mercedes pulled away in a scattering of gravel and Moran went through the gate as instructed. A tall, thin man was listlessly watering a flower bed with idle flicks of a long, green hosepipe. As Moran approached he looked up. The face was lightly tanned, handsome even, but lines around the eyes and mouth gave away his sexagenarian status.

'Hullo.' Summers' eyes were alert and enquiring, curious rather than defensive. 'And who might you be?'

Moran's warrant card came out a second time.

'Ah,' Summers nodded knowingly. 'This'll be either be something to do with my ongoing parking ticket battle, or something a little further back in time – 1981, perhaps?' He let the hose drop to the browning lawn where it lay, water pulsing from its spout like a severed artery. 'But I somehow doubt my parking fine is important enough to drag a Detective Chief Inspector out to the sticks, so it must be the latter – Laura, yes?'

Moran noted that he spoke her name with affection, and not a little sadness.

'Yes, quite right. Just a few questions, if you don't mind. A recap, I should imagine, after all those interviews back in the day.'

'I was only too happy to help,' Summers said. 'Laura was a lovely girl. The one that got away, for me. I think of her often. But look – let's have a sit down in the conservatory. More comfortable out of this heat. Can I fetch you a drink?'

'Just a glass of water, if I may?'

'Of course.'

Moran followed Summers around the building to a second lawn, landscaped to accommodate two long rose beds and delimited by a distant clump of laurel. A rockery lay snugly beneath the waxy leaves, and beyond this, he was able to make out an orchard of fruit trees. The gardens smelt pungently fragrant; the scent of the roses mingling with a rich, earthy aroma reminded Moran of a decade-old trip to Kew Gardens. He speculated briefly how much the land, never mind the house, might be worth.

Well out of your salary band, Brendan, that much is certain…

Summers ushered him into a wide glass conservatory and invited him to take a seat on one of the tastefully-patterned cane chairs.

'Make yourself comfortable. I won't be a minute.'

Moran did so and Summers reappeared presently with a jug of iced water and two glasses balanced on an ornamental tray that perfectly complemented the style of the chairs. Mrs Summers was evidently hot on her interior decor and design. He wondered if her husband's jurisdiction was confined to the sprawling outdoors.

'So, Chief Inspector, what can I tell you that I haven't already told your colleagues of yore a thousand times?'

Moran sipped his water, set his glass down. 'Let's begin with your relationship with Laura.'

A self-reproaching half-grin crept across Summers'

face. 'Well, there wasn't one, that's the truth. She was a friend. I liked her, and it's on record that I'd have liked to know her a lot better.'

'You fancied her.'

'Yes. I did.'

Summer's eyes were bright and alert. He didn't look like a man with anything to hide, but maybe he was just very good at the fine art of dissembling.

'And you socialised with her? Pub, parties, that kind of thing?'

'Yes. There was a group. We were all around the same age – most of us belonged to Brockford in some capacity. But there were one or two others. Friends of friends, you know, normal stuff.'

'So you knew Rita Dempster?'

Summers raised his eyes to heaven. 'Yes. She was a one.'

'Meaning?'

'Flirty, you know. She'd try it on with anyone, especially after a few drinks.'

'Including yourself?'

'Not my type.' Summers made a face.

'With local lads, then?'

'Rita? No way. She wouldn't have been interested. She was more ambitious than to settle for some spotty local.'

'Oh yes?' Moran sensed an underlying, unspoken, implication.

Summers wiped his brow. 'It's jolly hot in here, even with the door open. Shall I get a fan going? We've got a couple of big jobs on stands somewhere.'

'I'm fine, really.' Moran waved the offer aside. 'You were saying?'

'Rita? Yes, well, there was a rumour about her and a senior officer. I have no idea if it was well-founded, or–'

'Which senior officer?'

Summers hesitated, but only for a moment. 'I believe it was Wing Commander Akkerman.'

'Akkerman? Laura's babysitting host?'

'Yes.'

'I don't remember any mention of this in your interview notes.'

'No? I'm sure I must have referred to it, but–' Summers shrugged. 'It's a long time ago. Maybe I didn't.'

'No matter, you've told me now. So, this rumour. Was it widespread? Common knowledge?'

'Hard to say. I heard it, so others probably did too. Look, I'm going to set up one of these contraptions. You'll feel the benefit.' Summers sprang out of his chair, moving surprisingly quickly for a man of his age. A minute or two later he came back carrying a large fan on a tall stand. 'Here we are.' He bent, plugged it in and the blades whirred into life. Moran felt his hair ruffled by the moving air.

'That's better.' Summers took his seat.

'Rita and Laura weren't exactly best buddies,' Moran pressed on, 'or so my notes tell me.'

'No,' Summers agreed. 'But Rita rubbed everyone up the wrong way. Especially Isabel.' Summers smiled at the memory.

'Isabel – the Wing Co.'s daughter.'

'Yes. She was a strange one, right enough.'

Moran remembered Laura's diary entry. 'Can you tell me what exactly was strange?'

'Well, she wasn't one of us, really, I mean in the sense that she wasn't in the Service. She was only around because Akkerman was her father. Well, sort of.'

Moran frowned. 'What do you mean, sort of?'

Summers cocked his head to one side. 'I assumed you knew all this. Isabel wasn't his flesh and blood – she was adopted.'

Moran took a mental step back. 'Adopted?'

The ice in Summer's glass clinked as he took a sip. 'Yep. Common knowledge, because of the way she looked.'

'And how was that?'

'Well,' Summers shrugged. 'She was clearly from another part of the world. I didn't know the back story, and thought it best not to ask.'

'I see. And was Isabel around on that particular evening? When you and Laura met in the mess, before the squadron do?'

'No. At least, I didn't see her.'

'Did you own a car at the time, Mr Summers?'

'A car? No. I was more interested in flying than driving. Besides, I wasn't earning enough to pay the running costs, let alone buy one.'

'And did Rita own a car, d'you happen to remember?'

'I think she had some old banger. I can't remember the make.'

'So *she* could afford transport?'

'Well, I wasn't privy to her financial circumstances. Maybe her parents bought her a jalopy.'

Moran made a note. 'And Laura's colleagues? Can you tell me anything about them?'

Summers scratched his chin, fixed his eyes on a point somewhere beyond Moran's shoulder as he gathered his thoughts. He reminded Moran of the actor Bill Nighy. Maybe the physique and the hair, or the accent...

'There was the chef – nice fellow, Nick something. He was always either too busy or too knackered to socialise much. There was a Linda, or Lynn? A Margaret ... it's all so long ago. I can't remember much about them.'

'But you remember Laura.'

Summers paused, shook his head sadly. 'Yes. She was a lovely girl. Very chatty. Kind. It was desperately tragic what happened to her.'

'Do you remember seeing any vehicles outside Laura's lodgings that evening? Or anyone hanging around?'

'No, there were one or two cars parked, but I believe they were still in situ the next day.'

'Two, precisely,' Moran said. 'We have their registrations on record and we're satisfied they weren't involved.'

'It was raining, I remember that clearly,' Summers said. 'I said to Laura we should wait in her barracks, but she was worried about being caught with a man – there was some battleaxe in charge of the WRAF accommodation and she didn't want to be pigeon-holed as promiscuous, I suppose. She insisted she'd be all right, and virtually ordered me back to the mess. How many times have I wished that I'd stayed with her?' He shook his head again. 'I still dream about it, from time to time. Guilt, I suppose.'

'Even if you *had* stayed, there's no guarantee that things would have turned out any different,' Moran said. 'Whatever happened next may not have involved the driver. We can't be sure.'

'So many unknowns, eh? Listen, are you *any* further forward in all this? I mean, it's been forty years. Is there a realistic possibility you'll find out who did it?'

Moran looked Summers squarely in the eye. 'Oh, yes. We'll find out, all right. It's just a matter of time.'

Summers looked both surprised and impressed. 'Well, I'm encouraged to hear that, Chief Inspector. You will keep me in touch, won't you?'

Moran finished his water. 'You can be sure of that, sir. Oh, by the way, when did you leave the RAF?'

'1991. By then I'd flown every helicopter known to man. After Sea Kings and the Falklands, I'd had enough. Lucky to survive that – some didn't. So, I needed a change. Went into consultancy work.'

'You're retired now.'

'I am. The garden is my main project. Anna does everything else.'

'That sounds like a good arrangement.' Moran smiled

as he stood up.

'It works for us.' Summers held out his hand. 'Good luck with the investigation.'

Moran shook the proffered hand. 'It's not about luck, Mr Summers,' he said. 'It's about the detail.'

Moran was conscious of Summer's lithe figure framed in the garden gateway as he drove off, hand raised in half-salute. The guy seemed genuine enough.

Early days, though, Brendan…

His phone beeped; he answered it on hands-free. George McConnell's voice almost jumped from the speakers, interrupting his greeting.

'Guv? I think I might have a wee problem.'

Chapter Sixteen

'Well?' Tess' hands were on her hips. 'What did he say?'

'He said,' George replied evenly, 'that he'd let Charlie know straight away and not to panic.'

Tess' eyes widened. 'Not *panic*? *She*'s been *here*, in my parents' house, for God's sake, and you tell me not to panic?'

'It's probably a coincidence. She targets your parents' age group. That's how she operates. But we're wise to her now. We know, so it's OK.'

'It's *not* OK! And how can it be a *coincidence*?' Tess was standing by the window of her parents' lounge, looking out. Her mother was in the kitchen, preparing food, keeping out of the way.

Her father was standing in the doorway between them, hovering indecisively. 'I told you I shouldn't have said anything,' he muttered. 'Didn't I, love?' he called over his shoulder into the kitchen where the clattering of cooking implements threatened to drown his words.

Tess turned to face George. 'She knows where they

live, George. She's been here. In this actual room.' Tess stabbed a finger at the carpet.

'Look,' Mr Martin stepped in. 'She seemed perfectly reasonable. I'm sure she didn't mean any harm–'

'Dad – you have no idea.' Tess clapped a hand to her head. 'This is my worst nightmare.' She began to pace the room, gnawing a fingernail. 'The question is, George, why here? How did she know? How did she find out? Unless–' She stopped pacing, looked straight at him. 'She followed you. Oh hell, she *followed* you here.'

'I didn't see–'

'But you weren't looking. Why would you?' She sighed, rolled her eyes.

Mr Martin stretched out his arm towards her, waggled his hand. 'Look, Tess, don't upset yourself. You've been through enough–'

'Dad, this woman is a killer. That's what she does.' Tess gave George a look, challenging him to contradict her.

George felt a rush of helplessness. Everything had been going so well, and now…

'So,' Tess went on before he could reply. 'How do we find her? You've got Charlie's number?'

'I have her email address, if we need it.'

'Well, she's going to want chapter and verse on Chan's visit, that's for sure. And I need to decide what to do with my parents.'

'Excuse me. I *am* here, you know.' Mrs Martin wheeled herself into the lounge. 'And I'll tell you something for nothing: I'm not about to be ousted from my own home –

not by some confidence trickster, nor anyone else for that matter. I'm staying put, and that's that.'

'Mum–' Tess dropped her hands to her side. She appealed to George. 'Tell her, George.' She folded her arms, presented her back and looked out at the street through the big picture window.

'It's a serious matter, Mrs Martin. I think it would be better if we could move you to a more secure–'

Mrs Martin had manoeuvred her wheelchair into the centre of the lounge. 'Are you listening to me, young man? Policeman or not, I'll not be told what to do in my own home. We're staying put, and that's that. If Miss Chandra returns, well, we'll deal with that eventuality when it happens. Now, would anyone like a bite to eat?'

Tess made a gesture of futility. 'All right, Mum, have it your way. But I'm going to make sure there's a watch on the house, twenty-four seven.' She looked pointedly at George.

'Good,' Mrs Martin declared. 'That's that settled. Now, things always look better on a full stomach, don't they? So come along, young George, come and sit down and have some lunch.'

'Not before we've contacted DI Pepper, mum. She needs to know about this.'

George took his cue. 'I'll drop her an email. She'll have spoken to the guv by now.' He went upstairs, his mind racing, working through possible scenarios.

Tess was right. It was his fault. He'd been careless. He'd dropped his guard. He'd delivered Tess' parents to

Chan on a plate. That figure he'd seen on their walk, in the distance, in the trees – she'd been watching them. Thank God she hadn't done any damage. Yet. He grabbed his laptop and switched it on, tapped his fingers impatiently as he waited for it to boot up.

Come on, come on... It wasn't normally this slow.

She could have killed them both...

His virtual desktop appeared.

... and then where would he be with Tess?

He wiped beads of sweat from his forehead, clicked the email icon.

...and what's this going to do to her recovery?

Ye gods, what a mess.

George scanned his new messages. Quite a few; looked like they'd made some progress on the Laura Witney case. He'd have to read up on it before the end of the week, get up to speed.

Don't digress, McConnell...

The sound of heated conversation floated up from downstairs.

What to say to Charlie? He didn't have much intel. Chan came, she spoke to Mr and Mrs Martin, she left brochures ... and that was it. But why?

Just tell it as it is, George...

His finger swiped the trackpad.

Compose New Message...

Connie Chan raised her head as her laptop beeped an alert. She left what she was doing and returned to the bedroom. Her hands were a little sticky so she wiped them briefly with a tissue before turning her attention to the message.

User online

She opened the app, watched with satisfaction as the words appeared on her screen as they were written. She nodded with satisfaction as the email message took shape. McConnell and the female police officer now knew she'd been in the Martin house; it was only a matter of time before DI Pepper arrived on the scene, and in due course she knew the Irishman would follow suit. He wouldn't be able to keep away.

She turned her attention to the other messages in McConnell's inbox. There was a great deal of traffic regarding their current case, the Laura Witney murder. Chan sipped water from a paper cup as she read. She was hungry – hard physical work always made her hungry. But food could wait. This was more important.

Her eyes continued to scan the emails. This one looked interesting. From the bitch, DI Pepper to DCI Moran, cc'd to the team, dated yesterday:

Hello guv

Had a go at the Malaysian authorities again as suggested – this time they were slightly more helpful. They dug out a photo of the aunt. Prob taken around the late Sixties, before she left the country. Anyways, photo attached fyi. They also told me her father was South

Korean, the mother Malaysian.

Thanks for agreeing to take Val on btw – I think he'll be good for us both.

Kind regards, Charlie.

Chan clicked on the attachment, gasped, felt her insides turn over. She stared at the photograph. It had clearly been taken under duress. The background was a grainy, a high-ceilinged room, perhaps some state lockup, or sanatorium. The subject herself, unsmiling and obviously unhappy, was a girl in her early teens. Her mouth was clamped shut in defiance, her eyes dark with repressed anger. Chan reached out involuntarily, touched the screen. She had never seen a photograph of her before, never...

She stroked the stern face with the back of her hand.

Iseul ... auntie...

Chapter Seventeen

DC Bernice Swinhoe paused at the door of the tatty terraced house. Her search for one of Laura's ex-colleagues, Lynn Stamford, had eventually led her here after a frustrating series of dead ends. She'd finally tracked Stamford down via an ex-neighbour at her previous residence – a bedsit in Jesse Terrace – who remembered that Stamford had mentioned a road name, Argyll Street, before she'd moved a year ago. After checking with the council, they'd given Bernice the house number.

Bernice knocked, waited. A pair of youths passed by on the other side of the street. One of them whistled and winked. His mate, embarrassed, nudged him in the ribs, but this only encouraged a louder reprise. Bernice glared. They walked away, the whistler making a parting rude gesture just before they disappeared round the corner.

No damn respect…

Bernice fumed. The door behind her opened. 'Yes?'

She turned. 'Ms Stamford?'

'Yes.'

Bernice showed her warrant card. 'May I come in? I have a few questions regarding Laura Witney.'

'Not again.'

'I'm afraid so. We need to—'

'I know. I saw it on the telly. You'd better come in.'

Stamford led her into a small front room. It was plain, tidy, but characterless. Stamford sat down and indicated that Bernice do the same.

Bernice could see that Stamford was ill. Her face was grey, as was her thinning hair. Her clothes were functional, dowdy. This was the woman Laura had spoken of in her diaries, whose fiancé had been killed in some freak accident. A sad, bitter young girl, as the 1981 case notes had recorded. It didn't look as though her life had got any better in the intervening years.

Bernice cleared her throat. 'You said in your original statement that you were working on the night Laura was abducted?'

'I was.'

'Did you leave the kitchens at any point that evening?'

'I didn't, no. There were only two of us on prep that evening. Me and Margaret. Everyone else was at the party – even Nick, although he *was* with us till around seven, giving us instructions, you know, about what he needed done.'

'And you'd spoken to Laura earlier that day.'

'Yes, a little. She seemed fine. It was her birthday coming up, and she was thinking about what to do.'

'Socially, you mean?'

'Yes. Whether to have a pub evening out with everyone, or whether to go home to see her folks.'

'And how did you get along with Laura?'

'She was nice. Not like one or two others I could mention.'

'Please, do mention them.'

'Well, there was that Rita. She was a bit of a cow.'

'Rita Dempster?'

'I think so. I forget, it's a long time ago.'

'Yes – oh, are you all right?'

Stamford had sat back in her chair and closed her eyes. A tremor ran through her arms, and she gripped her knees involuntarily. After a moment she opened her eyes. 'I'm sorry. It happens more frequently, now.'

'Shall I call a doctor?' Bernice was concerned at Stamford's frail appearance. Her skin was the colour of chalk.

Stamford waved dismissively. 'It's all right. My sister's coming down at the end of the week to keep an eye on me. It's motor neurone disease, love. There's no cure.'

'I'm so sorry. Can I get you anything?'

'No. I'm all right, thank you. So, there was Rita, and Nick, and Margaret, and Laura. And in our wider circle there were, of course, some lads from the squadrons – mechanics and pilots – and others, casual acquaintances we met in the pub, or at parties, you know.'

'Do you remember someone called Isobel, or Isabel?'

Stamford made a face. 'Oh God, her. Yes, I do. The

Wing Co.'s daughter. Her and Rita were a right pair, used to feed off each other.'

'In what way?'

'Well, they were sarky, you know. Used to take the mick. I'm sure Rita got alongside her just to curry favour with the officers and bigwigs.'

'Like the Wing Co?'

Stamford nodded. 'There was a rumour that Rita was carrying on a bit. That's when she fell out – or seemed to – with Isabel.'

'Do you think the rumours had any substance?'

'Maybe. But then when Laura was … when we heard what had happened to Laura, it just changed everything. Everything else just seemed trivial, you know? We couldn't believe it. It hit me so hard – I'd already lost Jim the year before, and Laura was a friend I could talk to. Then she was gone, just like that. The place was never the same. Margaret left after a few weeks, then Nick. There was such a dark cloud over the place. I couldn't bear it. None of us could.'

'It must have been a terrible shock.'

'It was. And her poor parents. Can you imagine?'

'Lynn – may I call you that? Did you ever see Isabel again socially after Laura's death?'

'Not at that time, no. But I bumped into her years later in the town centre. She recognised me, made a bee line. She was handing out leaflets, tracts, whatever you call them, about some new-age community she'd joined, and you know what those types are like, always wanting to recruit you.'

'She'd joined a cult?'

'Whatever you want to call it, yes, I suppose.'

'Do you recall the name?'

Stamford took a deep breath and let the air out in a long sigh. 'No ... but I'm a bit of a hoarder, love. I keep all my old correspondence, tons of paper I'll probably never need again. I'll have a look, if you like; you might be lucky. But it'll take a while to root through it all.'

'If you find it, you'll let me know?'

'Glad to be of assistance. Paper shuffling is about all I'm good for nowadays, anyhow.'

Bernice thanked Stamford for her time. She considered briefly whether she should offer to help, but Stamford had appeared animated at the prospect of putting her mind to something useful and Bernice suspected that such therapy would be more effective if she left her to it.

Chapter Eighteen

The Incident Room whiteboard was filling up. Laura was in central position, the photo taken outside her barracks – the Dragon's lair, as Moran now thought of it – and marker pen lines radiated to photographs of Charles Summers, Rita Dempster, Lynn Stamford, Air Commodore Akkerman. There was also a placeholder for Isabel, Akkerman's daughter, in the absence of any photographs. Moran finished his new annotations and turned to face the assembled team.

'Good evening, all. First things first, I'd like to formally introduce you to Mr Valentine Savage, who has kindly agreed to offer us his expertise.'

All heads turned to look at the newcomer, who blinked and frowned under the scrutiny of so many eyes. He reddened slightly and bobbed his head in acknowledgement.

'Mr Savage has a strong track record in offender profiling, and, if he hasn't done so already, he'll be spending time with each of you. I'd be grateful if you'd give him all the assistance he requires.'

John Herbinson was lounging in his usual position by the door, watching the team's reaction. Moran caught his eye, but the gears of the Canadian's expression were set to neutral. Whatever his thoughts concerning Savage, he was keeping them to himself.

Moran waited for the team to settle. George's phone call was still at the forefront of his mind. He wanted to speak to Charlie again, find out what she'd decided to do about George's revelation, but his priority in this meeting was Laura. He tucked Charlie's problem to the back of his mind, cleared his throat and went on.

'Let's have a quick turn around the room – I'll go first. I caught up with Charles Summers today. Seemed steady enough. He answered my questions honestly, and one main fact came out that we didn't already know – Akkerman's daughter is fostered. She's an adopted child, not their own.'

A ripple of reaction spread across the room. There were one or two quiet asides to colleagues.

Moran held up his hand for silence. 'That may or may not be significant – we'll know more when we've found the woman and spoken to her directly. One other item of potential importance – Summers thought that Rita Dempster might have owned a car. So, however accommodating she might have been on my last visit, she neglected to mention it. I'll be popping over to find out more tomorrow. That's it from me. DC Swinhoe – do you have an update for us?'

'Yes, guv. I've spoken to Lynn Stamford. She's ill, and there's nothing much she can add to her original statements. But here's the thing. She mentioned the Air Commodore's daughter – *adopted* daughter, Isabel. Apparently she ran into to her – this was years after Brockford – and she remembered that Isabel gave her some kind of handout, some cult pamphlet. She's trying to find it for me – says she's a hoarder, so she'll have it somewhere. It may take her a while – like I said, she's a very sick woman, but she seemed to want to help. I'll call this evening to see if she's had any joy. Anyway, she also confirmed that Isabel and Rita Dempster had some kind of falling out.' Bernice shrugged. 'Seems like Rita was one awkward person to get along with.'

'Indeed. OK, thanks, DC Swinhoe. That sounds very useful. Bola, DC Collingworth?'

Chris Collingworth spoke up. 'So we've been trying to track down Akkerman's son – so far no joy, but the US is a big place. He could be using any name, so we've hardly got anything to go on. Akkerman said it might have been Philadelphia, but he wasn't sure.'

'It may be a low-value exercise, DC Collingworth. As we've already discussed, the son was only a baby at the time, so he'll hardly be able to tell us much about the days in question. If we can find him, sure we'll have a chat, but don't bust a gut over him.'

Bola had his hand up. 'I still think it's weird that Akkerman was so vague, guv. Surely he'd know more about his own family? Even if they were a bit dysfunctional – I mean, the wife had mental health issues and all, but you'd think the guy would take more of an interest in what his kids are doing with their lives.'

Moran agreed. 'You would indeed, DC Odunsi. So if the son is a dead end, the daughter's whereabouts may be more accessible – provided Lynn Stamford is able to give us a lead. Isabel ought to be able to shed some light on the family dynamic. And there's also the rumour that Rita Dempster and the then Wing Co. had a little ... how shall I put it ... history.'

'The potential revelation of sexual indiscretions are always a powerful motivation for aggression – I mean, where there may have been little or no aggressive characteristics in evidence beforehand.'

All heads turned once again to Valentine Savage.

Moran nodded. 'Thank you, Mr Savage. If I'm understanding you correctly, you're suggesting that, were the rumours to be confirmed, we should consider the possibility that Laura Witney somehow found out about this liaison, and that persons unknown took action to silence her?'

'Precisely.' Valentine Savage slid his glasses up the bridge of his nose with a practised flourish.

'That would be either Akkerman himself, or Rita Dempster, I'd say,' Chris Collingworth said.

'Quite possibly,' Moran concurred. 'It's a clear motive, at any rate. I'll be sure to mention it tomorrow when I speak to Dempster. And I suggest you dig a little deeper with our Air Commodore, too.'

'Will do, guv.'

Moran gestured to Herbinson. 'Any luck with the appeal, Mr Herbinson?'

'Negative. One or two crank calls. Nothing of any value. Ball's still in your court, Chief Inspector.'

'We're making progress, Mr Herbinson. It's early days.'

Herbinson's response was to reply to the room rather than to Moran directly. 'Early days doesn't mean that slow progress is acceptable. Time's marching on, ladies and gents,' he said in a louder voice, 'so I suggest you all march a little faster. We're the good, guys, remember? Not circus performers – at least, that's what I'm hoping. And I also trust that you're posting your updates on MS Teams, as requested? I can't overemphasise the importance of gathering our information in one place. If it's not written down, it's not done. We have to have all our ducks in a row, and it'll save *you* time in the long run. I'll be logging in to check daily, so don't skip it – we don't want anyone falling by the wayside, if you get my meaning?'

Herbinson gave them a long, hard stare before abruptly leaving the room, allowing his rhetorical question to hang in the air like an accusation.

Moran wrapped it up, a sour sensation churning in his stomach. Herbinson was beginning to get on his nerves. The Canadian's insistence on their recording every single activity and result on MS Teams had merit, he conceded, but the guy's attitude was patronising, his manner critical and his management style borderline boorish. It wasn't necessarily a cultural thing – Moran had met Canadians in the past and they'd all been friendly and, for the most part, pretty easy going. Whatever, Moran was all too aware that it was winding him up; life was difficult enough as it was without having Herbinson on his case.

Relegating Herbinson to the back of his mind, he headed for his office to speak to Charlie before calling it a day.

Chapter Nineteen

Chan was having a productive morning. She had discovered that Detective Constable McConnell was pleasingly careless with his communications, and the information she was now party to was going to prove priceless. One question had already been resolved: how to strike a devastating blow to the Irishman. Happily, McConnell's desktop WhatsApp had provided her with a number of possibilities, the front runner being some woman from a previous case with whom Moran had apparently established some kind of cautious attachment.

According to a gossipy message from one Bola Odunsi – Chan assumed he was a close colleague – Moran had recently made several personal visits to the house of a Mrs Alice Roper – visits unrelated to police work, so Odunsi had implied. McConnell had replied to say that he had formed the impression that Moran's intentions towards Mrs Roper might be interpreted as romantic, and Odunsi's reply had quoted another colleague, someone called Bernice, who had confided that Mrs Roper seemed very warm towards 'the guv'.

This was perfect. It would be a clean hit, and she would leave no trace. They would never associate the crime with her, and the Irishman would never know who was responsible for his loss.

Chan locked the laptop and sprang to her feet in a single, lithe movement. She loathed Moran and his team even more since she'd found out they'd been sniffing around in her past, exposing family secrets. *Iseul* ... her mother's estranged sister, who had been sent to England on some pretext...

Her mother had always been reluctant to speak of her absent sibling, but Chan had pieced it together. Her grandmother couldn't cope with two mentally agile offspring; her mother's IQ had been at the top of the scale, and so, Chan learned, had her sister's. There had been claims of some mental imbalance, but that was a smokescreen, Chan was sure. They'd sent Iseul away because she was precociously intelligent, difficult to manage. They'd sent her here, to this cold, inhospitable backwater.

How had she coped? Had she survived? Where was she now? These were the questions that had driven Chan to scour the UK from top to bottom in search of her estranged aunt. She was all the family Chan had left, and if Iseul was anywhere to be found, Chan was determined to find her.

The photograph had been a shock. Her mother hadn't kept a photo of her sister – at least, not as far as she knew

– but somehow Moran's police team had achieved what she, Chan, had failed to do. Now she had an image, a likeness of her missing family member. All she had to do was to imagine the weight of years on that sharply intelligent face to conjure a mental image of Iseul.

I will find you, auntie. I shall never give up…

First things first, though. She felt energised by the prospect of further action, especially as the action she had in mind promised to be highly satisfying. The intruder had reminded her that she was a little rusty, but had also whetted her appetite for more. She allowed herself a brief replay of the encounter. The man had been too slow, way too slow, and once she'd established that he was a loner who wouldn't be missed, it had been a simple matter to deal with him. He'd almost caught her by surprise – she was a little out of practice, after all – but he had turned out to be a weak adversary, whoever he was.

But Alice Roper … she would feel the full force of her vitriol. She would suffer before she died, and the Irishman's anguish would be all the more rewarding.

Moran pushed his front door open to the sound of his jangling telephone. Dropping his case and stick he made a grab for it before the caller rang off.

'Moran.'

'Oh, Brendan, I'm glad I've caught you.' Alice Roper's voice sounded tense.

'I'm just through the door. Is everything all right?' Moran's heart beat increased in tempo. Had Collier returned earlier? Was he there, even now, making threats?

'Listen. I know we rescheduled for tonight, but Peter's been playing up. I don't know what's got into him. He just hasn't settled at all today. He won't eat – and he won't watch any sport, which, as you know–'

'–is almost unheard of,' Moran interrupted. 'Is he ill, perhaps?'

'I don't think so – I don't know, really. He's not running a temperature. He seems all right physically. He's just very agitated.'

'I'm sorry to hear that,' Moran said. Part of him was relieved that Alice's state of mind had nothing to do with Mark Collier. Peter was a huge responsibility; an autistic man was bound to be difficult on occasion, surely? Moran had seen the film *Rain Man,* and although Peter's autism wasn't quite as severe as Dustin Hoffman's character, he was still likely to prove a handful from time to time. Moran searched for some words of comfort.

'Perhaps if you give Emma a call?'

'I did – she spoke to him, but it didn't make a lot of difference.'

'That is unusual.'

'So tonight, I'm afraid…'

'It's fine, Alice, please don't worry. I'm sure he'll be better tomorrow.'

'I do hope so. Let's reschedule, then – tomorrow evening, all being well?'

Moran laughed. 'Tomorrow sounds perfect. Call me if you're still worried later, won't you?'

'I will.'

'Good night, then.'

'Good night, Brendan.'

Moran replaced the receiver and bent to stroke Archie's head. The spaniel had placed a ball at his feet the moment he'd walked in, and was now looking up at him hopefully.

'It'll have to be later, boy. I should use this time to do a little work.'

He fixed himself a drink, went through to the lounge. He opened Laura's diary, removed the paperclip he was using as a bookmark, settled himself in the armchair and began to read.

Feb 11th

Still feeling crap but decided to go to work anyway. Not a good idea, as it turned out. Brain not working so burned the main course. Nick not happy but tried not to be cross cos he knew I was feeling rough. Worse thing was he asked R to salvage my mess and sent me home – well to my bedroom, anyhow. So here I am. Been in here since 3pm and feeling sorry for myself. Weather is still sh1t. Bored with reading. Bored with being ill. Hope I'll recover for birthday. Three days to go – touch and go. S'pose we could always celebrate the weekend after. I want something nice to happen. Is that too much to ask? One good thing – Lynn bought me the Dire Straits single! She knew I was ill and that I'm always humming this song! So sweet of her. Been playing it all day. Made me think of Charles. Is this a sign?

'...you can fall for chains of silver you can fall for chains of gold
You can fall for pretty strangers and the promises they hold
You promised me everything, you promised me thick and thin, yeah
Now you just say "Oh, Romeo, yeah, you know I used to have a scene with him..." '

Or maybe I'm still running a fever. Sleep now. Goodnight, dear D. x

'Goodnight, Laura.' Moran closed the diary, the by now familiar wash of melancholy washing through him, as 1981 gave way to 2021. Forty years gone, a lovely young girl's life brutally terminated. Had she been murdered to ensure her silence? And if so, by whom?

No mention in her innermost thoughts – at least so far – that she suspected Rita Dempster to have misbehaved with the Wing Commander. And even if she *had* known for sure about her colleague's upmarket dalliance, Laura didn't strike Moran as the kind of girl to go spreading malicious rumours. Quite the reverse.

Tomorrow he would revisit Rita Dempster, and this time his questions would be less agreeable. Rita was a straight talker. No point beating around the bush.

This time he would fight fire with fire.

Chapter Twenty

DC Bola Odunsi had been in the office since seven, and was feeling the pain of an unusually early alarm call. He knew there was a question mark hanging over his head and he wanted rid of it as soon as. He wanted to be seen to be keen. And he genuinely was; it was just that he wasn't a naturally early-morning person. He envied Bernice Swinhoe, who seemed to require very little sleep and who was always at her workstation before anyone else, regular as clockwork, Monday to Friday. He could see her tapping away at her keyboard out of the corner of his eye, bright as a button and fresh as a daisy.

He rubbed his eyes. More coffee required. But then, too much caffeine would only exchange his fatigue for a headache, and the last thing he wanted to deal with was another headache, because this POI trace was doing his head in as it was.

Christopher Akkerman, b. 12/06/1980. The baby of the case, now apparently emigrated to the Big Apple – according to Air Commodore Akkerman. The thing was, the guy was almost invisible. There was a birth certificate, a nursery record, but no school record – at least, not one they could find. No National Insurance number had ever been allocated, according to the Department of Work and Pensions, which in itself was odd, and there was consequently no tax record and no employment record. The invisible man? Maybe he'd changed his name?

'Morning Bols.' DC Collingworth announced his arrival with his usual swagger.

'Excuse me, that is *not* my name.'

'Yeah, but it suits ya.' Collingworth hung his jacket on the back of his chair with a practised flourish.

Bola pushed his chair back, the castors gliding over the new carpet tiles. A spark of static jumped from the chair arm to Bola's finger, and he flinched and swore under his breath. 'Are you *trying* to annoy me? Because if you are–'

'Language, please,' Collingworth said. 'There *are* ladies present.'

'Don't mind me,' Bernice Swinhoe didn't look up. 'Nothing I haven't heard before.'

'Can you make yourself useful and get me a coffee?' Bola pleaded. Five more precious minutes without Collingworth was worth having.

'Only if you say *please*.'

'Please? And when you come back, you can apply your fearsome intellect to the task of solving my little problem.'

'Oh, oh. That'll take way longer than I've got, that kind of problem.' He tried to catch Bernice's eye, but she wasn't playing.

'Two sugars.'

'OK, OK, I'm going. Anything for a quiet life.'

Collingworth sauntered off, and when he was out of earshot Bernice looked up. 'You cope with him really well, Bola.'

'You think?' Bola replied. 'I'm going to murder him one day, that's my big worry. End of promising career.'

She laughed. 'He'll be off to his sergeant's post soon, don't worry. He'll be some other team's problem.'

'God help them,' Bola muttered, and then broke into a grin.

Bernice grinned back. 'How's it going, anyway?'

'Weirdly, to be honest. I can't find any trace of this Akkerman guy past 1982.'

'The baby?'

'Yep.'

'Hm. You need to pump the Air Commodore about that. Like you said in the meeting, he seemed oddly unaware of what his kids were up to.'

'Yeah, for sure. But the guy had a load of trouble with his missus. Maybe the stress of it all broke up the family.'

'Right, but what was causing the stress? Was there something going on in the family unit that was causing her anxiety, or whatever it was she was suffering from?'

'That's my next angle,' Bola told her. 'I have the name of the hospital she was committed to. They might be able to fill in the gaps.'

'Good plan,' Bernice nodded. 'But here's your coffee.'

Collingworth reappeared with two steaming cups. 'Here you go, my man. Don't say I never do anything for you.'

'As if,' Bola said, with a covert wink in Bernice's direction. 'Stick it down on the mat, and let's get to work. Herbinson's gonna bawl us out or give us the chop if we don't come up with something soon.'

'You reckon? It'll be the guv who gets it in the neck, not us.'

'I wouldn't count on it, if I were you.'

Collingworth put the coffee down as instructed and glanced across the open plan as he did so. Valentine Savage was walking purposefully in their direction. The profiler was wearing a jacket that could be described as louder than appropriate, and sporting a crimson bow tie. 'Heads up,' Collingworth warned, 'geek approaching.'

'Great,' Bola muttered under his breath as Savage raised a hesitant hand in greeting. 'That is *all* I need.'

Rita Dempster expressed little surprise as she invited Moran into her flat a second time. 'This happened last time, too,' she told him, lighting a cigarette. 'I knew you'd be back. Is it a technique they teach you at detective training school, or what?'

'Not really,' Moran replied. 'It's only necessary when we believe someone isn't telling us the whole story. May I?' he indicated the sofa.

'Go right ahead,' Dempster said, exhaling a stream of blue smoke. 'Doesn't bother you, does it? I can vape if you'd prefer?'

'No, carry on.'

'Cheers.' She took another puff. 'So? What now?'

'Can you tell me about your relationship with Wing Commander Akkerman?'

Dempster hesitated for a second, cigarette poised between her lips and fingers. 'Wow. Haven't heard that one for a while.'

Moran nodded. 'Well? True or false?'

Dempster tapped ash into a cut-glass ashtray, shrugged. 'We had a fling, that was all. It was after a mess do. He was a little drunk, I was young and silly.' She looked up. 'He was an attractive man, an older man. I've always had a bit of a weakness for older men.'

'I see. Why didn't you mention this before?'

Dempster sniffed. 'Don't know. Bit embarrassing, I suppose.'

'Your embarrassment is a small price to pay to find out what happened to Laura Witney, wouldn't you say?' Moran raised an eyebrow.

'I suppose. If you put it like that.'

'And what did your buddy, Isabel, think of it?'

'My buddy? I hardly knew Isabel.'

'We've spoken to a few of your old colleagues; word is that you were something of a double act at parties, functions. Also that you might have had a falling out. Did she suspect that you and her father were seeing each other?'

'We weren't 'seeing each other.'' Dempster jammed her cigarette in her mouth and made inverted commas in the air with her fingers. 'It was a one-off, that was all.'

'But did Isabel find out, perhaps? The rumour machine was working overtime, or so we've been led to believe.'

'By whom? People remember things differently – especially after forty years.'

'And there's your car. Let's talk about that.'

For the first time, Dempster seemed flustered. 'My car? What do you mean?'

'You did own a car?'

Dempster stubbed her cigarette out, crushing the butt into the ashtray. 'I don't recall.'

'No? An old jalopy of some sort, so we've been told.'

'I forget. I might have, I don't remember.'

'Try harder.'

Dempster reached for her packet of cigarettes. 'Let's see. 1981. Did I have the car then, or was it the year after?' She drummed her fingers on her knee. 'I suppose I might have had it, yes. But I can't be a hundred percent sure.'

'Surely you'd remember driving it in and around Brockford?'

'My brain cells aren't what they used to be, Chief Inspector.'

'Well, what about the make and model? You say you might have owned a car the following year? Can you conjure a mental image? It was probably your first car –

and most people tend to remember their first car with some affection.'

Dempster took a new cigarette from the packet and twirled it between her fingers. She leaned back in her chair and closed her eyes. 'It was a Maxi. Red.'

'All right. Do you recall the registration number?'

'Seriously?'

Moran just looked at her, then said, 'Any letter or numbers will do.'

'I don't know.' She sighed. '4 something. Maybe D. Or E?'

Moran grunted, made a note, looked up. 'Did you give Laura a lift that night, Rita? Did you argue?'

'What? Are you kidding? Listen, I'm not answering any more questions without a solicitor.' She stood up, her face reddening. 'I didn't see Laura that evening. Like I said before. And I *certainly* didn't give her a lift. I can't believe you're accusing me of murder!'

'I'm merely trying to get to the truth, Ms Dempster.' Moran stood up. 'And I'm content to continue this discussion at the police station. Shall we say three pm? That'll give you an hour or two to secure the services of a solicitor, and to give some more thought to the details concerning your vehicle.'

Dempster went to the door, opened it, stepped aside.

'I'll see you later – don't go off anywhere in the meantime, will you?' Moran gave her a pleasant smile, and found his way out.

Chapter Twenty-One

'Hello? Is that Mrs Power?'

'It is. Who's calling?'

'My name is Detective Constable Odunsi, Thames Valley Police. I wanted to ask you a few questions concerning the nursery you ran – *Little Hedgehogs*?'

'Golly. That's a while ago. What do you want to know?'

'I wondered – do you still have a register of names from 1981?'

'Well, the archives are in my attic. I daresay I could root them out if you needed me to. But why?'

Bola explained.

Mrs Power clicked her tongue. 'The Akkerman baby – yes, I do recall. Unusual name, I suppose. That, and I seem to remember that Mrs Akkerman was rather difficult. We had a few Brockford babies – usually from the higher ranks. I'll see what I can find. But there's one thing I can tell you now.'

'Oh yes? And what's that?'

'The little chap was taken out of nursery rather abruptly. He was with us one week, and then the next, *pouf*, he was gone. We never saw him again. I remember that well because he was very friendly with another toddler, a little girl, and she was inconsolable.'

'And the Akkermans were still in residence locally? It's not as though they'd moved away?'

'No, no. I don't believe so. This would have been sometime in '82, as I recall. Brockford was still very much a going concern, and I used to see the father in the town on occasion, so the family were still there. Perhaps they decided to keep the little chap at home, for whatever reason. Like I say, the mother was a little…'

'Odd.'

'Yes. Indeed.'

'I'd be grateful if you could find the register for us, Mrs Power. Perhaps I could pop over to collect it?'

'I'll give you a ring when it's in my hand.'

'Thanks, I appreciate that.'

Bola signed off.

'Progress?' Bernice Swinhoe murmured as her fingers danced on her keyboard.

'Maybe. They took the kid out of nursery – it was sudden.'

'Back to Akkerman, then?'

'Yep. I reckon so.' Bola stood up and shrugged on his jacket.

'Shall I tell Chris to come and find you?'

'Maybe it might slip your mind?' Bola winked as he

walked past her workstation.

'OK. Got it. Have fun.'

'Always,' Bola said, making a beeline for the lift.

Collingworth emerged from the gents a minute later. Bernice smelt his aftershave approaching before the familiar voice disturbed her concentration. 'Hey, where'd Bola go?'

'Mm?' Bernice responded distractedly. 'Sorry, wasn't paying attention.'

Collingworth scanned the big room. That was strange; no sign of the big man. Canteen, maybe. Shaking his head in puzzlement, he went off to find his missing colleague.

Moran hung his coat on his office coat stand. He'd just seen Bola Odunsi hurrying off somewhere, looking purposeful. He hoped it was work-related. What was the time? Almost lunch. His stomach rumbled at the thought. Canteen, then a little preparation for Rita Dempster's interview. The phone rang.

'Moran.'

'Guv. It's Charlie.'

'Morning. What's up?'

'I'm at the Martins' house, guv. Things are getting a little … heated, shall we say.'

'Sorry to hear that. For what reason?'

'Mrs Martin is dead set against an officer *in situ*, or even keeping the house under obs. I thought we'd talked her round earlier, but she's digging her feet in – being rather awkward, I'm afraid. I mean, I get it, she wants her privacy respected, but she doesn't understand the threat.'

'Is George still there?'

'He is. It's all getting tricky – he's there for Tess, but, understandably, Tess is getting pretty wound up. George doesn't know what to do for the best.'

'It can't be good for her,' Moran said. 'She needs peace and quiet, not some stakeout bunfight going on under her nose, especially where her parents are concerned. But then, we can't be sure what our friend Chan might be planning.'

'Exactly. Guv, I wondered…'

Moran had seen it coming, but he let Charlie articulate her request anyway, prompting her with a low 'Mm?'

She sighed. 'I think your presence might be a calming influence, guv. I'm sorry to drag you into it, but the Martins remember you. I think you might be able to reason with them – the mother, especially.'

Moran was thinking about his three pm appointment with Dempster. Collingworth was on duty, and DC Swinhoe. They could handle Dempster, if he briefed them beforehand.

'As it's you,' he said. 'I'll see what I can manage, but your faith in me may well be misplaced.'

'I doubt that, guv.'

'I have some things to catch up on, but I can be with you by, say…' he looked at his watch, 'late afternoon is the best I can offer.'

'That's great. I really appreciate it, guv.'

'I can't promise to stay for long, but I'll do what I can.'

He signed off, drummed his fingers on his knee as he pondered the wisdom of what he had committed himself to. No, it was OK. Collingworth would be fine with Dempster – his interviewing skills were sound. And with Bernice Swinhoe there to balance things out, Moran was comfortable that they'd be able to handle it.

He got up, peered through his internal window. Bernice was at her workstation. No time like the present to break the happy news.

Chan's morning research had proved more fruitful than she could have hoped for. McConnell's colleagues had been diligently posting their updates on MS Teams regarding the cold case they were currently investigating, and one in particular had caught her eye. A DC Swinhoe had posted the following:

Lynn Stamford visit #1

Visited this ex-colleague of Laura's. POI unwell – Motor neurone. Confirmed Rita Dempster friendly with Isabel (then Wing. Commander Akkerman's adopted daughter). But also a falling out of some sort. POI encountered Isabel by chance some years later (unspecified year). Isabel pressed some tract re a cult onto POI, who kept the paper but has not maintained contact with Isabel. POI content to try to find the pamphlet – can't recall cult name but it may lead to whereabouts of Isabel. Action: BS to call back to POI to collect in 24hrs. Note: need to check re Isabel adoption papers. Rang POI after briefing – she thought Isabel's ethnic group might be Malaysian/Korean. (Check: Wing Co.? Which org from late fifties/sixties would keep archives?)

This was intriguing. An adoptee, born in the late fifties or sixties, origins in the Far East. And then there was the message from DI Pepper to the Irishman, the photograph of Iseul.

Isabel.

Iseul.

Chan's grip on the steering wheel tightened. Had the Irishman's team done the impossible? Had they found her long-lost relative? What were the odds?

Chan concentrated, allowed the half-remembered girlhood rumours of Iseul's instability, her mother's refusal to discuss anything regarding her sister or her fate to fill her mind...

Isabel, a POI in a murder investigation.

It *was* possible, surely?

But where had she gone to ground?

A cult.

Lynn Stamford.

The motorway traffic slowed and Chan touched the brake pedal. Junction 18, Bath. Always a little busier at this stage of the journey.

But there was plenty of time.

Time enough for two visits.

Chapter Twenty-Two

Bola Odunsi slowed as he pulled into Yattendon village. It was lunch time, so would he find the Air Commodore in the pub as before, or should he push on to the house?

Nah, let's check out the gaff...

He'd find it himself this time, without Collingworth jabbering in his ear. Bola felt more relaxed on his own, much more able to focus. Collingworth would bend his ear later, that was a given, but for now Bola was content to enjoy the moment. Talking of bending – sure, he was bending the rules a little, coming out on his own, but the POI was a septuagenarian, so what was the risk?

He took a right through Yattendon and cruised slowly along the lane. He came to a bend in the road, tickled the brake. There was a circular mirror inset into the hedgerow just on the bend on the opposite side of the road. That meant a driveway.

Sure enough, two mildewed, discoloured stone posts came into view as he took the bend. Blink and you'd miss it – as they had on their previous visit. The name of the house was partially obscured, inscribed on the nearest post. *The Willows*.

Bola turned hard left and found himself on a once-gravelled drive that was now more dirt than gravel. At the end of the gently curving track a squat, cubic house, whose sunken windows called to mind a stately home Bola had once visited on a school trip, awaited his arrival like a slumbering dog.

Could do with a little TLC, Air Commodore...

He parked adjacent to a double garage, and surveyed the property. The front lawn was wide and the grass was, like most gardens at present, browned by the summer sun and lack of rain. There was a stone fountain in the centre of the lawn, although there was no sign of running water. Perhaps it had been turned off in anticipation of imminent hosepipe bans. Having met the Air Commodore, Bola doubted that such a decision would have been taken by the man himself – more likely some eco-conscious gardener. Or maybe it just wasn't working properly and no one had seen fit to fix it.

Bola got out and approached the front door, a grand, oak affair with a large brass knocker. Even this was showing signs of neglect. It could do with rubbing down, a coat of linseed oil perhaps. Bola tutted under his breath. If he could ever afford a place like this, he'd make damn sure he looked after it properly.

The knocker produced a sonorous echo from within, and Bola imagined a large, bare hallway behind the façade, suits of armour ranged around its perimeter, portraits of long-forgotten family members adorning the walls, and a butler, perhaps, in full livery, pale, condescending, enquiring as to whom might be calling upon his employer at this hour.

When the door eventually opened, however, it was the familiar figure of the Air Commodore himself who greeted him.

'Ah, you again. Might have guessed. More questions? Am I right?'

'I won't keep you long, sir. Be as quick as I can.'

Akkerman looked him up and down. 'Very well. Better come with me, then.'

Bola followed Akkerman through the hallway, which wasn't nearly as imposing as he had imagined, and into a comfortably furnished lounge. Akkerman walked – a little unsteadily, Bola noticed – across the room to a large armchair which he'd evidently just vacated to answer the door. Without inviting Bola to do likewise he settled himself down, folded his hands, and lifted his chin enquiringly. 'Well, off you go.'

'Ah. May I?' Bola pointed to the nearest chair.

'I suppose,' Akkerman grunted. There was a cut-glass decanter on a side table next to him, half full of an amber liquid Bola guessed to be Scotch whisky. Akkerman reached out and poured a shot into a matching tumbler. 'Offer you anything? Suppose not, duty and so on.'

'Not for me, sir, thanks all the same.'

Akkerman took a slug of Scotch. 'All the more for me, then. Good show.'

Bola wasn't sure how to interpret Akkerman's manner, a curious combination of joviality and irritation.

Half-cut, by the look of him...

Should he begin the interview, or leave it for another day on the grounds of POI inebriation? But how would Akkerman respond to such an accusation? He could hardly say 'Sorry sir, you're clearly drunk, so I'd best come back tomorrow.' And the Air Commodore seemed, if not willing, then at least resigned to answering further questions, so he might as well press on.

'Sir, can I begin by asking about your son? We've been unable to find any record of him following his withdrawal from the Little Hedgehogs nursery in...' Bola consulted his notebook. 'April of 1982.'

Akkerman looked into his tumbler, made no reply.

'Can I ask where he went to school? We can't trace any record of him at the local schools, either. I–'

'Had his name down for Worth, the public school, you know. Damn good school, too, if you don't mind a bit of religion.'

'Yes sir, but that would have been later in life, I think? Where did he attend primary school?'

'She wasn't one for infant schools, his mother,' Akkerman said, taking another gulp of Scotch. 'Preferred home schooling.'

'Ah, I see. So Christopher was home-schooled?'

'That's what I said, wasn't it?'

Bola saw a challenge in Akkerman's eye, so he held his peace. They hadn't found a record of the son at either of the two GP surgeries local to Brockford, which was odd in itself, never mind Akkerman's assertion of home-schooling – a trend that hadn't caught on until the nineties, surely?

'We haven't had much luck finding out much about him at all, in fact,' Bola told him. 'Was he registered with a doctor – a GP? That would have been normal, but we–'

'All family health issues were handled by the medics at Brockford. That's the RAF way.'

'I see.' Bola scratched the side of his nose with his biro. 'So … did he attend university, college?'

'Decided to go his own way, that's all,' Akkerman stared glumly into his tumbler.

'Not academic, then, like his sister?'

No response. Bola tried again.

'Did he begin work somewhere? Near Brockford, or elsewhere?'

'Can't say, for sure. Bit of a rebel, Christopher. Unpredictable. Never shared much about his feelings.'

'But he must have told you where he'd decided to work? He'd have wanted you to know, surely?'

'Not a fruitful line of enquiry,' Akkerman said, shaking his head. 'I'd drop it, if I were you. You're supposed to be finding the perpetrator of a murder, am I right? Instead of asking a lot of pointless questions about my son.'

Akkerman's tone had changed to something closer to aggressive. Bola took a moment. How to play this? How could a man be so ignorant about his only son's life choices? Perhaps it would be best to move on.

'Can I ask when you moved away from Brockford, Air Commodore?'

'Oh, around eighty-five, six, as I recall. Wife was poorly by then. Thought a change might do her good, but...' He shrugged. 'Made her worse, if you ask me.'

'And do you remember when Mrs Akkerman was admitted to hospital?'

'Well, she'd had treatment before we moved, but as an in-patient? That would be around eighty-five.'

'Was your wife closer to Christopher, would you say, than yourself?' Bola eased the conversation back to where he wanted it.

'What's that supposed to mean?' Akkerman set his tumbler down and reached for a refill. 'Mothers and sons. You should know all about that. Of course they were close.' He drained the last drops of Scotch from the decanter and set it down with a *clunk*.

'And would Christopher have confided in her, written to her, perhaps?'

'Would you excuse me?' The Air Commodore got up, not without difficulty, and walked unsteadily towards the hall, tumbler in hand. 'Won't be a moment.'

'Of course.'

Bola sat back, breathed deeply. *Patience, patience...*

A minute passed, then another. A carriage clock on the mantelpiece ticked away the seconds. Apart from this discreet indicator of the passage of time, the silence was almost overpowering. Bola understood the attraction of living out in the sticks, but it wasn't for him. All the silence, all the *nothingness*, would drive him nuts. Better to hear the world passing by, feel the rumble of traffic, instead of this stultifying stillness.

Another minute passed. Had the old boy passed out in the toilet? Bola was about to get up to investigate when he heard the returning clump of the Air Commodore's feet in the hallway. No doubt he'd taken the opportunity to refill his glass.

Bola wet his lips in preparation for his follow-up question, but as Akkerman appeared in the doorway his mouth fell open wordlessly. Akkerman wasn't carrying a glass.

He was carrying a shotgun, and it was pointing directly at Bola.

Chapter Twenty-Three

'Ready for the three o'clock?' Bernice had popped her head up, not realising that Collingworth was on the phone. He waved her away and flashed three fingers at her. *With you in a jiffy, OK?*

It had taken only five phone calls to trace Nick McBrain, the Brockford chef, and Collingworth was very pleased with himself. Five calls to track a man down from forty years ago – not bad going. The guy was still active, running a gourmet pub called *The Flying Dutchman,* near Dartmouth, and better still, the conversation he was having with said chef was proving very revealing.

'So you knew Rita Dempster pretty well?' Collingworth pushed his chair back on its castors and dropped his feet onto his desk.

'Yeah, I suppose I did.' Nick McBrain still sounded a little bemused, understandably so. After all, it wasn't every day you got a phone call from someone asking questions about your previous life forty years in the past.

'Were you in a relationship?'

There was just the smallest hesitation before McBrain said, 'No. Not for want of trying, though.' The chef gave a disparaging laugh. 'She had a bit of a reputation, you know, so we all tried it on with her at one time or another. Unsuccessfully, in my case, but we were friends, in a way. She wasn't an easy person. Quite good-looking, though.'

'Do you remember her car?'

'Her car?'

'Yes, you know, *vroom-vroom.*'

'I do. It was a joint-owned car, bit of a wreck, but it did the job.'

'Oh, really? By whom was it owned?'

'Myself and Rita.'

'You bought a car together?'

'Yes. It made financial sense at the time. Her idea. Services wages were rubbish back then – probably still are – we shared it. Two weeks each in the month.'

Collingworth dropped his legs to the carpet, pulled his chair close to his desk. 'Make, model?'

McBrain chuckled. 'It was an old Austin Maxi. Just about roadworthy. Be worth a lot now, I imagine. Not many of them around these days.'

Collingworth could hear the sounds of a busy kitchen in full flow in the background. He strained to hear McBrain's voice above the din. 'A Maxi, was that?'

'Yes. Sorry about the noise, we're still on lunchtime service. Holiday period's always busier, we stay open later.'

'No problem.' Collingworth was on the internet looking

at a car collector's site. 'So, when did you sell it?'

'I left it with Rita after … after what happened. The place spooked me. I had to leave.'

'Yeah, I get that.' Collingworth was scrolling down the web page. Austin Maxi. Only a hundred and forty registered in the UK in 2020.

'She sent me a cheque a month or so later. I think it was a hundred and fifty quid or thereabouts.'

'Do you remember the registration?'

'Sure, it was 461 DLA. Easy. Mind you, it's probably scrap metal by now.'

Collingworth scribbled a note. 'Maybe, maybe not. OK. So on the night in question, when Laura was killed, where were you?'

'Sore point. I was supposed to be out at a mate's stag do, but Rita had lent the bloody car out, so I missed it. Had a right old go at her about that. But, to answer your question, I was working.'

'You were at Brockford all evening, all night.'

'Yep.'

'So who'd she lend the car to?'

'I forget. But it was usually the Wing Commander's daughter.'

Collingworth's neck hair was now standing to attention.

'Isabel Akkerman?'

'Yep, that's the one. And a right bloody shambles it was when I went to use it a couple of days later. Looked like there'd been a party in it.'

'Can you elaborate?'

'Well, it was just a mess. Bottles, discarded food packets, crisps, takeaway wrappers, you know. I told Rita to clean it up, but she just gave me a load of verbal about it not being her fault.'

'Did she tell you who was responsible?'

McBrain sighed. 'God, it's so long ago. I can't be sure, but if it had been Isabel, I wouldn't be surprised. She didn't give a damn for anyone.'

'What else can you tell me about Isabel?'

McBrain exhaled over the racket of raised voices, clashing pots and pans. 'I didn't have much to do with her. She was … too sarky for me. You know the type? Bright, though – I think she was going up to Oxford or Cambridge, I forget which. She was thick with Rita. I always thought she had some kind of hold on her. You know, Rita wasn't a pushover, far from it, but Isabel seemed to have her wrapped around her little finger.'

'OK, that's very helpful. One thing, didn't anyone ask you these kind of questions at the time?'

'No, I was never interviewed. Rita was, I think. Maybe one or two others closer to Laura.'

'It would have been helpful if you'd come forward.'

'Yeah, I see that now. But to be honest, I never made any connection at the time. We were all just so shocked. I guess we all thought it was some psycho from outside, you know? I mean, there are people you get on with, and people you don't, but you never think they're capable of murder, do you?'

'Clearly not.'

'You think Isabel Akkerman had something to do with it?'

'We'd like to talk to her. I don't suppose you're in touch?'

McBrain guffawed. 'Not likely. Haven't set eyes on the woman since eighty-one.'

Bernice Swinhoe appeared above her workstation a second time, gesticulating at her watch.

'OK, Mr McBrain. We'll leave it there for now. I'll probably be in touch again.'

'No problem. I hope you find what you're looking for. Laura was a nice kid.'

'I'm sure. Cheers.' Collingworth rang off.

'OK, Sherlock.' He gave Bernice one of his special winks – it didn't hurt to try. 'I'm ready for the big interview.'

Chapter Twenty-Four

'Good afternoon, Ms Dempster.' Collingworth entered the interview room with a cheery smile. Bernice followed close behind and shut the door.

Collingworth pulled two chairs out from under the table, slid one towards Bernice. 'Thanks for coming in. My name is DC Collingworth and this is my colleague, DC Swinhoe. This shouldn't take long.'

'It had better not,' Rita Dempster replied with a sharp exhalation of breath. She was wearing a loose-fitting, grey T-shirt and jeans, and her hair was scraped back into a ponytail. She'd remained seated as the two detectives entered the room, and now she looked at each in turn as she shuffled a pack of cigarettes from hand to hand. 'Can I smoke in here?'

'Nope. Sorry.' Collingworth placed a brown folder on the table, tapped his pen twice on the cover. 'Just waiting for your brief, then we'll begin.'

'I cancelled him. I've got nothing to hide. I'm not under arrest, am I? You get a solicitor involved, it makes out you've got something to hide, right? Well, I haven't, so ask away.'

'Fine.' Collingworth reached over and clicked the video recording button. 'Interview with Ms Rita Dempster, Friday 3.10pm. Officers present DC Collingworth, DC Swinhoe. Ms Dempster has elected to proceed without a legal representative.' He sat back, folded his arms. 'Now then, Ms Dempster. Why don't you tell us all about this car of yours? The one you shared with Nick.' He cocked an eyebrow. 'The one you lent to Isabel Akkerman.'

'On more than one occasion,' Bernice Swinhoe added.

'Car? I'm not sure—'

Collingworth interrupted. 'Nick didn't sound very happy about it. Long time ago, but he still sounded pissed off.'

'You spoke to Nick?'

'I did.'

'How is he? I can't believe you found him.'

'He's well, Ms Dempster,' Bernice said. 'But please answer my colleague's question.'

Rita chewed her lip. 'I might have, I suppose. Once or twice.'

'The occasion in question is the night of Laura Witney's murder, Ms Dempster.' Bernice leaned forward. 'February thirteenth, 1981.'

'Look, there's no way I'm going to remember dates.'

'I bet you remember that one,' Collingworth said. 'Nick told me that the car was in a state when he went to use it next.'

A shrug.

'Were you in the car that evening, Ms Dempster? With Isabel?'

'No. And I told DCI Moran the same. I had nothing to do with what happened that night. Look, I did let Isabel have the car, OK? And yeah, I gave it a quick clean.'

'Only after prompting from Nick – he was angry at the state it was in, wasn't he?' Bernice said.

'Tell us exactly what state it was in, Ms Dempster.' Collingworth's tone had hardened.

A sigh. 'Please let me have a fag. You could open the window?'

'No can do,' Collingworth said. 'Sealed units. All air conditioning in this building. Now answer the question.'

'She used to go out, pick up blokes. She was reckless like that.' Rita worried at the silver bracelet on her wrist, looked anywhere but at the two detectives. 'You know, the ash tray would be overflowing, cans of drink, a bottle or two. Other stuff, do I have to spell it out?'

'We get the idea. But on this particular occasion?' Bernice probed. 'Was there anything out of the ordinary?'

Rita went on fiddling with her bracelet for a few seconds, then looked up. 'The carpet was a bit damp. I thought it was booze, you know. I scrubbed it … couldn't get it all out – Nick was annoyed, anyway. It still stank of booze two weeks later.'

'It never occurred to you that it might be blood?'

'Blood? Not really. I didn't make a connection between Isa and Laura's disappearance – I mean, why would I? It looked like Isa had been partying, not murdering someone. She wouldn't have done that ... would she?'

Collingworth and Bernice exchanged glances. Collingworth's fingers drummed on the tabletop, a brief percussive flurry. 'We're still trying to establish the facts, Ms Dempster. And it might speed things up a bit if you'd concentrate on telling us the full story. Withholding information in regards to a serious crime is a crime in itself, right? So, let's move on. You sold the vehicle, I believe. When, exactly?'

Rita pursed her lips. 'Couple of months later, I guess. Put an ad in the local. Some bloke turned up, paid cash. I needed the dosh.'

'I assume you filled in the usual registration documents, sent them to the DVLA?'

'Yep. I remember doing that.'

'Do you also remember anything about Isabel that struck you as unusual when you next saw her?' Bernice wanted to know.

'I didn't see her again for a few days – until we all got together for a drink to talk about it, you know?'

'The murder?'

'Yeah.'

'Do you remember anything that Isabel said on that occasion?'

Rita gave Bernice a patronising look. 'Come on, love, this was forty years ago. We were all shocked. I mean, I never saw Laura as a true mate, really, but she didn't deserve that. Isabel was there, but I can't remember anything she said.'

Bernice turned on a hard stare. 'I want to know why you lent her the car, Rita.' She folded her arms. 'If I didn't know better, I'd say you were scared of her.'

Rita hesitated before answering. 'She was unpredictable. A bit fiery, you know.'

'But a car is a precious commodity, isn't it? Especially at that stage of your life, when there's very little spare cash around. I've been there, trust me. You were sharing it with a colleague. I'd have thought it was a big deal just to lend it out – and so often. Did Isabel offer you any compensation in return?'

A few seconds passed in silence.

'I'll take that as a no,' Bernice said. 'Look, we're going to find out anyway, so if there's anything you'd like to tell us – about your relationship with Isabel–'

'She was going to shop me to Akkerman's missus.' Rita had lowered her voice, as though she didn't want anyone to hear.

'About?'

'I had a little fling with the Wing Co. She found out. That's it.'

'We're aware of the rumour. Thanks for confirming it. So, she used that to get you to do what she wanted?'

'I'd have been chucked out if anyone had found out. Akkerman's wife was as straight as a die. Prissy, proper, everything above board, you know the sort? She was best friends with the big boss's wife. If it had all come out, I'd have been out on my ear.'

'Isabel was angry that you'd got involved with her father?'

Rita looked surprised. 'Angry? You're kidding. She thought it was funny. I reckon she loved the thought that the great Wing Commander had blotted his copybook.'

'But, her *father*?' Collingworth looked perplexed.

Rita was shaking her head. 'She was adopted, right? She *hated* her foster-father, *and* his wife. I reckon she'd have loved to have seen him dragged through the mud, but it was more practical for her to lean on me. She probably found other ways to get her own back on the Akkermans. To be honest, after I left I was glad to see the back of her. She had a screw loose, that one. I'm glad I never saw her again.'

Chapter Twenty-Five

The Martins' front door opened before his hand reached the bell, and Charlie Pepper greeted him with a rueful smile. 'It's good of you to come, guv. I really appreciate it.'

'I'm not sure I'll be able to help much, but I'm happy to try.' Moran could see Tess Martin hovering nervously in the hallway behind Charlie. As he caught sight of her she ducked back into the lounge. Moran took a mental deep breath. 'Shall we join the party?'

Moran could feel the tension in the atmosphere. Charlie preceded him into the lounge, announcing his arrival like a butler proclaiming the arrival of a royal dignitary. Moran wondered how he was going to live up to the opposing expectations of the rooms' five occupants.

George was sitting on the sofa, his expression wavering between a sort of forced bonhomie and stoic resignation. Tess was sitting on the arm of the sofa, while Mr Martin stood, benignly proprietorial, beside his wheelchair-bound wife, who was glowering disapprovingly in

Moran's general direction.

'Hello, Chief Inspector,' Mr Martin offered his hand. 'Nice to see you again. Mary and I were pleased when we heard you were paying us a visit.'

'I'm afraid it'll be a fleeting one,' Moran confessed. 'But I wanted to make sure you were both happy with the necessary arrangements.'

'Arrangements!' Mrs Martin barked a short laugh. 'Dear, dear. We don't need any arrangements, Chief Inspector. We're quite able to take care of ourselves without putting anyone to any trouble, least of all the police. You're all busy enough as it is, without worrying about the likes of us.'

'Love, if you'll just–'

'We've good locks on the door, a telephone, and Jim was handy with his fists when he was younger.' Mr Martin's attempt at conciliatory interjection was swept aside. Moran bided his time, waited for Mrs Martin to finish.

'The problem is, Mrs Martin, that we're not a hundred percent sure at this stage what Connie Chan's – Ms Chandra's – intentions might be. You could well find yourselves playing a leading role in helping to remove a very disturbed woman from the community and into safe custody. All DI Pepper and her team are asking is that you remain vigilant, and allow one of two of her officers to keep an eye on your road – and your property of course – because she may even decide to target one of your neighbours, which I'm sure you'd agree would be undesirable, and unfortunate. We just don't know for sure what this woman might do.'

'There's Mrs Jackson,' Mr Martin said. 'She's on her own. Doesn't keep very well. It'd be terrible if anything happened to her and we could have stopped it.'

The muscles in Mrs Martin's face worked as she considered Moran's statement along with her husband's supplemental observation. 'Well, I suppose … under the circumstances, if it's not too intrusive. I wouldn't want to think we've missed a chance to help. And Peggy Jackson, she's had such a bad year already…'

Charlie Pepper was looking at Moran with a mixture of wonder and amusement. It was a look that said *he's been in here less than thirty seconds and he's got a result.* Moran pressed home his advantage.

'That's very good of you, Mrs Martin. Of course, I was absolutely certain we could count on your assistance. You've both been tremendously helpful, and I'm sure we'll have this whole unsettling business tied up in very short order.'

'I don't know what we would do without our police force, Mary, I really don't,' Mr Martin said, puffing out his chest. 'When our Tess joined up there wasn't a prouder man in the whole of the county, I can tell you that, for sure. And hasn't she done us proud? I'll say.'

'Dad–' Tess, her cheeks colouring, dismissed her father's panegyric with a wave. 'I was only doing my job. And now I think you should listen to DI Pepper's advice very carefully, don't you agree, George?' Tess nudged

George in the ribs.

'Aye, definitely,' George said with an emphatic nod. 'Just like we've been telling you for the best part of—'

Tess nudged again, not so gently this time, and George took the hint, lapsing into watchful silence.

'We're all ears, pet,' Mr Martin told his daughter. 'So, DI Pepper, what would you have us do?'

'You worked your magic, guv, as I knew you would.' Charlie walked side by side with Moran to his car.

'Your faith in my abilities is commendable, DI Pepper, if a little misplaced.'

'Guv, they were putty in your hands.'

Moran clicked his key fob. 'Folk of a certain age tend to respond better to mature male officers. It's one of those quirks of the job. If I could have persuaded DCS Higginson to come with me today he'd have pulled the same trick, I'm sure – or anyone of my vintage, for that matter.'

'You're *way* too modest, guv. Higginson would have freaked them out.'

Moran grinned. 'Maybe. Anyway, the Martins are on your side now, and that's what matters.' A thought occurred to him. 'By the way, where's DS Luscombe got to? I expected to see him today.'

'Tidying up a few loose ends, guv. He'll be here tomorrow.'

'Good. Keep me posted. Now,' he glanced at his watch 'I must be off.' But then his face fell as, horrorstruck, he remembered what he had forgotten. 'Oh, *no*.'

'Guv? What's up?'

Moran bit his lip, restrained the curses that were lining up in his mind and demanding to be yelled out loud. 'I'm supposed to be at Alice Roper's for dinner. In half an hour.'

Charlie's hand went to her mouth. 'Oh, God. That's my fault. I'm so sorry – give her a call, tell her you're running late.'

'Late? I won't get there before nine from here. *Damn*.'

'I know,' Charlie said quickly. 'Get someone over there with some flowers. That'll do it.'

Moran thought for a moment. One name came immediately to mind – Bernice Swinhoe. Alice knew her. She'd be an ideal ambassador. 'Brilliant. Thanks, Charlie. Don't let my personal problems hold you up. You'd better get in there and keep the *entente cordiale* going.'

Charlie grinned. 'Not *another* French speaker. OK, if you're sure.'

'I'm sure. One quick call and I'm off.'

Bernice answered after two rings. Moran made his plea and it was received with good natured grace, as he knew it would be. Marks and Spencer were still open, and their blooms were usually good quality. She could pick some up on the way.

He felt a great sense of relief. The flowers would set the stage for his late arrival. Alice was an understanding person – and she *had* rescheduled their evening twice already, after all.

Moran found his way back to the M4 in a lighter frame of mind. His visit to the Martins had gone well and his slip of memory had been countered.

He called up Spotify on his iPhone, selected a favourite Miles Davis album. The smooth sound of jazz filled the car. He cruised into fifth gear, hummed along to the trumpet solo.

All was well.

Chapter Twenty-Six

Alice Roper checked the table for the umpteenth time. Spotless. Scarlet tablecloth, John Lewis matching brass candles in position, freshly-laundered napkins, brand new place mats. It all looked fine. No, it looked *lovely*. Pleased, she retreated to the kitchen, checked the oven temperature. *Down a touch, Alice, I think...*

She went through to the lounge. Peter had calmed a little since this morning, but he still wasn't himself. He was watching the Tokyo Olympics – swimming, this time, but he didn't seem as engaged as he usually was.

'Are you all right, Peter?'

'Yes.'

There was nothing odd about the monosyllabic response. Alice was used to that, as she was used to all Peter's quirks and habits. Learning to manage Peter when she had assumed his guardianship following her sister's mysterious disappearance in 1976, had taken a lengthy period of adjustment. She had studied autism, read all the books, but it had been in the day-to-day, practical business of dealing with him, befriending him, gaining his trust, that her understanding had reached a level where she felt able to cope.

She had learned not to treat Peter as some sub-intelligent being, but rather to assume intelligence, instead of a lack of it. She had determined to presuppose absolute comprehension and act normally. It had been tempting at first to adjust her vocabulary as if speaking to a small child, but she quickly found that Peter responded far more positively to an adult lexicon.

In short, she treated Peter as a neurotypical man, not the opposite, and allowed him full human credentials. Consequently they enjoyed a close relationship, with only a few troubling incidents over the years disturbing the status quo. Yes, minor wobbles were not unknown, even now, but by and large, as she had told Moran, they rubbed along very well as a team.

But this last few days Peter had seemed preoccupied, unsettled – clingy, even, which was almost unheard of. He rarely took any interest in her daily tasks around the house, but this morning had insisted on following her every movement, from room to room, even to the extent that he had declined his usual late afternoon TV in favour of keeping her close company as she prepared the evening meal. It had taken all her powers of persuasion to settle him so that she could get on and concentrate on the job in hand.

She left Peter to it and returned to the kitchen. She glanced at the clock. Plenty of time.

Chan slid the car into a tight space, engaged the hand brake. She had a good view of the woman's house, exactly as she'd wanted. The front room curtains were open, as was a window. Not many people around; rush hour was coming to an end and pubs would be filling up with Friday night drinkers, anaesthetising themselves after yet another week of slavery in some office, factory or shop. Chan felt a mixture of pity and resentment. Why did the British find it so difficult to take control of their lives? Why did they settle so compliantly into a life of submission and mediocrity, like so many laboratory mice?

No matter. Chan banished the distraction from her mind. Tonight's mission demanded care, concentration and precision. Let the mice be mice, and the cats rule over all.

She retrieved a khaki wallet from the glove box, untied the knot. Which to use? She favoured the fillet knife over the chef's. Better for the task in hand. She ran her finger gently along the blade; the forged steel felt clean under her flesh. Yes, this one would do nicely. She slipped it into the leather sheath under her armpit. Her jacket would hide the weapon, and it would be easy to retrieve in an instant.

Chan settled back in her seat to watch the house. A woman appeared at the open window, looked out, and turned to speak to someone else in the room. That would be the autistic brother.

Chan had learned a great deal by examining the case

notes. An amazing story; the missing police detective, Alice Roper's long-lost sister, tracked down to a northern city after all this time. And Alice's selfless care of the brother. Just the two of them, living together in a strange partnership. How sweet, how selfless.

How vulnerable.

And how attached to this odd household the Irishman seemed to be. How perfect, therefore, was this opportunity to make him pay.

But first a reconnaissance of the terrain, to ensure she had a choice of exits. Chan stepped out of the car, slipped on her sunglasses. She locked the vehicle and began a casual walk up the road that ran adjacent to the house. Good access from the back garden into the road; some camouflage at the rear, too. Probably not necessary, but an essential part of preparation.

She passed an elderly gentleman walking his dog, one of those curious little creatures shaped like a German sausage. 'Good evening,' he smiled as he passed by. Chan kept walking. Any engagement could always jog the memory, and that was undesirable.

At the end of the road she found herself beside the entrance to the University campus. Water glinted through the bordering bushes and trees in the evening sunlight. If necessary she could lose herself in the University grounds. She entered the gate for a closer look.

Twenty minutes later, satisfied, Chan retraced her steps to the car. The curtains in Roper's front room were closed now. Perfect.

Time to meet Alice…

She locked the car, walked across the road and unlatched the small gate, checking for passers-by as she approached the front porch. There was no-one around. No witnesses. She pressed the bell, heard it ring somewhere inside.

Waited.

The door opened. Alice Roper looked her up and down, a nervous, surprised reaction to an unexpected visitor.

'Oh! I'm sorry. I was expecting someone else.'

Chan registered this as one of the possible obstacles to her mission for which she had already prepared – the expectation of visitors other than herself. That meant she would have to work quickly, as the unknown visitor might arrive, possibly imminently.

'How can I help you?' Alice Roper prompted, her smile a little nervous, perhaps, but still unsuspecting.

Chan went for the direct approach. She stepped forward and pushed Alice into the hall, swung the door behind her. Alice gave a cry of surprise, held both hands out in front of her. 'What do you think you're doing? What do you want?'

'I want your blood, Alice.' Chan reached for her knife, withdrew it in an easy, relaxed motion.

Alice Roper's face drained to a chalky white. She leaned against the wall for support. 'Peter!' she shouted hoarsely. 'Peter! Get out! Get out now!'

The blare of the TV drowned her voice.

'Your friend, the policeman. He humiliated me.

Detained me against my will when I was weak, vulnerable. Like you are now.'

'I don't know what you're talking about.' Alice had rallied a little, some colour had returned to her cheeks. Her eyes were darting this way and that, looking for something to defend herself with, something she could use as a weapon. They always did that. But they were never quick enough. Chan stepped forward, went for Alice's arm. It was good to let them feel pain, but superficially at first. That way, they could anticipate what was coming, how bad it was going to be. She felt the point of the filleting knife part the flesh in Alice Roper's forearm as her victim reflexively raised her hands. Blood issued from the wound and Chan moved forward again.

'Hullo?'

Chan spun at the sound of another voice – not the brother, but … a woman's voice. The front door hadn't closed properly, she now saw – it was ajar.

And it was opening.

'Hullo? Is anyone in?'

Bernice had left the office in a hurry and made a beeline to Marks and Spencer in Woodley. She'd chosen a mixed bunch – without carnations, as the guv had instructed. Alice apparently didn't like carnations. Of course, all the mixed bunches had carnations; in the end she'd persuaded the woman on the till to let her take the carnations out and replace them with roses, if she paid an extra £2.50. The queue forming slowly behind her was getting restless, the shoppers muttering to each other, getting really shirty. Bernice ignored them, bit her lip as the till lady repackaged the flowers for her.

This was all taking much longer than she'd wanted. She had things to do at home, her flatmates were cooking her dinner for a treat, and ... well, frankly, it wasn't the most convenient time for her to be rushing around town delivering flowers. But hey, it was the guv, and he'd been good to her. She could hardly say no.

And then, traffic was bad. Of course it was, it was Friday. London road was badly snarled up, and there were achingly slow four-way traffic lights on the Wokingham Road due to resurfacing. Progress was so glacial that Bernice began to wonder if the guv would make it back from Chepstow before her, after all. She'd finally squeezed through an amber light and found herself with a clear road ahead.

Five minutes later she was parking outside Alice Roper's house. She checked the flowers – they'd wilted a little even during the journey from Marks. Oh, well, they'd just have to do. If Alice popped them in water they'd revive quickly enough. She checked her hair in the mirror.

Almost as wilted as the roses...

Bernice fussed it into some semblance of order, got out and walked quickly over to the house. She saw immediately that the gate was unsecured and the front door ajar. Alice was probably doing something in the garden – she was always pruning and planting, digging and dead-heading.

As Bernice reached the porch she thought she heard Alice' voice – Peter was probably playing up, or, more likely, hyper-focused on the TV and ignoring entreaties to come through for dinner. She could hear the TV bellowing some sports commentary at maximum volume. Bernice grinned. Alice deserved a medal for taking on her brother's care. The woman was a saint, really. Bernice doubted if she'd have the patience.

She knocked softly. 'Hullo? … Hullo? Is anyone in?'

Chapter Twenty-Seven

Bernice experienced a moment of discombobulation as she took in the scene in the hallway. Alice was facing her with a shocked expression, clutching her left arm. Immediately in front of her was a dark-haired woman in jeans and leather jacket, half-turned towards her. The woman was holding a knife – Bernice saw the blade as it caught the light – and it was swinging in her direction. In her peripheral vision she saw Peter appear in the lounge doorway, his eyes quizzical, confused.

Later, as she tried to recall the details of what happened next, she found that she couldn't remember, only that she had felt a strange sense of coolness and calm as the woman completed her turn and faced her.

The knife came up and the woman lunged. Bernice dropped the flowers, turned sideways on and the knife caught in the fabric of her jacket and blouse, tearing a gash in the material and grazing her skin beneath. She felt a sharp pain, as though she'd been stung. Her subconscious reassured her.

It's all right. A knife wound feels like a fist, a punch, not a cut. It's superficial. You're still OK...

Her back was flat against the wall; there was nowhere to go, and the knife was coming at her again. But then it wasn't. Alice had aimed a kick that struck the woman's leg behind the knee, altering the knife's trajectory enough to bury it harmlessly in the wallpaper next to Bernice's head. The woman gave a cry of frustration, raised the knife for another try.

Bernice imagined that her training must have kicked in automatically at this point, because all she could remember later was aiming a punch at the woman's head that connected with her cheekbone, made the woman reel back, strike her head on the door jamb. The woman hesitated for a split second, dazed, and Bernice followed her punch with a kick aimed at her midriff, but the woman shifted her weight, moved aside in one agile movement and the kick missed its target.

'Get back, Peter,' Bernice heard Alice tell her brother in a hoarse whisper. 'Go back into the lounge. Stay away.'

But Peter kept coming, and Bernice saw that he was carrying a brass poker. He held it up in front of him, waved it at the woman.

'Get out. Get out or I'll *kill* you.'

The woman bared her teeth, her eyes darted from side to side, sizing up the situation. She was hefting the knife in a loose grip, moving the blade this way and that, selecting which of them to attack first, calculating who posed the greater threat...

Peter raised the poker, took another step forward.

The woman snarled, backed away, and, still facing them, flung the door fully open. A second later she was gone. Bernice went to follow but felt Alice's hand on her shoulder. 'No! Call the police.'

Bernice pulled away. 'I *am* the sodding police. Stay here. I won't be long.'

Bernice dashed to the gate in time to see a red Mini rev its engine and move off in the direction of the University. She caught a glimpse of the number plate, ran back along the path to the house. Alice was sitting on a Windsor chair in the hall by the kitchen, nursing her bleeding arm; Peter stood over her like a guardian angel, stroking her hair, the poker abandoned on the floor. With shaking hands, Bernice fumbled for her mobile, called the car registration in, and went to tend to Alice's injuries.

'There's a first aid kit in the kitchen,' Alice said, 'just above the sink, left-hand cupboard. I'm fine, really I am. It's just a cut.'

Peter began to moan, a long, sustained note of agitation.

'Hey, it's all good, Peter. It's OK now,' Bernice put her hand on his arm. 'You were fantastic. Very brave. You scared her off. I mean, *wow*, how amazing were you?'

'I didn't *like* that lady,' Peter interrupted his lament with a frown. 'Why did she want to hurt us?'

'I don't know, Peter,' Bernice said. 'But she won't be coming back, don't worry.'

Alice's wound proved to be deep, but, as far as

Bernice's first aid knowledge went, it didn't look as though it needed stitches. It was a clean wound, made by a razor-sharp weapon. She cleaned and bandaged the injury, watched carefully and slightly suspiciously by Peter, who refused to leave Alice's side, even for a moment.

Bernice shuddered to think what might have happened if she hadn't come to the door. She had a pretty good idea regarding the identity of the would-be assassin. It had to be Connie Chan, the woman Charlie Pepper's team were searching for, and the perpetrator of a number of murders across England and Scotland. But how had she found Alice's address? Had Chan followed her? Or…

Better leave the post-mortems till later, DC Swinhoe…

When she was satisfied that Alice was comfortable she found a quiet spot in the garden and made a cursory check of her own injury. She had a long graze on her ribcage but quickly established, as she'd anticipated, that it was superficial. She tucked her blouse into her trousers, fished out her mobile and called Charlie. It went to voicemail, so she left a message detailing everything she could remember about Chan's appearance and the car she was driving. Five minutes later the doorbell rang, making them all jump and setting Peter off again with his mournful sonic lament.

Bernice told Alice to stay put, checked the caller's identity from the front room window, and went to greet the new visitor.

Moran's face reflected his puzzlement when he saw her.

'DC Swinhoe? Still here?'

Bernice did her best to arrange her expression into a welcoming smile. 'Let me tell you, guv, Interflora never had a delivery like this one.'

Chapter Twenty-Eight

As soon as Moran arrived at Atlantic House he called the team together. The previous evening's events were spinning around and around in his head, a never-ending pirouette of self-reproach. How had Chan found Alice? Why was she targeting her? What was the connection? It had to be himself, surely. Which meant that Chan was on a serious revenge trip. They'd been blindsided, always assuming that Chan would want to lock horns with Duncan Brodie, the residential care homes magnate, her original target, or the Martins. Well, she'd obviously put Brodie on ice for the time being in favour of action closer to home.

Thank God Alice was all right. Thank God Bernice had turned up when she had. He didn't want to contemplate how things might have worked out, otherwise. Uniform had completed a comprehensive search of the area – including the campus – which resulted in, predictably, ASNT. Chan was never going to hang around after her aborted mission.

But the important thing was that no real harm had been done. Alice's injuries were superficial. He'd spoken to her first thing this morning, and although her arm was a little sore, she was otherwise in good spirits, good-naturedly accepting that there would need to be a uniform presence in and around the house for the foreseeable future – an inconvenience that he'd swiftly arranged.

Peter, however, was more unsettled. Alice had spent a restless and constantly interrupted night dealing with her brother who had eventually succumbed to fatigue just before dawn. It would take a while for him to settle – hardly surprising, given the severity of last night's attack. Moran was full of admiration for his autistic friend. He couldn't imagine how much courage it had taken to stand up to such a threat. He was sure now that Peter's willingness to confront Chan had been the turning point of the encounter – she probably hadn't reckoned with such determined opposition.

The main question, however, remained: how had Chan known about Alice? How had she become aware of his connection to her? As the team filtered into the IR and took their seats, Moran went over the facts again for the umpteenth time. He was pretty adept at spotting anyone tailing him, as were the whole team. They were trained to be observant. DC Swinhoe had assured him that she hadn't been followed, and he believed her. She was a sharp as a needle; it was unlikely that anyone would have been able to tail her without her knowledge.

Which begged the question: was there an information

leak? And if so, where was the most likely hole?

'Morning everyone.' Moran stood directly in front of the whiteboard, did a swift head count. One or two missing – Herbinson being the most obvious, but he could live with that. Chris Collingworth, Bernice, DC Delaney, the runner, looking flushed from his usual four-mile jog to work. Bola? ... no, no Bola. Moran frowned. He wasn't on a Code 11 today, so far as Moran knew. Whatever DC Odunsi's faults, lateness was not usually one of them. He looked at his watch.

'OK, let's make a start. You'll all have heard about last night's incident. Before we press on with the Laura Witney updates, I want us all to have a brief brainstorming session regarding Connie Chan. You'll all be aware that a specialist MIT has been assembled in Birmingham with the specific purpose of finding Chan, headed up by our very own DI Pepper. Well, it seems that Chan has turned the tables; she is no longer the hunted, but the hunter. And I want to know how she has established her hunting grounds.'

'Are we talking some kind of information leak, guv?'

'Potentially, DC Delaney. Yes, that's exactly what we're talking.'

All heads turned immediately to DC Collingworth.

'Now wait a *minute*.' Collingworth held up both hands in a gesture of innocence. 'I might have gone off the rails a bit on a previous occasion, I admit, but I'm not in the habit of sharing confidential info with on-the-run psychos, OK?'

There was a general low murmur of acquiescence, one or two pithy comments. Collingworth's unfortunate encounter with the security services had achieved almost mythical status, and team members rarely lost an opportunity to rag him about it.

Moran waited for them to settle. 'We're not looking to blame anyone necessarily, DC Collingworth. We just need to figure out how Chan knew where to go, who to hit.'

'Mrs Roper – she's a friend of yours, guv, right?' Collingworth shot back with an air of feigned innocence.

They all knew by now that Moran had formed a friendship with Alice Roper. It was old news. Nevertheless, Moran found any reference to his private life, particularly regarding Alice, acutely embarrassing. Well, he'd just have to deal with it, put his emotions to one side. He replied with a simple affirmative. 'She is, DC Collingworth.'

'Which means that Chan's trying to get at you, guv, to hurt you in the worst possible way.' DC Delaney went for the obvious answer.

'It looks that way, yes. But, as you all know, I keep my private life exactly that, which is as it should be. I don't telegraph my social life to any Tom, Dick or Harry. So, I repeat, how did Chan know where to look?'

Bernice Swinhoe said, 'It comes down to three possibilities, guv – number one, intuition, number two, someone told her, or three, access to data.'

'All right. Intuition only gets you so far, agreed? So if we rule out an informant, and I think we can, that just leaves the possibility of a data breach.'

'You'd have to be damn clever to hack into our systems these days,' Collingworth observed. 'Everything's nailed down under firewalls.'

'There are sophisticated hackers out there, we know that.' Moran was thinking aloud now. 'It's a possibility we shouldn't discount.'

'She could do a lot of damage if she *has* hacked in,' Bernice said. 'Especially as we've got to log everything in triplicate these days.'

'Too right,' one of the other detectives piped up. 'Shouldn't we alert the IT guys, guv? They'd be able to check for unauthorised access, surely?'

'I'll make sure that happens.' Moran acknowledged the suggestion.

The door opened and Herbinson came in, nodded, took a seat at the back. Moran's heart sank.

Great ... that's all I need.

'Guv? George is away right now, yes? At Tess Martin's parents'?'

Moran knew that look on Bernice's face. She'd tested a theory and was ready to share it.

'He ... is,' he replied, cautiously.

'And Chan was in the house, wasn't she? Speaking to Mr and Mrs Martin? And we don't know what she was up to, why she just waltzed in and went away again? No sign of her in the area since. But ... George has his laptop with him, right? Because he sent me an email yesterday.'

Moran clapped a hand to his forehead. 'Thank you, DC

Swinhoe. I'm half-asleep.' He raised his eyes to the roof and began to pace up and down, the assembled team almost forgotten, shaking his head at his own blindness.

Brendan Moran ... you old fool ... how could you miss something so obvious?

His head was pounding. He took out a handkerchief, wiped the sweat from his brow, suddenly remembered where he was, and spread his hands in appeal before their upturned faces. 'That's *exactly* what Chan was doing. She *knew* George was there. She watched for an opportunity, popped in when the senior Martins were on their own. And I'll bet there was a point during her visit when she was left alone. If she knew what she was doing she wouldn't need much time.'

'Toilet request,' Collingworth suggested. 'We use that one all the time when we want to case the joint.'

'Yep.' Moran was thinking of the horrendous implications if they were right. Chan might have access to personnel files, case notes, personal communications, anything. Everything.

'Am I hearing this correctly?' Herbinson spoke up from the rear. 'We've been careless enough to let a wanted criminal hack into one of our computers, and potentially into the whole police network?'

'It's just a theory at present,' Moran growled. He was in no mood to be ticked off by Herbinson today. 'You'll have a report on your desk as soon as we can follow this up.'

'You'd better,' Herbinson shot back, 'or this damn

circus is going to shed a few clowns.'

Chapter Twenty-Nine

There was a brief, uncomfortable silence following Herbinson's departure. Someone muttered 'bloody Mussolini.' under their breath.

'All right. Let's move on.' Moran clapped his hands for silence. 'DC Collingworth, DC Swinhoe, let's hear your interview report from yesterday.'

Moran listened as the detectives spoke in turn, Bernice correcting Collingworth on the occasional detail, much to her colleague's annoyance. When they'd finished, Moran summarised.

'So, Isabel Akkerman looks to be firmly in the frame. You're following up the other woman today, DC Swinhoe? Moran consulted his notes. 'Lynn Stamford?'

'Yes, guv. Hopefully we'll get a lead on Isabel's whereabouts – if Stamford's been able to find the pamphlet.'

'OK, let me know as soon as you have that, please.'

'Will do, guv.'

'Lastly, anyone seen DC Odunsi today? He's not Code

11, as far as I'm aware.'

'I'll call him, guv,' Bernice offered. 'I'm sure he's on his way.'

'He'd better be. When he does show his face, can you tell him I'd like a word?'

'Sure,' Collingworth replied with a barely concealed smirk. 'Happy to.'

'I'll bet. Anyway, right now I could use a strong coffee and a bacon sandwich. I'll be in the canteen if anyone wants me. Carry on.'

'Wow. I've never seen the guv so angry,' Bernice said to Collingworth as they made their way along the corridor to their office.

'Hardly surprising,' Collingworth replied with another of his irritating winks. What did they mean? Was he flirting, implying complicity, or what?

'Maybe it's all getting a bit much for him,' Collingworth went on. 'Time catches up with us all.'

'He seems totally on the case to me,' Bernice replied. 'I said he seemed angry, not despondent.'

'He's too old, if you ask me. Herbinson's got his card marked, you watch.'

'He might not be in his prime,' Bernice said, feeling her cheeks flush, 'but there's plenty of life in the guv yet. He's in good shape –physically, at least. Have you noticed he's hardly used his stick since we've moved here?'

Collingworth turned down the corners his mouth. 'He's in denial, that's what. He'll reach a point where he'll just fold up, mark my words.'

Bernice held her tongue, trapped the stinging reply that had formed so readily on her lips. No point letting Collingworth get to her. 'I'm calling Bola.'

'Sure. Whatever. I've got notes to write up. Catch you later.'

Bernice watched him saunter to his workstation. God, he really knew how to wind her up. She found Bola's name in her mobile's contact list, called his number, waited for a response. Ten rings, voicemail.

This is Bola Odunsi. I can't speak to you right now...

Bernice killed the call. She felt the first pangs of disquiet. Bola was always in the office, always available. She lingered indecisively in the corridor. It was probably nothing. He'd been fine yesterday; they'd conspired together to cut him loose from Collingworth for a bit of peace and quiet.

Maybe that had been unwise. Had she seen him since? She couldn't remember. Surely he'd returned to the office after his appointment with the Air Commodore? Wait, he might have gone straight home ... but no, it'd been a lunchtime appointment.

The more she thought about it, the more uncomfortable she felt. She had what Moran invariably described as a gut feeling. Something was wrong.

She went through to her workstation, rifled through her top drawer. Her address book was at the back, out of plain sight. She flicked through to O, found the address.

'Back in twenty minutes,' she told Collingworth. 'Call

me if you need me.'

'Oh, sweet promises,' Collingworth grinned as she passed his workstation.

'In your dreams,' she snapped over her shoulder.

Bernice had walked all the way to her car before she felt another pang of disquiet. Bola had gone off solo. Now she was about to do the same. Bad idea. She leaned on her car, twirled her keys.

Come on, Bernice, you know what to do...

She went back to the lift, found her way to the canteen. Moran was still there, sitting alone at a corner table, finishing his bacon sandwich.

'Hello, DC Swinhoe. How can I help?'

She made her plea. The guv was busy, had a lot going on, but she just felt this was right.

Moran listened to what she had to say. 'No reply, eh? And we last spoke to our friend when? Yesterday? Yes, it is rather odd, I'll grant you that.'

'I know you're pretty full-on, right now, guv, but I–'

Moran didn't let her finish. He was already getting to his feet. 'Come on, then. Let's pop over to Yattendon. The county air will do me good.'

Bernice felt a burst of relief. 'Thanks, guv. I appreciate it.'

'We have to look after our own, DC Swinhoe, that's always been my priority.'

'I mean, it's probably nothing, guv.' She heard herself wittering on as they walked to the lift. 'It was only the Air

Commodore he went to talk to, and–'

'I've learned to expect the unexpected in this job, DC Swinhoe,' Moran said. 'Just imagine how dull life would be otherwise. You all right to drive? I'll carry on thinking – that's all I was going to be doing, anyway.'

Chapter Thirty

Bernice drove slowly through Yattendon. Bola had mentioned that they'd interviewed the Air Commodore in the pub the last time they'd been here, but there was no sign of Bola's car in the available spaces by the village shops. Onto the house, then.

Moran was resting his head on the headrest, eyes closed. She forked left, motored down the lane at a sedate 20 miles per hour, checking house names on gateposts. She found it eventually hugging a bend in the lane, and turned into the driveway.

The first thing she saw was Bola's car parked four-square in front of the house. Moran stirred beside her.

'Well, now we know,' he said. 'Stay here, I'll do a quick recce.'

Moran got out and approached the front door. He didn't knock, just peered through the letterbox. Bernice watched him anxiously. What if Chan was here? What if she knew all about their current case, was tracking each of them in turn? What if she'd hurt Bola? Or worse?

Moran disappeared around the side of the building. She waited in a state of near-panic until he reappeared, gave her a wave.

She leaned over and opened the window as Moran bent to speak to her. 'We have a little situation, I think. I can see into a drawing room. The Air Commodore is in there, and someone – I assume DC Odunsi – is sitting with his back to the window. Akkerman has a gun – I think it's a shotgun but I can't be sure. I didn't want to push my luck in case he saw me.'

Bernice swore under her breath and muttered a quick apology. 'Want me to call the ARU, guv?'

'If we're going to do this by the book, we probably should. But that'll take time – forty minutes or so at the very least, and we don't know how much time we have.'

'Hell, this is my fault.'

'How so?' Moran frowned.

'I let Bola go off without Chris yesterday.'

'DC Swinhoe, you are not responsible for your colleagues' conduct. DC Odunsi knows the rules.'

'I know, but … wait.' Bernice had spotted a movement in the mirror. 'Someone's coming.'

Moran turned to look. A woman in a long winter overcoat was wheeling a decrepit bicycle up the drive towards them.

'Right-oh,' Moran said. 'Let's go and have a word.'

The woman cocked her head quizzically. 'And who might you be?'

Bernice allowed Moran to make the introductions. She

noticed that in spite of the warm weather, the woman was also wearing a scarf.

'My name is Miss Hines,' she said, after Moran had finished explaining their presence, 'the Air Commodore's housekeeper, for my many sins.' She raised her eyes to heaven. 'I have to warn you that he doesn't much care for visitors.'

'Yes, we've established that,' Moran said. 'In fact, Air Commodore Akkerman seems to have taken a strong dislike to one of our colleagues. I'm afraid we're going to have to ask you to postpone your housekeeping duties today. I'm sorry you've had a wasted journey.'

Miss Hines shook her head vehemently. Bernice wondered if the array of clips holding the housekeeper's hair in place would withstand the sudden turbulence. 'Oh, the Lord and his saints preserve us. What's the old fool done, now? He's not fetched his gun again, has he?'

Bernice glanced at Moran.

Moran nodded. 'I'm afraid so, Miss Hines. He's done this before, has he?'

'Oh, yes. He pulled that stunt on me once – he won't again, I can assure you. I know how to deal with him, you just wait here...'

'Hold on – are you quite sure?' Moran had been ready to physically restrain Miss Hines, but she had already begun to wheel her bicycle purposefully towards the house. 'He won't harm me,' she called back to them, 'don't you be worrying.'

'Guv – is this a good idea?' Bernice made as if to

follow.

'Possibly not.' Moran let out a stream of air from puffed cheeks. 'But she obviously knows the old boy well.'

Miss Hines propped her bicycle against the porch and produced a set of keys. She opened the front door and marched in. Bernice and Moran walked cautiously towards the open door. They could hear Miss Hines remonstrating with the Air Commodore.

'Now, what in God's name do you think you're up to?' They heard her voice echo in the hall. 'This poor gentleman's all in, look at the state of him, would you? Now give that horrible thing to me this instant, and let's all get on with the business of the day.'

Akkerman's voice came back to them, protesting feebly, sounding to Bernice like a recalcitrant schoolboy who'd been caught stealing apples.

'You're upset, I can see that,' Miss Hines was saying. 'But so is this young man. Just look at him! You've not kept him up here all night with no food or drink to sustain him, have you? God have mercy on us all. Give that dreadful thing to me, right this minute!'

They heard footsteps and Miss Hines reappeared, carrying a broken shotgun at arm's length. 'Here you are, it's all yours.' She handed the weapon to Moran. 'He just needs to be spoken to firmly, that's all.'

Bernice shook her head in amazement. 'Who needs the firearms unit, guv?'

'Think she'd be interested in a part-time position?'

Moran stage-whispered, removing the cartridges and tucking them into his trouser pocket. 'You'd better see to Bola. I'll put this in the car.'

Bernice followed the sound of voices until she found the drawing room. Bola was standing up, rubbing his calves. The Air Commodore was sitting a few feet away, muttering to himself; he seemed oblivious to their presence. Miss Hines reappeared with a tray carrying two mugs, gave the first to Bola and the second to Akkerman, folding the Air Commodore's fingers carefully around it. 'There you are. Now, when you're ready, I think you owe us all an apology.' She stood back, hands on hips.

Bernice went to Bola's side. 'Hey. You OK?'

Bola straightened up with a grimace. 'So, apart from being starving hungry, thirsty, stiff as a board, and totally knackered, I've never felt better. But mostly, I just feel pretty stupid.' He sipped appreciatively from his mug and smacked his lips. 'Man, I needed that.'

They left Miss Hines to deal with Akkerman and repaired to the kitchen. Ten minutes later Miss Hines came in, rubbing her hands. 'That's him tucked up in bed. He'll be out for twelve hours at least, mark my words.'

'I'm very grateful, Miss Hines. You saved us a lot of bother,' Moran told her as he came in. 'May I ask how long you've been the Air Commodore's housekeeper?'

'Well, he was just a Wing Commander back then, right enough, but it would have been January or February 1984 when I first came to him. And if I don't get a sainthood at the end of it, I'll be having words with the man upstairs.'

Bernice smiled, but a more serious thought had occurred to her. 'So, you would have known *Mrs* Akkerman?'

'Oh yes, poor woman, I knew her. And young Isabel.'

'And the boy, presumably?' Moran chipped in.

Miss Hines frowned. 'Boy? No, it was just the two of them plus the girl, and Mrs A didn't keep well, not at all.'

Bola cleared his throat. The coffee was obviously doing its work. 'There was a son, surely? His name was Christopher. We've been trying to trace him.'

'No, no. As I said, it was just the two of them, and Isabel, but she upped and left home shortly after I arrived.' Miss Hines selected a fresh apron from the kitchen drawer, slipped it over her head, fastened the strings. 'They were a quiet, orderly couple. Well, it's the RAF, you see? The discipline. He was a stickler back in the day, although you'd never know it, the way he is now. But Mrs A loved her garden, sure she did. Oh, she'd have spent all her life out there. Used to talk away to herself, she did, at the foot of the vegetable garden – out there all the time, in fair or foul weather. An emotional woman, I'd say. She'd have tears in her eyes so often. But then, one day, off she went to that hospital.' Miss Hines crossed herself. 'And the poor soul died not long after, God love her. Well, I carried on a bit for the Air Commodore, and when he moved to Yattendon he took me on full time, more or less…'

'The Air Commodore seems … ah, reluctant to talk about his family, Miss Hines.' Moran dangled the suggestion.

'Oh, well, I can't say I blame him. He'll be missing his poor wife, of course he will. He finds it hard to talk about her, naturally he does. And Isabel, well, she was a difficult one. I don't think they ever saw eye to eye, even after all they did for her. She's not been to see him for years, can you credit it? Not since she went off to her studies. Ungrateful, I call it, when she'd been rescued from a difficult life in … some foreign place, bless me, I've no idea where. I've often said, why don't you remarry, there's no shortage of wealthy, capable widows around these parts. And then I could retire in peace. But oh no, he won't make the effort. All he wants is to drink with his cronies up the road.' She jerked her head in the direction of the pub. 'And here's me, breaking my back for him day in, day out.'

Bernice had been listening carefully, filtering the housekeepers' words, separating the wheat from the chaff. One phrase Miss Hines had used had stuck in her mind.

…used to talk away to herself, she did, at the foot of the vegetable garden – out there all the time, fair or foul weather…

They finished their coffee, and thanked Miss Hines again for her timely arrival.

'You'll not be pressing charges, I hope?' She threw Bola a worried look. 'He doesn't mean anything by it, you know? It's just his way. He's a poor soul, really, that's all he is – his glory days are behind him, so they are, and he finds that difficult. He's a poppet, really …well, most of the time.' She fell silent. Bernice wondered if she might bolster her plea with a flutter of her eyelids, but she just peered over her spectacles and awaited Bola's reply.

'No,' Bola reassured her. 'I'll let it pass this time.'

'Oh, that is good of you. Now, if you'll excuse me, I must get on.'

Outside, Moran called Bola aside. 'DC Odunsi. I think you'd better get yourself home, take some time out. I'll see you in my office on Monday morning, nine sharp, if that's convenient?'

'Look guv, I'm sorry about this. I didn't think–'

'–And that's the problem,' Moran interrupted. 'You didn't think. Anything useful to tell me before you sign off?'

Bola pursed his lips. 'Only that Akkerman was very reluctant to talk about the son. That's what set him off. I had no idea he was going to–'

'Quite. I'll see you on Monday.'

Bola turned without a word and walked back to his car.

'Hey,' Bernice called after him. 'Take it easy, yeah?'

'Sure.'

They watched Bola swing the BMW in a wide circle before accelerating away.

'Don't waste any sympathy on him, DC Swinhoe,' Moran advised. 'He's only got himself to blame.'

'I suppose.' Bernice still felt guilty, but dealing with that guilt would have to wait. Right now, the implications of Mrs Akkerman's emotional state as described by Miss Hines were pointing to an unpleasant possibility – a possibility she felt she should share. 'Guv? What Miss Hines was saying. About the wife?'

'Yes. I picked up on that, too.'

'I think we should have a sniff around Akkerman's old house.'

'The vegetable garden in particular?' Moran gave her a sideways look.

'Yes,' Bernice replied, 'the vegetable garden.'

Chapter Thirty-One

Connie Chan was working hard to control her conflicting emotions. Emotional reaction inevitably led to weakness, and there was no way she was going to allow her stupid miscalculation to faze her. Mistakes happened; it was how you dealt with the aftermath that mattered. There would be further opportunities to settle with Alice Roper, and by then she hoped to have assistance, because now her focus had temporarily shifted to follow the unexpected lead unwittingly provided by the police, a lead she fervently hoped would result in a momentous meeting.

The possibility that this woman, Isabel, might actually be her estranged relative was almost overwhelming. It was hard to contain the sense of excitement bubbling in the pit of her stomach, but contain it she must; the Irishman and his team would be on full alert. She had been seen, and at close quarters. They would be thinking hard about how she had penetrated their defences, considering how to trace her movements and neutralise her, as if she were some verminous quarry. If ever there was a need for caution, it was now.

Nevertheless, she was still one step ahead. Stamford had been reluctant to help, naturally, but had succumbed to gentle persuasion. Now the question was whether 'Isabel' Akkerman had remained faithful to her ... calling, for want of a better word. She was apparently with an oddball religious sect based outside the small village of Wisborough Green – just a stone's throw, Chan had noted, from Duncan Brodie's derelict old school, the scene of her humiliating encounter with the Irish policeman. There was some synchronous providence at play here, Chan reflected; it didn't matter whether it was fate or some other unknown channel of predetermination. Her persistence had been rewarded, albeit from the most unexpected quarter.

She eased the car to a halt by temporary roadworks and took the opportunity to consult the map. Satnav would have been quicker and more efficient, but she couldn't take the risk that others might track her via the orbiting satellite. And on the subject of risk, it was also time to change her car. She couldn't be sure that the Mini, as anonymous as it was among so many, and even with yet another change of number plate, hadn't been compromised at Alice Roper's house.

She memorised the route, then caught sight of the tract she'd taken from Lynn Stamford's house. The paper was creased, the print beginning to fade, but the cult's logo and strap line were still clearly visible:

Simplicity – live life the way nature intended

What would she find? A group of middle-aged naturists? Some communal New Age idyll? Chan had no idea, and it didn't matter, so long as Isabel was there. She would liberate her aunt from whatever powers of indoctrination had ensnared her, bring her to her senses, and reconnect her with her lost bloodline. Isabel would be a worthy partner. She would help Chan avenge her name – it was also her family name, after all. If the police were right, Isabel was in possession of a fine set of skills. She had done what she had done and simply walked away, unscathed and unsuspected. That took skill, intelligence. Confidence.

But Chan was sure the net was closing in, and she had no reason to believe that Isabel had any inkling that her past crimes were about to catch up with her.

Don't worry, auntie. I'm coming to warn you. I'm coming to set you free…

The lights changed to green and Chan slipped the Mini into gear. She felt at peace as she drove through the quiet Sussex village, a growing conviction that she was working out her destiny.

Together she and Isabel would make a life for themselves. They would be content. They would be strong.

They would hide away from the world, and never be found.

'I think it's best if you press on with your appointments, DC Swinhoe. I'll sort out the archaeology and keep an eye on progress.'

'If you're sure, guv?' Bernice indicated and turned into the Atlantic House car park, killed the engine. 'I was planning to pop over to Lynn Stamford's place. See if she's managed to dig out the paperwork Isabel gave her.'

'I'm absolutely sure,' Moran said, as he heaved himself out of the car. 'The way the wind's blowing, I'll be a lot happier when we've at least *some* idea where we can find this woman.'

Bernice was relieved. There was a niggling worry at the back of her mind, and she wanted to put it to rest. 'And … the Air Commodore, are we going to let him be for now?'

'Well, according to Miss Hines he'll be good for nothing until tomorrow. But we'll need to speak to him again, for sure.' Moran leaned on the open car door. 'Let's wait until we've done a little excavating. Let me know if Stamford turns up anything useful.'

'Will do, guv.'

'See you later.'

Bernice watched Moran limp towards the front doors. She thought about what Collingworth had said, and reflected that maybe, for once, there was a grain of truth in her colleague's pessimistic predictions. Moran looked for all the world as if he were carrying a load much too heavy to bear. He'd lost weight, the bags beneath his eyes were more pronounced, and his hair was a shade or two greyer around the temples. Bernice wondered, taking into consideration everything the guv had been through, what reserves of determination kept him going, why he didn't just throw in the towel, set sail into the sunset of a richly deserved retirement. God knows, he'd earned it over and over. Duty or loyalty, she suspected, played a part.

And maybe a little fear. A shying away from an unmapped future, a clinging on to the way things have always been. Retirement was a significant life stage, she understood that, and it was not always welcomed with open arms. She thought about Alice Roper. That would be a good place for the guv to end up. He just needed a little nudge in the right direction.

File under 'work in progress', Bernice...

She swung the car onto the road and set out for Lynn Stamford's address. Should she call first? No, perhaps not; Lynn was unlikely to be out and about, not in her condition. Motor neurone was a brutal illness, debilitating and deadly; it didn't lend itself to mobility past a certain stage, and Bernice was pretty sure Lynn Stamford had already passed that point.

Saturday shopping traffic was unusually thin, and it was just short of ten minutes later that Bernice turned into Argyll Street and pulled up outside the house. There was no sign of life, but that didn't mean that Lynn was out. She was probably sitting alone in her living room as before. Bernice couldn't imagine how she would feel herself under the same circumstances. What must it be like for the poor woman, who, having already experienced devastating personal tragedy, now had to face the unpleasant effects of a long drawn out terminal illness? Bernice shuddered at the thought, helplessness and pity bringing an unexpected tear to her eye.

Oh God, this is no good. Come on Bernice, pull yourself together...

She went to the door and gave two short raps on the knocker. It had taken a while for Stamford to answer before, so for the first minute Bernice wasn't unduly perturbed, but when twice that time had elapsed she began to feel a creeping dread in her stomach. She peered in through the net curtains, but they were thickly patterned and she couldn't make out anything in the room with any clarity, except the squat shapes of furniture. She knocked again, louder this time, waited with folded arms and compressed lips.

'She's a cripple in that 'ouse – you'll be waitin' forever.'

Bernice turned and saw the same two kids cycle past, one riding hands-off, the other performing a wheelie as he called out. They skidded to a halt, laughing.

'Disabled is the word I think you're looking for,' Bernice shouted back, feeling herself reddening. 'Go on, piss off and learn some manners.'

'Bloody fuzz,' the hands-off yelled back. 'Oink oink!'

They disappeared around the corner. Bernice went to the window a second time and tapped.

Nothing.

She stepped over the low wall separating Stamford's

house from her neighbour, rang the bell.

'Hello?' A middle-aged woman answered the door immediately. 'Can I help?'

'You don't by any chance have a key for next door, do you?' Bernice showed her warrant card.

'For Lynn? Sure.' She unhooked a small keyring from somewhere nearby. 'Here you are. Is everything all right? I haven't seen her for a few days.'

'I hope so.' Bernice took the keys. 'I'll pop these back in a moment.'

'I'm off out now, so just slip them through the letterbox,' the woman said, closing the door behind her.

'Of course. Thanks.'

Bernice hopped back over the wall and selected the Yale from the keyring. As she inserted it, she hoped that Stamford hadn't put a chain across from the inside, but the door swung open without restriction. She stepped into the hall.

'Lynn? Hello?'

She took another step. She could tell immediately that something was wrong, something in the atmosphere was out of kilter.

'Are you in? It's DC Swinhoe.'

She entered the lounge. Her heart gave a lurch and her hand went to her mouth.

Lynn Stamford was spreadeagled on the floor, her head lying in a mess of congealing blood.

Oh *shit*…

'Lynn? Can you hear me? Lynn?' She bent, felt for a

pulse. It was faint, but it was there. Bernice fumbled for her mobile.

'Hello? Yes. Ambulance, please. I'm a police officer.' She gave the address, and turned her attention to her casualty.

'Lynn. It's all right. I'm here. You're going to be OK.'

She cradled Stamford's head; the eyelids twitched, half-opened. 'A woman...' Stamford tried to say more but couldn't get her breath.

Bernice put her ear to Stamford's mouth, listened hard as the injured woman described her attacker. 'Don't speak. It's OK. I've called for help.'

'Took it.' Stamford's slack mouth dribbled saliva and blood. 'The pamphlet. But I–'

'Shh. It doesn't matter.'

Bernice could hear sirens in the distance. Lucky Lynn. Hopefully they were headed this way...

Stamford took a wheezy breath, tried to sit up.

'Careful, take it easy – everything's going to be fine.' Bernice heard herself babbling. The woman was in a bad way. What kind of person could do this to an invalid?

Stamford tried again. 'A copy. Have copy. Phone.'

'You made a copy? Thank you Lynn. Now, don't talk any more.'

The sirens were directly outside, now, footsteps in the hall. Thirty seconds later the paramedics had taken over.

Bernice watched helplessly as they rechecked vital signs, made Stamford comfortable, strapped her into an EMS stretcher and loaded her out to the waiting ambulance. She felt a strong compulsion to go with them, but she needed to speak to the guv, pronto; she had a strong suspicion as to why this had happened. The description fitted, and the motive, however speculative, also made sense.

She found Lynn's phone by her bed in the next room. It was unlocked; Bernice found the photo app and scrolled to the latest. There it was, an image of a creased tract with an undemanding invitation:

Simplicity
Come and find us at

The Old Manor,
Wisborough Green,
West Sussex.

Chapter Thirty-Two

'Yes, I can see that it's logical,' Moran agreed. 'Chan's been in the area, and I accept that she may be keen to check out Isabel, given what we know regarding the aunt, but what her intentions might be if and when she finds her is anyone's guess. Have a seat. You look all in.'

Bernice collapsed into a chair. 'Thanks, guv. I just felt for Stamford. She didn't deserve that.'

There was a knock on Moran's door. They both looked up as Collingworth came in, uninvited and clearly fired up.

'I've got it.' He beamed at them.

'The plague?' Bernice volunteered, 'I could do with some good news.'

'Not offended.' Collingworth mocked up a blank expression. 'But to the point. You'll like this.'

'Enlighten us, DC Collingworth,' Moran invited. 'Please.'

'Austin Maxi. Rare. Only a hundred and forty still registered. It's taken me five hours and–' he consulted his wrist watch, '–seven minutes precisely to find the needle in the proverbial.'

'You traced Dempster's car? Excellent.' Moran was genuinely surprised.

'It's with a collector. A retired mechanic, collects old models and does 'em up. Makes 'em roadworthy. Sometimes he sells 'em on, most times he hangs on to 'em – much to his missus' disappointment. He's running out of room but that doesn't stop him. So she says. She's considered divorce, but–'

Moran held his hand up. 'All right, we don't need his marital options on the table as well. The question is, how quickly can we get forensics on the job?'

'Already sorted, guv.' Collingworth glanced at Bernice but she looked away before he could wink. 'They collected it an hour ago. As soon as they have anything they'll give me a buzz.'

'Great work.' Moran was impressed. 'Let's just hope there's enough left for them to find something.'

'Fittings and carpets are all original, so the guy told me,' Collingworth said. His cheeks were glowing with satisfaction; Bernice couldn't bear to look at him.

'If there's anything to find, they'll find it.' Collingworth concluded.

Moran inclined his head. 'Let's hope so. Now, I think a break from automobile research is called for this afternoon, DC Collingworth. I'd like you to keep an eye on a little gardening project we've set in train.'

As Collingworth, hands in pockets, gave ear to Moran's

update, Bernice was thinking hard. What was Chan planning to do when she found Isabel? How would she approach her? How would Isabel respond? Whatever the answers to these imponderable questions, it was imperative not to waste time. Isabel was now the prime POI, and they had an address.

She chewed her lip as Moran wound up his summary of their morning activities, Collingworth absently massaging his stubbled cheek as he absorbed the information.

'OK. And DC Odunsi? I take it he'll be joining me?'

'Not for the time being.' Moran picked up his desk phone, began to dial a number. 'I'm sure you can cope without him. Chat to the present owners, keep an eye on Forensics. Let me know how it's going.'

Collingworth departed with a mild air of dissatisfaction. Bernice was about to speak when Moran raised his hand and spoke into the mouthpiece.

'Ah, Mr Savage? DCI Moran. Is this a convenient time to talk?' Moran fell silent, listened to the response. 'Yes. If you can spare a few minutes? Good. Yes, now is fine.'

'Isabel may or may not be living in Wisborough Green,' Moran advised. 'It's, what, eight or nine years since Lynn Stamford was handed that pamphlet. Chan may draw a blank, if indeed it is her intention to pay Isabel Akkerman a visit on the off-chance that she might be her relation.'

'I'm convinced that's exactly what she's doing, guv,' Bernice replied. 'She lost no time securing the information from Lynn – once the possibility had occurred to her, she was on it in a flash. I mean, she might have taken *any* other course of action, right? She could have turned her attention back to Duncan Brodie; she could have targeted you directly, or returned to Alice Roper for a second try.'

'I think the latter unlikely,' Moran shook his head. 'Uniform are keeping a close eye.'

'Sure, but Mrs Roper has to go out from time to time, doesn't she? There'll be other opportunities, no matter how careful we are, and Chan knows that. But anyway, she's left her calling card in no uncertain terms by attacking Lynn.'

'Um, if I might?' Valentine Savage had been listening intently to the exchange of views.

'Go ahead, Mr Savage.'

'Val, please.'

Moran grunted, and Savage went on. 'As far as religious cults are concerned, if one becomes indoctrinated – ensnared, if you like – statistics show that it's very difficult to back track. Once you're committed, involved, absorbed into the fold, so to speak, those unfortunate enough to succumb to the process of proselytisation find that they're rather … stuck.'

'Trapped, you mean?' Moran suggested. 'Unable to leave, even if they wanted to?'

'Such associations tend to be long-term, yes.' Savage adjusted his glasses, blinked.

'But does that square with what we know about Isabel?'

Bernice wanted to know. 'I mean, she's feisty, manipulative, secretive, not averse to a little blackmail. She doesn't sound like the kind of person gullible enough to fall into the clutches of a cult.'

'I'd have to agree,' Moran nodded. 'It doesn't add up.'

Bernice' impatience drove her on. 'But ... however unlikely it sounds, we still need to check it out. What if she *is* there? What if we miss an opportunity to bring her in? Shouldn't we get ourselves down there ASAP?'

Moran considered the options. 'The last thing I want is to go in like the Magnificent Seven,' he said. 'If Chan makes an appearance, we'll find out. She'll have to make herself known to the ... well, to those in charge. She can't just waltz in – I imagine there's some procedure to follow to gain entry. So, yes, we ought to follow up, but protocol demands that I speak to DI Pepper before we do anything.'

Bernice sighed. 'Understood, guv.'

'Mr Savage?' Moran wanted to know if the profiler had any further wisdom to impart.

'I'd agree with you about the profile,' Savage said. 'From what I've been able piece together about Isabel's character, a cult seems an unlikely long-term place of residence for someone of her temperament. But then, she may have changed. Forty years is a long time. Perhaps she's found rest for her soul.'

'Well, if she has,' Moran said drily, 'I wish she'd share it around a little.'

'Indeed.' Savage rubbed his chin. 'I think we have to

remember that she is still only a Person of Interest at this time, and has a right to be protected from whatever dubious motives Connie Chan might be harbouring.'

'The way the evidence is stacking up, I think the scales are tipping in favour of a 'suspect' label.' Bernice frowned.

'I needn't remind you that PACE guidelines should be strictly adhered to when it comes to labelling a suspect,' Savage shot back. 'Until we have concrete evidence that Isabel Akkerman is guilty of any offences, she should be treated as we would treat any other vulnerable member of the public.'

'Thank you, Mr Savage,' Moran said, 'for reminding us of our statutory obligations. Shall we take a break before the team briefing?'

As Savage left the room, Moran gave Bernice a look she interpreted as a query. And she was thinking the same.

Was Savage just one of those types known for sticking rigidly to procedure, or was there another reason for his apparent reluctance to convert Isabel Akkerman's status to that of suspect?

Chapter Thirty-Three

It was getting late and Moran was weary. How nice it would be to pop over to Alice's, pour two large glasses of Sangiovese, and relax in each other's company – *chill*, as the younger detectives on the team would have put it. He felt a strong urge to be there for her, to provide the reassurance she badly needed.

But that wasn't going to happen; not tonight, at least. There was too much going on.

Chris Collingworth had added yet another layer to an already event-packed twenty-four hours when he'd telephoned an hour earlier with the news that the remains of a child had been found in the vegetable garden of Air Commodore Akkerman's former property near Brockford. Forensic pathologists were examining the remains, but it seemed highly likely that they belonged to the mysteriously absent Christopher Akkerman.

It would have been easy to speculate concerning the cause of death, but Moran was content to leave that to the pathology lab. He was pretty sure he knew what they were going to say, and he was already mentally constructing a timetable for the following morning, which would now involve, as a matter of priority, a formal interview under caution with Air Commodore Akkerman – minus shotgun.

George McConnell and DI Pepper had just arrived, and Charlie understandably wanted to share information with the team as soon as was practicable. As for George, Herbinson had insisted that he be recalled immediately with specific instructions to deliver his laptop directly to Digital Forensics. Chan's window into Thames Valley's various databases and information would soon be pinpointed and permanently shut down. How much data had already been stolen was a matter Moran had briefly considered, but put out of his mind in favour of more pressing priorities.

He had gathered the team members together for an informal meeting. Pizzas had been ordered and the mood was, if a little tense, at least a bit more upbeat than the last official briefing.

'I know it's late. I know it's Saturday, but things are beginning to hot up,' he began. 'We've made good progress on the Laura Witney case, but over the last few hours the lines between our investigation and DI Pepper's have become rather entangled. DC Swinhoe?'

Moran gave the floor to Bernice, who gave a summary of their visit to Yattendon, and then went on to describe the assault on Lynn Stamford, together with her description of the attacker. Then there was a twenty minute break in proceedings as the pizzas arrived, and Moran took the opportunity to speak to George.

'I'm going to get a roasting for this, amn't I?' George said miserably as he tackled another slice of Margherita.

'The laptop?' Moran made a face. 'It was legitimate to take it with you. It was password protected. Chan must have had some serious software to bypass the firewall and all the other cyber-security gubbins that I don't pretend to understand. I think you can make a case that it wasn't negligence; you were hacked, that's all there is to it. It's not as though you left the machine in your car while you were in the pub, eh? I'll support you all the way, George. You know that.'

George wiped tomato from his beard with his handkerchief. 'I appreciate that, guv.'

'And how's Tess?'

George shrugged. 'Slightly more relaxed now we know Chan wasn't planning to hit on her parents. She's transferred the worry to yours truly now.'

Moran laughed. 'Women are good at that. Onto the next problem.'

'I heard that.' Charlie was sitting on a nearby desk, eavesdropping. She wiped her hands on a paper napkin. 'And while we're on the subject of problems, may I tell you all about mine?'

'Go right ahead,' Moran invited her. 'I think we're finished.'

Charlie went to the front of the room and clapped her hands. 'OK guys, I'll try to keep this short. We have good reason to believe, as DC Swinhoe has already outlined for us, that Lynn Stamford's assailant, in all likelihood Connie Chan, will attempt to make contact with your POI, Isabel Akkerman, at a Sussex address owned by some kind of New Age cult. Rightly or wrongly, Chan probably thinks that Isabel may be a relation of hers, an adoptee who was sent to the UK in the late sixties, early seventies, and fostered by the then Wing Commander Akkerman and his late wife. Chan has recently confined her activities to the south, and has apparently chosen to leave Scotland for another day – I'm referring to Duncan Brodie, the man she was with when we apprehended her in Sussex a few months ago.

'We still believe she intends to target Brodie at some future point. However, this latest development presents us with a strong opportunity to catch her. She's already made one mistake, and came close to being apprehended yesterday.' Here Charlie paused and glanced at Bernice Swinhoe, who smiled grimly in return. 'So, she's rattled, and now, on top of that, she may well be emotionally compromised. We can't be a hundred percent sure, but that's where the evidence is pointing. Chan's been searching for her relative since she came to the UK – or so we believe – and now she thinks her search may be over.

'The messy part of all this is that the woman she's searching for is also your prime POI, possibly even your prime suspect. So we need to tread carefully, We want a double result here; Chan's been giving us the runaround for too long, and Laura Witney's murderer has been at large for forty years.' Charlie paused to allow the team to take this in.

'I've been in touch with Sussex. We're all agreed that a covert approach is the best way forward. We don't want to spook either Chan or Isabel – if she's there. If Chan's been and gone, we have a fighting chance of tracking her movements post-visit – CCTV, or perhaps contact information left with … what are they called?'

'Simplicity,' Moran reminded her.

'Right. If your Isabel turns out not to be around, Chan might leave a number or at least some way of getting hold of her. If she's really that keen to get in touch with Isabel.'

'She was keen enough to beat up a woman suffering with motor Neurone disease,' Bernice said quietly.

Charlie winced. 'Point taken, DC Swinhoe. So, to conclude, Sussex are beginning surveillance shortly and are under strict instruction to let me know of any significant comings and goings from Simplicity's HQ. Apparently it's a pretty big site – extensive grounds, large eighteenth century house. Think Downton Abbey for oddballs.'

'Speaking of which,' DC Collingworth stage-whispered to George, 'where's that Savage bloke? Wasn't he supposed to be here?'

Moran overheard the question and frowned. He had indeed invited the profiler to elaborate on his earlier comments regarding Isabel, but Savage was nowhere to be seen.

'He left a good half-hour ago, guv.' DC Delaney had also heard Collingworth's remark. 'I saw him chatting to two blokes outside the car park – then he went off in that little sports number of his – I'd say he was in a hurry.'

Chapter Thirty-Four

Moran had slept badly. His first thought on waking had been Alice, so he called her as he was preparing his morning coffee. She sounded a little distant. He stirred his coffee automatically, pitched an open question. 'How's Peter today?'

'He's all right, Brendan. He spends most of his time looking out the lounge window, checking every car that pulls into Green Road.'

'He'll be right as rain, just give him a little time. How's the arm?'

'Oh, I hardly notice it. It throbs a little, that's all.'

Moran took a cautious sip of coffee. It was too hot, scalded his tongue. He set the mug down, put the mobile on speaker, and began to prepare Archie's breakfast – the spaniel was on a low-calorie diet following a bout of canine pancreatitis, as if he hadn't enough to worry about. 'Alice, is there something you're not telling me?'

'It's nothing.'

'I think it's something. Just come out with it.'

A pause. Moran set Archie's bowl down and the little spaniel tucked in, tail wagging nineteen to the dozen. At least someone was happy. Alice said, 'It's just that Mark was supposed to be coming back yesterday. You remember?'

Moran's heart sank. Of course. Now he recalled the threat, Collier's promise to take further action if Alice hadn't complied with his demands. Which, he assumed, she hadn't. With everything else on his plate, it had gone clean out of his mind. 'I'm sorry, yes, of course. But he hasn't turned up?'

'Not a sign. Which is odd. He made no bones about it; he was coming to see me Saturday, and woe betide me if I hadn't done what he'd asked.'

'Something must have happened to delay him. Or perhaps he's decided not to bother you anymore.'

'Unlikely.'

'And you haven't complied with his request?'

'After everything else that's happened this week? No, of course I haven't.'

'You're angry that I forgot.'

Alice sighed. 'No, not really.'

The flatness in her tone gave the lie. Should he go over now? There was so much to do.

She read his mind. 'It's all right, Brendan. You're busy. I understand. Everywhere I look I see a policeman, so I can always call for assistance should Mark decide to turn up.'

'If you're sure. I'll come over later.'

'Only if you've time.'

He signed off, dissatisfied with the conversation. His watch told him it was almost eight – time to find out what had been happening in the leafy suburbs of Sussex.

Bernice arrived at the same time. Moran fell into step beside her as she walked towards the entrance to Atlantic House. It was a little cooler today, the sun obscured by light cloud which the forecasters predicted would worsen by late morning. The hot spell was coming to an end.

Bernice was wide awake and bristling with energy. Moran envied her. 'Charlie called me ten minutes ago, guv. The only traffic in and out of Simplicity in the last eighteen hours has been a Tesco delivery van and a postman.'

'No sign of Chan?'

'Not yet. She may be biding her time, checking the place out. But if she is, she's doing it very covertly. The Sussex surveillance team haven't had a peep.'

'She's good, we know that. But so are the Sussex lot – or so Charlie claims. I'm making the assumption they're covering all points in and out.'

They called the lift. 'When do we make the decision to go in for Isabel?' Bernice acknowledged a colleague on her way out as the lift doors opened.

'How long do we give Chan to make an appearance, you mean? My guess is if she hasn't made herself known by this afternoon, she's probably decided against a personal visit.'

'I suppose she could just make a phone call, ask for Isabel.'

'That's assuming they're contactable via that medium,' Moran said. 'Simplicity implies a shedding of life's unessential items. Telephones may well be on that list.'

'That's true. There's no phone number on Lynn's pamphlet.'

'Any news of her, by the way?'

Bernice stepped out of the lift. The smell of bacon drifted along the corridor from the canteen. 'I called late last night. She's stable. No skull fractures, which was the big worry, but they're keeping her in for a few days just to make sure the concussion isn't going to cause any complications.'

'Well that's not bad news, at least.' Moran forced a smile. 'How are you fixed to interview Air Commodore Akkerman, by the way?'

'I … can do, guv. Sure. But I did think, maybe I should get down to Sussex, see if I can … I mean, I do think someone should check Simplicity out.'

Moran shook his head. 'Chan knows your face. Probably best to stay away for now. Let Sussex continue surveillance – for the moment.'

'You're the boss, guv.'

Moran smiled. 'Sometimes I wish I wasn't. In the meantime, you and George can tackle the Air Commodore, see if you can draw him out. He must know what happened; I suspect he's buried it deep in his subconscious.'

'You don't think he's responsible for his son's death?'

'I doubt it very much, but see how you get on. The fact that he knows what happened makes him an accessory in any case, so he won't get off scot-free. Could you give Forensics a call, see what they've managed to establish? I've arranged for Akkerman to be collected – he's due in at eleven, so make sure you have all the facts beforehand.'

'Will do, guv.'

'Let's catch up at midday.'

Moran went to his office, hung his jacket behind his chair. There were three missed-call post-it notes stuck on his writing pad. The first was from Herbinson, demanding an update about George's laptop. The second was from Miriam Eborall, the senior Forensics officer. The third was from Charlie. *Call me ASAP when you're in. C.*

That didn't bode well. Moran found his mobile and dialled Charlie's number.

Air Commodore Akkerman was dressed smartly in slacks and a navy blazer. He made no attempt at conversation as Bernice led him along the corridor to the reserved interview room. George met them outside. 'Morning, Air Commodore.'

Akkerman looked at George and grunted an unintelligible reply. Inside, George motioned for him to sit down. After the introductory formalities had been observed, Bernice opened with a simple question. 'You know why you're here today, Air Commodore?'

'Something about my former residence,' Akkerman grudgingly conceded, avoiding eye contact. 'Some nonsense about what was found.'

'A child's body can hardly be described as nonsense, Air Commodore,' George said, matter-of-factly.

'Let's talk about your family, Air Commodore,' Bernice jumped in quickly to settle the mood. 'Yourself, your wife, Isabel, and Christopher. How would you describe the family unit? Loving? Strong?'

Akkerman made no response.

'Happy? Busy, perhaps?'

'Happy?' Akkerman looked up. His eyes were rheumy, bloodshot. 'There's a word I've not applied to my situation for a long, long time.'

'We know there were problems,' Bernice pressed on, encouraged. 'When did they begin? Was it when Isabel arrived?'

Akkerman bowed his head; Bernice couldn't tell whether he was considering a reply, or had just reverted to silence.

'Difficult age, early teens,' George offered.

Akkerman looked up again. 'Yes, but one hopes they grow out of it.' He glanced up at the ceiling; a frown of concentration had appeared on his brow.

Bernice made a tactful signal to George. *Wait...*

Presently, the Air Commodore seemed to reach some conclusion. 'I feel I ought to apologise for that business the other day – with your colleague. Nice enough chap. It's been hard, you see, to live with all this, but … I

suppose the truth'll come out now, whatever. Am I right?'
The question this time was monotone, resigned.

Bernice felt a weight slip from her shoulders.
Akkerman's initial attitude had seemed a fragile defence,
and now the barrier was coming down. 'Please. Take your
time.'

Akkerman did. Finally, after a full minute's silence, he
began to speak. 'It was the wife's idea, really. We'd been
trying for children for a long time. No joy. Went for all
the usual tests and so forth. None of them showed any
issues with either of us, but the months went by, and still
nothing. One day, Jane made a suggestion – she'd read
something about unwanted children in the Far East. How
we could help, solve two problems in one. So, the
fostering process began. I was busy, didn't think about it
too much, but it kept her happy.

'It took a considerable length of time to finalise, but
eventually the day came. We went to meet Isabel – Jane
named her – and brought her home. Language was the
first hurdle, but she was bright, picked up our lingo pdq.'

'Did you know much about her background?' Bernice
gently prompted.

'Enough. Half Korean, half Malay. Problems in the
family. It was thought best for all parties to bring her to
the UK, settle her into a new life.'

'And how did you all adapt, those first few years?'

A long pause.

'There were ... difficulties. She was headstrong,
demanding. Jane struggled. School was a trial – teachers

complained about her attitude. Her behaviour.' Akkerman ran a hand through his grey hair. 'She was sent home, as often as not. Disruptive, they said.'

'In what way?' George asked.

'She had a cruel streak,' Akkerman said, looking George straight in the eye. 'She knew how to hurt people.'

'Do you think that might have been the reason her birth family couldn't cope with her?' George sat back in his chair, encouraged by the relaxed conversation that was developing.

'Maybe. Hardly a selling point though, so not surprising they played it down.'

'Your wife must have found it hard,' Bernice said.

'Yes.' Akkerman lowered his head again, looked down at the mottled plastic of the tabletop.

Thirty seconds passed. There was a brief, inappropriate muffled burst of laughter from outside the room as a group passed noisily in the corridor. Akkerman remained silent. Bernice wondered if the well had run dry. She was about to prompt him when he looked up.

'Still loved her, though. That was the thing.'

'Of course,' Bernice said. 'That's understandable.'

'When a child is so wanted, you see,' Akkerman carried on as though he hadn't heard, 'all the affection that's invested, all the love. You can't take that away.'

'And … how did things change when Christopher was born?' Bernice noted that George was maintaining a nice, easy tone. Thank God it wasn't Collingworth sitting next to her. She gave silent thanks for Moran's considered approach to staff deployment.

Akkerman smiled sadly. 'Ah, Christopher. The boy who came out of the blue. We were both astonished, but there it was. After everything we'd tried had come to naught – we could hardly believe it. Jane was cock-a-hoop.'

'And Isabel...?'

'Hated him from the start.' Akkerman's tone changed dramatically. His face flushed, and as he combed a stray lock of hair from his forehead, Bernice saw that his hand was shaking. 'Wouldn't accept – *couldn't* accept – that a new-born needed attention, care, time. God knows, Jane tried everything, as did I, but it was never going to work.'

'Christopher was just a few months old at the time of Laura's murder, that's right, isn't it, Air Commodore?' Bernice cut gently to the chase. 'Do you remember the events of that night?'

Akkerman gave a deep sigh. 'Of course I do. I was due to collect Laura, but there'd been a row. Isabel insisted that *she* should babysit. Why should we employ someone from outside? Why couldn't a family member look after the baby? Didn't we trust her? I remember her shouting, carrying on. Jane was almost at the end of her tether. And I ... well, you see, the truth was,' he spread his hands in helpless appeal, 'we both knew that she was ... unreliable. We didn't feel it would be *safe* to leave her alone with Christopher.'

'So what did you do?' George asked.

'Well, it all turned nasty. Isabel said – in Jane's hearing, mark you – that I only wanted Laura Witney to come round so I could do to her what I'd done to Rita Dempster. Then she said I'd better explain myself to Jane, and in the meantime, *she* would go and collect Laura, give us time to sort out our family mess, as she described it.'

Bernice folded her arms. 'She confronted your wife with your infidelity.'

'I'm not proud of it. It was a silly indiscretion, it meant nothing. But somehow, Isabel knew.'

'So she took your car? To collect Laura?'

'No. She'd borrowed a car, that much I do recall – we wouldn't let her have one, you see. Didn't trust her. You have to understand that she used people for her own ends, Detective Constable. She bent people to her will. That was her *raison d'étre*.'

'But … she didn't return with Laura. And so…'

'And so I went to look for her, as I explained to your colleague a few days ago.'

George nodded. 'Can I ask when you saw Isabel again, Air Commodore?'

'She didn't come home until the early hours. I don't know, sometime around first light. I didn't speak to her until later in the day.'

'And by then, you'd heard about Laura?'

Akkerman swallowed hard, nodded stiffly. 'I wonder, might I have a short break? Visit the rest room?'

'Of course.' George paused the recording. 'I'll order some coffee. The toilets are just along the corridor.'

George collared the constable outside. 'Pop along with the Air Commodore, would you? Keep an eye.'

Bernice joined him in the corridor. Everything in the building was new, still smelt faintly of freshly applied paint. 'That went better than I was expecting.'

'Aye. He's had time to think everything through, that's my take on it. We're not quite at the crux of the matter yet, but we're getting there.'

'DC McConnell?'

They both turned, instantly alert to the urgency in the PC's voice.

'Yes? What is it?' George was already striding towards the toilets.

'It's the old fella. I think he's having a heart attack.'

Chapter Thirty-Five

'I like your style.' Isabel Akkerman climbed elegantly into the passenger seat of the Audi S3 as Chan fired the engine and revved the accelerator experimentally 'So much nicer than that revolting van you showed up in. I knew you were too pretty to be a postman.'

Chan was glowing. 'I like to travel in comfort. And I like to change my car often.'

'Oh, so do I, so do I,' Isabel purred. 'But where are you taking me? This is all very mysterious.'

'Just somewhere we can be private. Alone.' Chan shot out of the car park and screeched onto the main road. The owner of the Audi had left a mobile phone and purse on the back seat. 'Would you pop those out of the window when we're clear of the traffic? There's a lay-by coming up in half a mile. That will do.'

'Of course.'

Chan turned her head. 'I'm so glad you agreed to come.'

'How could I refuse? I'm intrigued. Perhaps you can

help me put things in order, about my childhood … my past.'

'Your mother, and father. Do you remember them?'

'They are … shadows. It was a difficult thing, to be exiled, sent away. I was very young, I didn't understand what was happening to me. I think I blotted them out, to protect myself.'

Chan was following signs to the M25. She overtook a slow lorry, was rewarded by a blaring horn. 'But we look very alike. There is a family resemblance, don't you agree?'

'Perhaps,' Isabel conceded. 'But you are pretty. The lines on my face, not so much.'

'Your age is of no consequence. You are healthy, your lifestyle is good. Living at Simplicity has been a positive thing for you, I think. But you must try to remember.' Chan felt encouraged. 'I will help you.'

'And if we are … related? What then?' Isabel asked.

'Then we have each other. Is that not enough?' Chan smiled. 'We are two of a kind, I think.'

'Birds of a feather?'

Chan guided the Audi around the roundabout, took the M25 exit, put her foot down. 'Oh yes, we are alike, auntie – can I call you that?' Before Isabel could respond, she added, 'We are alike … because I know, you see.' She risked a quick sideways glance. 'I know what you did.'

'The Post Office van,' Moran repeated. 'I thought you said Sussex knew what they were about?'

There was a pause on the end of the line. 'I was wrong. Sorry.' Charlie sounded more distracted than annoyed. 'They sent someone in to check, guv. Apparently Isabel Akkerman *was* in residence until early this morning.

'When Chan waltzed in and stole her away,' Moran said. 'Did we get a name, a contact for this Simplicity lot?'

'An Alastair Catton is in charge. He was very helpful, so I'm told. He confirmed that Isabel has lived there on and off for a number of years. It's a community, but fairly loosely bonded, not like one of those…'

Moran helped Charlie out. 'Weirdo cults.'

'Yeah, I suppose. I mean, they mostly keep themselves to themselves on the manor estate, but members are free to come and go as they please. They do have get-togethers, meetings and what have you, but they don't spend time doing head counts or worrying about what their neighbours are up to. I suppose it's a loose kind of hippy-type arrangement. They farm, cultivate, try to avoid modern shortcuts, stick to the basics. That's the vibe. Nothing overly sinister, as far as I can make out.'

'Maybe I'll sign up when all this is over,' Moran said. 'But in the meantime, do we have any decent intel regarding Chan's arrival and exit, or any leads as to where she might be heading?'

'I'm on my way there now, guv. I'll let you know.'

'I'd suggest a quick call to traffic, check out any stolen vehicles early this morning.'

'Already done, guv. There's three so far. We're waiting

on updates.'

Moran sighed. 'OK, Charlie. Thanks. Oh, before you go, any news of Val Savage?'

'I've not heard a thing, guv. Bit odd, I'd say.'

'So would I,' Moran agreed. 'Just when he might be able to help, he goes AWOL.'

'I'm sure he must have a good reason.'

'I'll reserve judgement,' Moran said. 'Let me know how you get on.'

He stabbed the red icon to end the call.

So, Bernice's hunch had been spot on – and for whatever reason, Isabel Akkerman had agreed to go along with Chan's game plan.

Whatever that might entail.

He allowed himself one consoling thought; at least both fugitives were now together, which meant that he and Charlie could combine forces. But where to start? They had no clear notion where Chan was headed. If she had settled on any permanent or semi-permanent base, its location was still a mystery.

Moran looked out through his internal window. Bernice was making her way towards his office at speed.

This didn't look like good news, either.

Chapter Thirty-Six

Valentine Savage knew the routine. Question, repeat, question, repeat. Each time he replied he tried to provide the same answer, precisely as before. He hoped it might discourage them from the endless cycle. Even though they'd allowed him to sleep for three hours – a generous concession, the one with the prominent Adam's apple and Roman nose had declared – he didn't feel any better for it. The spare room in this nondescript house was front-facing onto a main road, and evidently a thoroughfare for HGVs en route to the M4. Every two minutes from four till seven, he had felt the building shake, jolting him awake.

Now it was mid-morning and he was exhausted, wrung dry. He made another appeal.

'Look, I've told you everything I can remember. Everything I suspect might be happening. What more do you want?'

'Well, we'd like to know where our asset has been taken, for starters,' Roman Nose said. 'Someone pipped us at the post, Val. And, according to you, that someone is a highly unstable, potentially murderous loose cannon.'

'Not an ideal situation for us to be in,' his colleague added, a larger man with cauliflower ears. Definitely a rugby player, in his earlier years. He looked at Val and approximated a friendly smile. 'What with the big job looming on the horizon.'

'And Ixora not being the most co-operative or predictable asset on our payroll,' Roman Nose said. 'I'd be a lot more relaxed, Val, if you could make a sensible suggestion or two as to where this Chan woman might conceivably be billeted.'

'Well, there are a number of possibilities.' Val moistened his lips. 'I wonder, might I have another coffee? With brown sugar, if you have it?'

'All in good time, Val. Let's just get that grey matter on the case first of all.'

Val delved deeper into his consciousness. He had to come up with something. 'There's a Scottish background, but I, ah, I don't think she'll travel that far. Not at present. My guess is that she's in the south somewhere, possibly somewhere in the Home Counties. Her fixation ... this strong desire to connect with a family member, is what has been motivating her, driving her on – that and her financial needs. Now she *has* made contact, however, her next move is difficult to predict.' He shook his head, tried to clear the fog. 'What will she do next? It's hard to say.'

Roman Nose sighed. 'Mr Savage. You were asked to do a job, keep us informed if the investigation seemed to be straying in Ixora's direction.'

'But I did,' Val protested. 'I've told you everything.'

'You're supposed to be ahead of this game, Val, that was the deal.' Rugby Man leaned his bulk forward in his chair. It didn't look robust enough to hold him.

Roman Nose threw his hands into the air. 'So, what you're telling us, Val, is that she could be *anywhere*.'

'They might get a trace on the stolen vehicles. If you let me go back to the office, I'll see if they've been able to–'

'Plural,' Rugby Man said. 'Exactly. That's the point. By now, she'll have changed cars several times. This kid changes cars more often than I change my shirt. It'll take weeks for the boys in blue to catch up.'

'We don't have weeks, Val,' Roman nose said.

Rugby Man nodded slowly. 'We have precisely two days.'

Val rubbed his eyes. 'I really need that coffee.'

Roman Nose shook his head. 'You'll be needing something a lot stronger than coffee if we don't find her.'

'My best suggestion?' Val opted for the honesty card – he didn't have much else to play. 'Keep close tabs on Moran. He's got a nose for this kind of thing.'

Chapter Thirty-Seven

Moran was frustrated that he hadn't spent more time on Laura's diary. He'd resolved to set aside at least an hour a day studying its contents, but his discipline had fallen by the wayside over the past forty-eight hours. There was only one remaining entry, and this he wanted to read and reread in the hope of spotting something that no one else had. He was pretty sure that Isabel Akkerman was the killer, but 'pretty sure' wouldn't cut much ice with the CPS.

Feb 12th

Still snotty. But no temp ... hurrah. Wing Co. has asked me to babysit tomorrow eve – groaaaannn. But at least I have an excuse now re Charles. Don't want to put him off totally but — oh I dunno.

Actually managed to function at work so Nick was pleased. Best batch of Hobart rolls ever. Yes! Tick in box. Everyone else is going to the do tomorrow – even Lynn –

good on her. Hope it's fun. Me ... not in the mood really. Feet up, sip a Babycham. Watch TV. Homely girl, that's me. Save my energy for Saturday night and birthday Yay!!

Let's hope the little prince doesn't play me up ... but Mrs A apparently says he's good and sleeps from 6pm so that's cool.

PS - Oh yeah, Charles is trying to wangle me a flight in a Pembroke (birthday treat!). That would be a mazzz zingggggg.
Nite dear diary xxx

Moran read and reread the entry. Laura would be dead less than twenty-four hours after she'd penned this final update. His desk phone rang, and he picked it up automatically.

'Moran.'

'Didn't you receive my message?'

'Ah. Mrs Eborall. Yes, I did, but–'

'I haven't time to continuously chase up non-responding officers.'

'No, I'm sure. Please accept my apologies, Mrs Eborall. We've been rather–'

'The car. It's old, so there's a multi-layered story. We've found traces of blood – not on the current seats, but on the originals that were removed by ... just a moment–'

Moran pictured Mrs E adjusting her glasses and peering at the documentation.

'A Mr Jeff Flowers. I believe he is the current owner. An enthusiast. He kept the original seats wrapped in cellophane in a garage. The passenger seat had a four-inch tear, and rather than repair it he replaced both front seats.'

'That's wonderful news, Mrs E–'

'I haven't finished. The blood is old, but we've been able to conduct our usual DNA tests and now have two available profiles. One was considerably trickier than the other – a smaller stain to work with.'

Mrs Eborall launched into a technical explanation, but Moran was no longer listening.

Two profiles. Laura and her killer. She'd managed to injure her killer, spill their blood. Which gave them a chance – no, more than that; the CPS would rubber-stamp the evidence without a second thought. Moran's heart thumped behind his ribs. Good news ... at last.

He could see through the glass that DC Swinhoe was making urgent signals from her workstation. George McConnell was on his feet, shrugging his jacket on. Moran cut into the Forensic Lead's crisply delivered monologue. 'I'm sure you have everything under control, Mrs E,' he interrupted. 'We'll get the DNA samples run through the database as soon as we can. I'll send someone over. Thanks again.'

'But I–'

Moran replaced the receiver, allowed himself a small grin of satisfaction.

Bernice met him at his office door. 'Guv, Akkerman's

awake. He's out of immediate danger. The medics say we can speak to him. Ten minutes, max.'

'That should be enough to finish your interview.' Moran grabbed his coat. 'You and George, get yourselves over there pronto. I'll see you there – I have a quick call to make first.'

Collingworth appeared from the direction of the canteen, alerted by the commotion. 'Hello? What's up?'

'You're going to collect DNA samples from Mrs E and get them checked, please, DC Collingworth. First against the database, and we also want to match a sample with Laura's DNA. Quick as you can. They're ready now. And well done again for the car – excellent work. I might even mention it in despatches.' A thought occurred to him. 'Who knows, you might even get free tickets to the ice hockey.'

He made a bee line for the lift, leaving a startled Collingworth in his wake.

Alice Roper's house was ten minutes from the Royal Berkshire Hospital. He wanted to show his face, try to smooth over his gaffe, his lapse of memory concerning Collier. He was relieved the guy had been a no show, but the nagging question was why? Alice had seemed convinced that Collier meant to see his plan through. Had he had a change of heart? Unlikely, from what Alice had said about Collier's background and character.

Still, no news was good news for the time being. The important thing was to show Alice that he was concerned, that he hadn't forgotten about her. Just a few minutes out of his day, that's all.

'And when I say ten minutes, I mean ten – absolutely no longer.' The consultant, a petite black woman of around thirty-five, gave them a stern look. 'He's had a close shave. I don't want him getting worked up.'

'We'll go softly-softly,' George assured her. 'We just need a wee chat, that's all.'

The consultant gave George an appraising look, glanced at Bernice for confirmation, who nodded vigorously. 'Really quick. Promise.'

'OK,' the consultant conceded. 'He's the last bed on the left – but I don't want to hear any raised voices.'

'Scout's honour,' George said.

'You were a Scout?' Bernice whispered as they walked along the ward. 'Somehow I can't see you in a pair of shorts and a woggle.'

'My woggle's none of your business, DC Swinhoe.'

Akkerman was lying on his back with his eyes closed, his arms straight down by his sides and his breathing assisted by means of a nasal cannula.

'Air Commodore,' Bernice began. 'I'm glad you're feeling a little better. We're sorry, but we have to ask you a few questions.'

Akkerman grunted a response.

'You were telling us about Isabel. After the night of Laura's murder. You didn't see her until later that that day.'

'Correct.' Akkerman winced at the cannula's intrusion,

shifted his head to one side, took a breath.

Bernice was about to speak when Akkerman said, 'We knew. We both knew. There was something about her that day. She was … nervy, excited almost, you might say.' He paused, and his hand went to adjust the cannula. Finding it impossible, he let his arm drop back to the bed, and took another deep inhalation. 'We knew she'd been out and about, driving. We knew she was angry that night – angry with us.'

'And … resentful that you'd chosen an alternative babysitter, perhaps?' George asked.

Akkerman closed his eyes. 'We should have spoken up, I know that now. Perhaps if we had done … but the thing was, you see, Jane pleaded with me. Isabel was her daughter. In spite of everything, she loved Isabel. She is my *first* child, Dennis – that's what she said to me. How can we lose her? How can we betray her?' Akkerman opened his eyes and stared at the ceiling, searching for a place and time somewhere in the past imperfect, a past he had no way of altering. 'God knows how many times I've regretted the decision to stay silent.'

'Isabel's behaviour worsened?' Bernice checked her watch. Two minutes left.

Akkerman gave an affirmative grunt. 'That's putting it lightly. Girl became unmanageable. She and Jane were in constant conflict. Jane wouldn't let her near Christopher, until…' Akkerman sighed and turned his head away.

'Go on, sir,' George said quietly.

With great difficulty, Akkerman shifted his position, lay

half on his side. Bernice could almost see the events replaying behind his watery eyes. When he spoke again, it was close to a whisper.

'Until that ... awful night. We were both in. Isabel was in her room. Later she told us she'd heard the baby crying, that he was disturbing her studies. Oh, she studied hard, yes, that was a priority for her. We hadn't heard a thing downstairs. It was all quiet. Christopher was sleeping soundly. And then we heard her calling out.

'We rushed upstairs and she was in his room, cradling him in her arms. 'He woke, but then he closed his eyes,' she told us. 'Look, how quiet he is now.''

Akkerman took a rasping breath. From the corner of her eye Bernice could see a nurse gliding across the polished ward floor towards them.

'His lips were blue.' Akkerman's voice was shaking. 'We tried to resuscitate him, but–'

'Isabel had smothered him.' George's simple statement elicited a silent nod.

'I'm afraid you'll have to leave it there.' The nurse was standing over them like a vulture waiting patiently for its carrion.

'One more minute, and we're gone,' Bernice told her.

'I won't ask you why you didn't report it, sir,' George said. 'I think we've covered that already.'

'Isabel was leaving shortly for Cambridge. If we'd told the police what she'd done, we'd have lost both ... both children.' Akkerman looked at George with bloodshot eyes. 'You can understand that, can't you?'

'I'm trying hard, Air Commodore.' George turned to the nurse. 'We'll need a formal statement at some stage, when your patient is well enough.'

'Of course.'

'If you could let us know when the Air Commodore is fit to be discharged.' Bernice gave the nurse her contact details. 'We'd be most grateful.'

Chapter Thirty-Eight

'You shouldn't have come,' Alice said, before he'd had a chance to speak.

Moran felt like a doorstep salesman. Alice's body language told him she wasn't planning to invite him in. A feeling of panic, of something important slipping away, began to clutch at his insides.

'It's fine. I've put aside thirty minutes. Everything's under control.'

Is that what you think, Brendan…?

'Well, that's good to hear.'

'And Peter? Is he–?'

'The same. He retreated to the kitchen when he heard the door.' Alice folded her arms. 'How did that woman find us, Brendan? What did she want with us? We're nothing to do with her. We're…' Alice' face crumpled.

Moran reached forward, put his hand on her forearm. She flinched.

He withdrew his hand immediately, remembering too late the injury inflicted by Chan's knife.

'We *are* going to find her, Alice. I can't tell you how sorry I am about what happened.'

She took a breath, lifted her chin. 'I don't want to spend the rest of my days as a house prisoner. If this is … if this is what happens when you befriend a policeman, then…'

Moran's heart sank. He felt like a drowning man; he was on his own, with no one to pull him out of the water. In desperation he changed the subject. 'Still no sign of Collier?'

'No. But that could mean anything. He'll be back, I'm sure. Just when I least expect him.' Their eyes met, and Moran glimpsed the internal struggle. She wanted to protect Peter. She wanted security, continuity, safety. And these basic needs, the needs most folk took for granted, were in danger of being compromised by their potential relationship.

'And I'll be ready for him,' Moran assured her.

'But will you? You're so busy, Brendan. You're like a magician balancing plates on sticks, rushing from one crisis to the next. I don't want to be just another crisis for you to take care of.' She paused. A motorbike droned past along the main road, shattering the quiet street with its staccato racket. 'Oh, just come in for a bit. Peter will be pleased to see you.'

Moran went in as invited, unsure as to how he had won this temporary reprieve, but pleased nevertheless to have a further opportunity to make things right between them … somehow.

Peter was sitting at the kitchen table. As Moran entered

he looked up. 'Hello Brendan. I wondered who was at the door. I didn't want it to be the lady. The bad one with the knife.'

'It's all right, Peter. She won't be troubling you again. I give you my word.'

Alice glanced at him as she filled the kettle. The look was both a challenge and a question. *How can you be so sure about that?*

'I think about her a lot,' Peter went on. 'Sometimes when I'm asleep.'

'She can't hurt you now, Peter. You won't see her again. Ever.'

'Brendan's keeping an eye on us, Peter,' Alice said briskly as she passed Moran a mug of tea. 'So don't you worry.'

'All right,' Peter sounded unconvinced. 'I'll try not to.'

'Let's think about Collier,' Moran said, taking a sip of tea. 'He went off to visit this property he wants to sell. So, where exactly is it?'

'Oh, somewhere on the Welsh borders.' Alice sat down next to Peter.

'Only a couple of hours away, then. It's not as if he's likely to have been held up by some travel complication. If it had been the Isle of Skye or somewhere more remote, I could understand his being delayed.'

'I suppose one of the potential buyers showed up,' Alice speculated. 'So perhaps he's taking the opportunity to make a closer inspection of the place. Or show someone around.'

'I'm surprised he's had any interest at all,' Moran said. 'If the place is as run down as you say it is.'

Alice shook her head. 'Investors – entrepreneurs – see the potential in a place, don't they? Especially if they're rolling in money. They can see past the shortcomings of a property all the way to how it could be after an injection of capital. The first fellow to enquire certainly falls into the entrepreneurial category – you've probably heard of him. Duncan Brodie, the care homes millionaire.'

'Brodie?' Moran's eyes widened, his brain immediately beginning to interlace a series of new connections: Brodie – Scotland – the senior citizen murders – Chan …

'*That's* how she knew about it,' he said aloud.

'You're spilling your tea, Brendan.' Peter pointed at Moran's wavering mug.

'What? Oh.' Moran set the mug down. His thoughts continued to hurtle along the new route. 'Where exactly is the property? Welsh borders, you say?'

'Yes. What is it, Brendan?' Alice was taken aback at Moran's change of mood.

'But where exactly?'

'I have it written down somewhere, 'Alice muttered. 'Shall I go and look?'

'Please.'

The Welsh borders. Close to the M4. A derelict property. A hotel. A stone's throw from the Martins' house in Chepstow.

'It's near Chepstow,' Alice echoed, handing him a slip of paper. 'Here you are. Out in the sticks, though.'

'I have to go,' Moran was on his feet. 'I'll call you. Don't worry – everything's going to be fine.'

'But what–?' Alice's face was a mask of puzzlement.

'I know what's held Collier up,' Moran said. 'And I suspect he's found more than he bargained for.'

Alice held up her hand, signalled for Moran to wait. 'But how do you know? How can you be sure?'

'Because I know where Chan is,' Moran said patiently. 'She was all over the Brodies' affairs in Scotland. She'll have known what Brodie was interested in, what he was looking at for future projects. She'll have figured out that this place is perfect for her.'

'Be careful, Brendan.'

'You know me.'

'Yes. That's what I'm afraid of.'

Chapter Thirty-Nine

'An interesting choice,' Isabel Akkerman said as Chan completed her security checks. 'I wouldn't have expected to find a hotel out here.'

'It's temporary. I've made three rooms habitable. There is water – cold, but fresh. I have power.'

'You *have* been a busy bee.' Isabel stepped into the lobby and wrinkled her nose. It smells a little damp.'

'I have dehumidifiers for my living area.'

'You're *very* well organised.' Isabel was at the disused reception area. As Chan watched she ran a finger along the counter, held it up for inspection. 'But you need a housekeeper, my dear.'

The excitement Chan had felt earlier had been superseded by a wary curiosity. There was something about Isabel, something different. Chan couldn't figure it out, but she intended to, in time. However, the important thing was that Isabel was here. Her age and ethnicity seemed to fit, but to be absolutely sure there was one vital requirement still to address: a DNA sample.

But that request could wait. First of all they had to get comfortable with each other, talk, find the common paths, if any existed. What did Isabel remember? She'd already claimed not to remember much, but that was no reason to give up. Her early years would be deeply ingrained in her subconscious. What was needed was the right touch, the right questions.

'My living area is clean. The rest of it ... doesn't matter.'

'Economy *and* a sense of priorities. Good.' The older woman came towards her, took her chin in a slim, strong hand. 'You say you know what I've done, darling? Oh, I think not. You don't know the half of it.'

Chan wasn't going to be intimidated. She allowed Isabel to look deep into her eyes. 'Tell me, auntie,' she whispered. 'I want to know everything about you. I want to know what happened.'

'Take me to your rooms, my lovely, and we'll talk.' Isabel dropped her hand and stood back. 'But I think we'll begin with you. The newspapers are saying the most terrible things about you. I want to hear the truth from the horse's mouth.'

'That's right,' Moran repeated. 'Chepstow. It used to be the Borderlands Hotel. Now it's derelict. Brodie had his eye on it, he was in negotiations with Mark Collier – I'll tell you more about him when I see you.'

'I'm on my way.' Charlie's voice was steady but Moran could feel the tension, even through the car speakers.

'What about backup? Shouldn't we be in touch with our Welsh counterparts?'

'Well, hang on a second.' Moran was thinking aloud as he guided the car down the slip road onto the M4 at Junction 10. 'We've got one suspect, no previous use of firearms as far as we know, one member of the public, still at this stage a POI, an unknown quantity in terms of volatility.'

'No firearms, maybe, in Chan's case,' Charlie said, 'but pretty handy with a knife.'

'Point taken.' Moran overtook a lorry. Smart motorway speed restrictions were still in force, but that wasn't a major concern right now. He put his foot down until the needle reached eighty, settled in the fast lane. 'But I still think calling in an ARU would be a little excessive. I'm not sure about getting the Welsh involved. This is better handled by a select few.'

'Just you and I?' Charlie sounded sceptical. 'Is that wise, guv? I can call Luscombe–'

'I think we'll be better served by stealth, Charlie. And let's remember, this is only a theory, albeit a fairly robust one. If we call in the cavalry only to find an empty building, the boyos will take a dim view.'

The speakers fell silent for a moment as Charlie collected her thoughts. 'Yes, I suppose. But the hotel does fit, guv. It sounds like a perfect refuge. My worry is what she's planning to do with Isabel Akkerman.'

'Our theory that she's been looking for her relative, her aunt, since she arrived in the UK, is sound enough. Hers is a cathartic mission. Her childhood experiences have left her rootless, resentful. She knows that her aunt was sent to the UK to be fostered, and the timelines fit. She wants what we all want, I guess – a sense of belonging, of family. She lost that when her parents were killed, and she's been kicking off about it ever since.'

'But she has no way of knowing if Isabel *is* a bona fide relation, unless–'

'Unless she does a DNA test. Quite. I'd guess that that's exactly what she intends to do, provided she's reasonably certain of Isabel's provenance.'

'And she'll only come to that conclusion by talking to her.'

'Yes. Which is precisely what will be going on now. She'll be probing, testing the waters, seeing if Isabel remembers anything, if they share any common thread.'

'Could be a volatile situation, guv.'

'Given the two personalities we're dealing with, I have to agree.'

'If Chan wants this so badly but it turns out that Isabel has no familial connection – what then?'

'Your guess is as good as.' Moran flicked his wipers on as thick raindrops began to plop onto the glass. The forecast was poor, the warm spell coming to an end in typical British fashion: thunderstorms, floods, high winds. 'If Isabel *is* responsible for Laura Witney's and Christopher Akkerman's murders, then they both share a murderous track record. Both are manipulative, clever, and sharp as a razor's edge, as my ma used to say.'

The speaker crackled, a burst of static. Ahead, the sky darkened and a blue flash lit the horizon. 'You still there, Charlie?'

'Yep. I'm driving now.'

'Weather's turning. Take it steady. You want the postcode?'

'Yep, that would be handy.'

Moran spoke it from memory. As he did so he glanced in his rear view. There was a dark blue VW Scirocco several hundred metres behind, keeping its distance. He was sure it had been behind him since joining the M4. A junction was approaching. He signalled to leave and the car behind followed suit. At the last instant, he cancelled the indicator and stayed put in the slow lane. The VW did the same, swerving a little as it made the adjustment.

'Just a by the way,' Moran said, 'but I think I'm being followed.'

Chapter Forty

Bernice was about to leave Atlantic House when her conscience got the better of her. She backtracked to the office, went to her desk, picked up the phone, and dialled a number. As she waited she wondered what to do for lunch. The canteen was closed on a Sunday and she hadn't eaten anything since breakfast. She'd just have to pick something up on the way.

'Hello?' Bola's voice sounded like he'd been asleep.

'Bola. It's me.'

'You?' A pause. 'Ah, DC Swinhoe. Sorry, I was zoned out there, watching a film.'

'I just wanted to see how you were.'

'How I am? Passing the time like a prisoner on death row, is how I am. Waiting for the axe to fall tomorrow morning.'

'It won't be as bad as you think, Bola.'

'No?'

'Come on, you know the guv. He'll be reasonable.'

'You think? I reckon my luck's out. He's had my card

marked for a lo-ong time, and I just gave him an excuse to wave it in my face.'

'I feel bad. I should have said something.'

'Not your fault,' Bola said. 'Collingworth getting on my … irritating the hell out of me isn't your problem.'

'Chris is everyone's problem.'

Bola laughed. 'Ain't that a fact.'

'Look,' she said, 'the guv's asked me to nip down to Sussex, speak to the manager of this Simplicity place, see what we can dig up about Isabel Akkerman. She's bang in the frame for the murder, by the way.' Bernice went through a quick update for Bola's benefit.

'OK. So she killed the kid too? Man, that's so bad. What kind of a person would do that?'

'A seriously screwed-up person, that's who. But listen, why don't you come with me? I could do with the company.'

'I don't know. Moran told me to sit it out at home till Monday.'

'You don't have to do anything. Watch the countryside go by.'

'Well … maybe. I guess there's no harm.'

'You can say you wanted to make sure I was supported. That'll go down well.'

'It won't make any difference to the final verdict, I don't reckon. I'll be back in uniform by ten tomorrow.'

'Rubbish. Think positive.'

Bola sighed. 'OK. I guess the film can wait. Want me to come over?'

'I'll pick you up. Sit tight. With you in fifteen minutes.'

Bola gave a low whistle as they passed between Simplicity's gateposts. 'Would you look at that. That's some pile.'

And it was – an eighteenth-century country manor once owned by some long-forgotten Sixties pop star, Bernice had read, encompassing seventy-eight acres of formal gardens, paddocks, ponds and light woodland. It had been inherited by the late pop star's nephew, Alastair Catton, who had converted the property and its grounds into a communal retreat for those seeking alternative lifestyles – whatever that might entail. Here and there, dotted about the grounds, some half- hidden by trees and some nestling beside open water, lay a scattering of log cabins, lightly fenced, within the boundaries of which several varieties of vegetable garden could be discerned, little fertile oases presumably tended by the residents. Bernice could see a few of these at work now, some bent in attitudes of inspection, others fetching or carrying produce to and fro in large wicker baskets.

'Center Parcs for the spiritually-minded?' Bola broke into her thoughts. 'Not a bad place to live, eh? If you're into self-sufficiency and all that jazz.'

'Maybe.' Bernice found a parking space in front of the manor house and brought the car to rest. 'It's certainly peaceful.'

She was struck by the purity of the air as they walked towards the entrance. It felt clean, unprocessed. She wondered about the ethos of the cult, what revelatory belief systems or dynamic spiritual agenda had encouraged so many to exchange their regular lives for something so counter-cultural. Perhaps Mr Catton would be able to enlighten them.

They were met at the door by a youngish man in T-shirt and jeans. Bola looked at Bernice with an expression that suggested he might have been expecting a butler in the style of Downton Abbey, instead of a clean shaven youth in denim and cotton.

The man wasn't particularly forthcoming, though; a brusque 'follow me,' was all they could get out of him until, when pressed, he looked over his shoulder and said, 'Mr Catton is happy to welcome you, but as there are other duties he must attend to this afternoon, he can only afford you ten minutes max. He's sure you will understand.'

'Of course,' Bernice replied, thinking, *Is he now*? 'We'll try not to detain him too long.'

The young man came to a halt outside an imposing oak door. He knocked and turned the wrought-iron handle, pushed the door open a crack. 'Do go in.'

Bernice opened her mouth to thank him, but he was already walking away along the carpeted corridor. She pushed the door and it swung open surprisingly easily.

A middle-aged man was sitting at a pedestal desk in front of a wide window that looked out onto the grounds. He was wearing a crisply laundered white shirt, a navy blue jacket and, incongruously, a battered black baseball hat emblazoned with a familiar logo, the prism and diffused spectrum of Pink Floyd's *Dark Side of The Moon.*

He looked up as they entered. 'Ah. The policemen.' He affected to make a closer inspection. 'Mea culpa,' he tutted. 'Police *officers*, begging your pardon, ma'am. Eyes aren't quite up to the mark these days.'

'That's all right,' Bernice said. 'Mr Catton?'

'Yep, that's me,' he said. 'Always disliked the name, but there we are. I'm stuck with it.'

'And you're in charge here?' Bola asked. 'Of the...' he searched for a less contentious word than *cult*. '...estate?'

'The estate? Well, in a manner of speaking. We don't really have a concept of 'in charge' here. The property and grounds came to me many years ago, but I've always considered myself a facilitator, or custodian if you like, rather than conferring the status of owner upon myself. After all, we don't get to keep our worldly possessions forever, do we? All of us being, if you'll forgive the Biblical analogy, creatures of dust.'

Bernice was struck by Catton's attitude. He wore an air of calm, balanced serenity. She estimated his age to be somewhere around the late forties mark, early fifties, perhaps, and he looked to be in excellent health. His body language was languid, almost yogic in its execution. He had what she'd heard described as an *aura* about him.

'Do you know Isabel Akkerman well, Mr Catton?' Bernice felt a little light-headed. She pressed on before she fell under whatever spell it was that Catton was casting.

'Please, do sit down.' Catton indicated two chairs facing his desk, but oddly placed in the centre of the room; Bernice wondered if he had personal space issues. 'I think you'll find them comfortable.'

Bola was first to move. 'Thanks.' He lowered himself into the nearest chair and Bernice followed suit.

'I wouldn't say well,' Catton continued. 'We pass the time of day on occasion. But most of the residents just get on with things. We don't engage in too much social interaction. Folk come and go as they please – we maintain a flexible arrangement here.'

'We'd like to take a look at her lodgings, if that's not too much trouble?' Bernice was enjoying the chair. It *was* wonderfully comfortable.

'It's all about placement,' Catton said, as though reading her mind. 'Ensuring all physical objects are arranged in the most ergonomic positions for line of sight, linear relativity and relational aspect.'

'I see,' Bernice lied. She could feel herself getting flustered, but Catton stepped in to mask her embarrassment.

'If I may ask … your interest in Ms Akkerman is apropos of…?' Catton's question was pitched casually as if, whatever its content, the answer was of little consequence.

'We'd like to speak to her in relation to a serious incident that took place a number of years ago,' Bola explained. 'We know she's not here at present, but as my colleague has explained, we'd like to take a look at her rooms if you'd be kind enough to point us in the right direction.'

'I can't see any problem with that – provided you're respectful of Ms Akkerman's property.'

'Of course. I wonder, did you happen to notice her visitor? It would have been early this morning.'

Catton spread his hands and Bernice was struck by the fingers – long and articulate, a musician's fingers. 'I'm afraid not,' he said, 'I spend the first hour of my day in the gym and pool.'

'We believe the visitor arrived in a Post Office van,' Bola went on.

'The postman? Well, the Royal Mail would scarcely draw anyone's attention, would they?'

'Well, no, that's true,' Bola admitted. 'But we believe Ms Akkerman may have left the premises *with* the van driver.'

Catton considered this briefly. 'Well, it's hardly a crime, is it? Our residents are free to do as they please.'

'But generally speaking, outsiders … or visitors, I mean … are they required to report to you?'

'As a rule, yes. I have staff who keep a watchful eye; we don't allow just anyone to saunter in and wander about the place unsupervised, if that's what you mean. It's a big bad world out there, sadly. I'm sure I don't need to tell *you* that, of all people. But a Royal Mail vehicle … well, there's no need to check, is there?'

Which is exactly why Chan chose to nick one, Bernice

thought. 'No, you're right, of course. How about CCTV?'

Catton shook his head. 'Such apparatus would not sit terribly well with Simplicity's ethic.'

Bernice put on a sympathetic expression. 'No, I imagine not.' This wasn't going anywhere – not that there was anywhere it could go, the bird having long flown. They might as well get on with the search. 'Well, if you wouldn't mind showing us–'

'Indeed. Happy to oblige.' Catton stood up and slid his chair underneath his desk. Bernice studied his movements as he came around his desk and walked across the heavily-piled carpet towards them. There was something about the way the man carried himself that fascinated her.

Catton went past them to the door. 'If you'd care to follow me, I'll take you straight there. But I'm afraid I'll have to leave you to it. I have a few urgent matters to attend to.'

'No problem, sir,' Bola said. 'We'll make sure everything is left as we found it.'

They walked with Catton across an expansive lawn in the direction of a crazy-paved path which in turn led to a gap in a wide, sculpted laurel hedge. Catton strode along the path, passing a fountain and pond guarded by stone cupids and populated, Bernice noticed, by large, dappled fish, lying motionless just below the surface of the murky water like submarines on some covert Cold War mission.

'Just round the next corner,' Catton called over his shoulder. 'One of the smaller cabins, but there's only her, so it's all she needs.'

Bernice was fascinated by the setup. She had a hundred questions she wanted to ask Catton, but as they weren't relevant to her mission she had to park them at the back of her mind.

Isabel's cabin was nestled between two stunted crab apple trees. A short bark-topped path led directly to her front door. Bernice wondered how Chan had sniffed it out, but as soon as Catton unlocked the door and she caught sight of a pile of unopened letters on a low bookshelf, she had her answer. The address on the first envelope read:

Ms. Isabel Akkerman,
Simplicity 9

'I'll leave you to it,' Catton said. 'Just shut the door on your way out, if you don't mind.' He lingered on the threshold, one hand on the latch. 'I will have to tell Isabel about your visit, obviously.'

'That's not a problem, sir,' Bola said. 'Thank you for your co-operation.'

With the smallest inclination of his head, Catton departed. Bernice watched his retreating figure until the laurels swallowed him up.

'Interesting guy.' Bola was smiling broadly. 'I think he took a shine to you, DC Swinhoe.'

'You think?' Bernice tore her gaze away, reddening. 'Different rather than interesting, I'd say. As for the shine bit, you have a good imagination.' She picked up the letters, began riffling through them.

'Just an observation,' Bola said. 'That's all.'

'Well, carry on observing,' Bernice said tersely, waving a hand at the cabin's interior. 'She may be back any time.'

'I doubt it,' Bola replied, walking through to the living room. 'I reckon her and Chan have a lot of catching up to do.'

'That rather depends on Isabel's identity. If she turns out to be the long-lost aunt, then maybe. Otherwise, who can say?'

'Who indeed?' Bola opened a desk drawer, started pulling stuff out – train tickets, bills, nothing of any significance. He scrabbled around the interior, allowing his fingers to trace the contours of the wood. Nothing. He moved to the next drawer, repeated the operation. 'Aha.'

Bernice turned. 'What?'

'False back. Shorter inside.' Face screwed up in concentration, he tapped once, twice. Something clicked. 'Oho. What have we here?' He withdrew a thick, rubber-banded envelope.

Bernice came and stood next to him. Bola undid the band, pulled out the contents. Three passports tumbled onto the desktop, along with a laminated pass, or ID card of some sort. Bernice picked up the card and examined it. The photo showed a middle-aged Asian woman with short, jet black hair. Even though the photograph was small, the eyes were piercing, dark and intense. She read the name aloud. 'Yoon-suh Mook.' She showed the card to Bola. 'What language is this, any idea?' She showed the card to Bola.

'Hm. Looks Korean to me. Ah, yeah, see here?' He pointed to a signature in the bottom right-hand corner of the card. 'Ri Son-gwon – he's the Minister for Foreign Affairs.'

'How the heck do you know that?'

Bola lifted his chin, affected a professorial air. 'When it comes to world affairs, I like to keep myself informed.'

'South Korea, I assume, the north being off-limits?'

Now Bola was frowning. 'No. Not south, as it happens. Interesting.' He flicked through the pages of the three passports. 'Did you hear about that diplomatic incident a few weeks back? About the North Korean scientist?'

'Nope, but I guess you're going to enlighten me.'

'Guy was travelling to the UK for some conference or other. What the heck was his name?' Bola rapped the passport bundle with his knuckles. 'Tang, that's it. Seo-Jun Tang.'

'You amaze me, Bola.'

'He vanished, that's what the incident was all about. Things got a bit heated. North Korea blamed the Americans, of course.'

'And was it?'

Bola shrugged. 'It all went quiet. Heard nothing since, so who knows? Guy was some hotshot boffin, they reckon. The Koreans wouldn't say what his specialism was.'

'Maybe he defected. Is that still a thing?'

Bola nodded vigorously. 'You bet it is. It's all going on

– we just never get to hear about it. Anyhow, look, what about these?' Bola waved the passports. 'Same person – Isabel, we presume. Different names.'

'What would Isabel be doing with a North Korean ID card signed by the Minister for Foreign Affairs and three flavours of passport?'

'That,' Bola replied, 'is what used to be called the sixty-four thousand dollar question.'

Chapter Forty-One

'They're going to find you. That's why I brought you here. The Irishman, DCI Moran, he's getting closer. He won't give up. But you're safe now.'

They were sitting in Chan's living area, which used to be the hotel's bridal suite. The only sounds were the background hum of the generator a few doors along, and the spattering of rain on the windows.

'Safe?' Isabel crossed one leg over the other, rested her head on the sofa. 'How nice to feel 'safe'. Now, I'm curious. You're not a natural blonde, are you?'

Chan suppressed a frisson of irritation. She didn't want to discuss cosmetics. She wanted to get down to basics, talk openly, but Isabel had a knack of skirting around the subject, never allowing herself to be pinned down, changing the subject just when Chan felt she might be about to open up. Moreover, Isabel had failed to show the slightest appreciation that Chan had saved her from the ever-tightening noose of the Irishman's investigation.

'Of course not, auntie.' Chan pulled at the wig,

shrugged it off and shook out her own shoulder-length dark tresses. 'See?' She threw the wig down. 'Better?'

'Oh that's much nicer, much more in keeping with your … ethnic background. Now then,' Isabel sipped from a bottle of mineral water, 'you've made quite a name for yourself, haven't you? *The silent assassin*, the press call you. 'Chan regularly visits the elderly, but her motives are far removed from the inevitable necessities of home care, provision of medication, nursing and the like. Instead, she targets the vulnerable, smothers them in their beds, steals their money, and moves on to her next victim with scarcely a backward glance." Isabel beamed. 'Daily Express. Not a bad summary, is it?'

'I do what I have to do.' Chan frowned. Was Isabel making fun of her? She'd taken the trouble to memorise the journalist's prose. That was strange … oddly prescient.

'Oh well, we're all driven by our basest needs, I suppose. But what you do is more of a hobby, wouldn't you say? To me, it smacks the teeniest little bit of amateurism – oh, I'm not putting you down, dear heart. I'm just interested, that's all.'

'I want to know!' Chan's patience suddenly gave out. 'Are you Iseul? Is it you? You *must* tell me. Tell me remember, please. Tell me you remember my mother, your own sister. I have a photograph, let me show you.' She went to the black attaché case, took out the treasured image of her parents, gave it to Isabel.

As the other woman examined the snapshot, Chan went

to her laptop, found the police photograph of Iseul, the true image of her mother's sister. 'And this is you, isn't it? See? It's old, but look how you were.' Chan searched Isabel's face, the eyes, the nose, the shape of the chin, compared the two. 'It looks so like you. Auntie, talk to me. Who are you?'

'Who am I?' Isabel's face lit up in a predatory smile. 'I'll tell you, my lovely, if you are prepared to listen.'

'He's not answering,' Bernice said. 'Straight to voicemail.'

'Try DI Pepper?' Bola suggested.

'Good plan. Wait.' Bernice stabbed at her iPhone as Bola switched on the wipers. 'Holy Moley,' he muttered, 'get a load of those thunderclouds.'

Bernice held the phone to her ear. The sky was darkening ahead of them on the motorway, brake lights winking as the traffic slowed. 'Here it comes,' Bola warned. Large droplets spattered on the windscreen until, in a rush, the rain came down in a furious torrent. Bola tickled the brakes and they slowed to a near standstill.

Bernice's phone speaker clicked and Charlie's voice said, 'DI Pepper?'

'Ma'am? It's Bernice Swinhoe. Can you hear me?'

The rain was bashing on the roof; Bola shrugged. *What can I do* Bernice pressed the phone hard to her ear.

'Yep, just about,' Charlie's voice said. 'What's up, DC Swinhoe?'

Bernice explained what they'd found at Simplicity.

'OK, so Isabel might be a tougher nut to crack than we supposed – among other things.'

'It looks that way, ma'am.'

'It's Sunday, DC Swinhoe. You can cut the ma'ams.'

Bernice moistened her lips. She always felt a bit nervous when speaking to Charlie. 'OK, sure. So, the guv is on his way to Wales, is that right?'

'Yes, and so am I,' Charlie replied. 'But he's got an hour on me at least. There's an incident three or four miles ahead – someone's had a shunt, emergency services have just shot past on the hard shoulder. So I'm at a standstill, and over the last half-hour it's turned into monsoon season.'

'Yep, same here. Cats, dogs, and the rest of Noah's ark.' Bernice pressed the mobile even harder to her ear.

Charlie said, 'You'd best get back and see if Val Savage has showed up. I now have a sneaking suspicion he's working for several masters, at least one of whom we know nothing about. And if you do happen to see him, I'd suggest you tell him what you've found and ask some searching questions about the two guys DC Delaney spotted him chatting to before he went AWOL.'

'You think something's happened to him?'

'I'm not sure, DC Swinhoe, and that's the honest truth, but from what you just told me, I suspect it's no coincidence that Savage was conveniently available to both my investigation *and* to yours.'

'All right, ma'am … DI Pepper,' Bernice corrected herself. 'I'll let you know if he shows up. But what about you? I mean, you'll need backup for Chan … won't you?'

The car lurched forward as traffic began to move again. Bola reset the wipers to medium.

'DCI Moran says no, at least not immediately,' Charlie said. 'Don't worry, I'm sure everything will come together. Speak later. Bye.'

Bernice signed off. She hoped Charlie was right.

Chapter Forty-Two

To Chan it felt as though she had been living through some kind of dream sequence, an unscheduled and unexpected series of revelations that she could never have conceived or predicted, even in her most outlandishly imaginative moments.

Isabel wound up her story with a patient smile, took a fresh sip of water. 'So, you see, sweet girl, my life has been rather eventful. One gets used to it, in time, but you can probably see that we're really very different animals, you and I – very different indeed.'

Chan, not without difficulty, found her voice. 'But ... you say you were born in Korea – *North* Korea. I thought ... not Malaysia, not like...' Her world was beginning to crumble piece by piece as Isabel chipped at its edges, sawed away at the hope she had invested, the certainty with which she had gone about her search.

'Poor love.' Isabel took a deep, admiring breath. 'You are so pretty, and you do have certain ... attributes that I find very appealing, but, sadly, I must be candid. It wouldn't be fair otherwise, would it? To keep you hanging on, I mean. It would be cruel. I may be a lot of things, but cruel isn't one of them. And another thing I am surely not is your relation, your estranged auntie. Wouldn't it be lovely if it were true? But then, how many fairy stories come true, after all?'

'I saved you,' Chan said, a last, pointless statement. 'I saved you from them. From prison, from humiliation.'

'Did you? And what makes you think I'm such easy prey for your Irishman and his crew?' Isabel tucked her legs underneath her, made herself more comfortable. A thought struck Chan like a hammer blow.

She's enjoying this. She's says she's not cruel, but...

Chan suspected that the conversation was moving inexorably towards some fixed point, to a conclusion that, should she fail to recognise the signs, might end badly for her. For the first time in her life she felt a wave of raw fear run through her body, from the nape of her neck to the tips of her toes.

'You're not Iseul,' Chan said. 'I can see that. I was mistaken.'

Isabel's casual demeanour was undergoing a subtle change; to Chan, she was becoming less like a woman, more like a coiled snake. She could sense the other woman's hidden power, now humming louder in her ears than the distant rumble of the generator.

'You're right, sweetie. I am not Iseul. I am *Ixora*. Do you know what that means?'

Chan shook her head.

'The needle flower. Sharp and pretty, as someone once said.'

Chan began to assess her options. A small knife was fastened to her ankle. It was always there, because it was prudent to be prepared. She was wearing a split skirt, so access wasn't an issue, but she had a feeling that a knife would prove inadequate for whatever was about to happen. Her combat skills were sound, but something told her that direct physical contact with Isabel would be a mistake on her part. She recalled her first impressions. *There's something about her … something twisted…*

'Ixora,' Chan repeated, more to buy time than anything else. 'It suits you.'

'Well, thank you.'

Chan considered making a break for the door, but the snake was tight now, like a spring at full tension. She could read the body language, if nothing else. Best just sit tight. Keep talking.

'So … what happens now?'

Isabel returned a leisurely smile. 'It's a bit of a cliché, my lovely, I know, but I've told you everything about myself, haven't I? I do go on a bit once I get started – it's one of my failings. I've had slapped wrists for it on many occasions.'

Chan's voice sounded small and childlike. 'A cliché?'

'Just so,' Isabel said. 'I've told you everything. And now, I'm afraid, I'm going to have to kill you.'

'I won't tell anyone.' Chan's bladder was rebelling. She was going to wet herself.

'Well, of course you're going to say that. I'd probably say exactly the same.' Isabel sighed, looked at her with something akin to affection. 'Yes, we're both killers, honey pie. But you ... you're an amateur – a gifted one, I'll not deny – whereas I ... *I* am a professional, in the truest sense of the word. And so, I'm afraid your game of happy families has brought you to an unscheduled dead end.'

Chan moved her hand slowly down her leg. 'We don't have to finish like this, Isabel. I can help you – work with you, even. I have much to offer.'

Isabel laughed. 'You don't know what you're saying, little one.'

Chan had reached the knife handle. Her hand closed around it. At that exact moment, the lights went out.

Chapter Forty-Three

Chan blinked. As soon as the lights cut out she had made her move, not towards the door as Isabel would have expected, but around the sofa where her antagonist had been sitting, to gain an advantage; she needed to be behind Isabel, not in front of her.

She crouched in the darkness, took three long, even breaths, focused on her training, tried not to dwell on the growing awareness that she was competing in an uneven match. Isabel's mocking tones echoed in her mind.

You ... a gifted amateur ... I ... am a professional...

Her night vision was kicking in. She could make out the shapes of armchairs, the dressing table, the desk. But where was Isabel? She gripped the knife tightly, scanned the room from left to right. And then felt a soft breath on the exposed skin of her neck...

A sharp, stinging sensation in her lower back galvanised her into action. She pelted for the door, gulping air in a sob of terror. Her hand closed around the door knob. She yanked it, propelled herself forward, ran for her life along the thinly-carpeted corridor.

She passed the lift, paused at the staircase. Her heart would surely give her away, so fast was it beating. Her bare feet made scarcely a sound as she scampered up the stairs to the first floor. Isabel would expect her to make for the exit, and although her instincts were screaming at her to do just that, she knew that her only hope was to use her brain, try to keep a step ahead.

On the first floor landing she paused again. Her lower back felt wet, sticky. She probed with her free hand, winced as she found the wound, an area of parted flesh just above her buttocks. It was deep, and she was bleeding profusely. It would have to wait, she couldn't afford to stay still. She moved cat-like along the corridor, casting backward glances every few paces, alert for the shadowy shape of her tormentor.

Presently she reached the tall plate-glass window at the corridor's end, but as she stood stock-still, unsure which bedroom to choose or even whether she should attempt to break the window and climb out, a new thought occurred to her and quickly assumed centre-stage in her panicked thoughts. It nibbled at her wavering composure, paralysed her into immobility.

Who had stopped the generator? Who had turned the lights out?

Moran cut the engine and turned off the lights. The rain was still beating down, drumming on the thin metal roof like a military tattoo. He'd slavishly followed the satnav until, at some point five or so miles back, the signal had abruptly shut off, leaving him peering into the soaking gloom like a sailing ship's captain with a defective sextant. The car that may or may not have been following him was nowhere in sight; it had disappeared somewhere between Bath and Bristol, and right now was not the time for idle speculation. If they turned up again, so be it. He'd deal with that eventuality if and when it happened.

Driving slowly, he'd followed his nose along narrow lanes, past wooded areas and bleak, open spaces, until he chanced upon a battered signpost that read

orderlands Ho el

He'd almost missed it, but his headlamps had picked out the faded lettering just as he was about to turn back and retrace his route to the main road he'd left fifteen minutes earlier. Muttering a prayer of thanks, he gingerly steered along the thin track the sign had indicated.

Now, as he squinted through his windscreen he could make out, to his immediate right, a wide patch of open ground, at the end of which loomed the twin-gabled shape of a large building. Running alongside the grassy enclosure was an overgrown driveway leading to a smaller outbuilding that Moran assumed to be a storeroom or garage.

Talk about isolated...

The larger building lay in complete darkness, its inverted, rectangular windows staring out into the night like unblinking eyes. He checked his phone. Surprise, surprise. No signal.

A gust of wind rocked the car from side to side and the rain bore down with renewed ferocity.

He sat quietly for a few minutes, testing his theory. Brodie, Collier. A hotel up for sale. Chan, lurking somewhere in the background, picking up snippets of information, filing them away for future reference. It was more than possible she'd come here; it was highly likely.

He rummaged in the glove box for a torch. He had a raincoat folded in the boot, but there wasn't much point – he'd be soaked through after twenty paces. What else? He was unarmed, but there was always the tool box, just in case.

He opened the door and the elements roared into the car like the wrath of the Valkyries. Head bent against the deluge, he opened the boot and pulled out a wrench, slipped it into his pocket and took a few tentative steps towards the parallel trackway leading to the hotel.

Eyes slitted against the driving rain, Moran scanned the building as he approached, checking for any telltale glint of light, but there was nothing to suggest it was anything but a long-unoccupied derelict. As he drew closer the wind dropped, the hotel's bulk affording some respite from the elements. He hugged the brickwork. Even if Chan was in residence, it was unlikely she'd have spotted his arrival – visibility was down to a metre or so at best.

He tried the main entrance. Unsurprisingly, the door was securely fastened. He skirted around the building, looking for a likely candidate – a broken window, or tradesman's entrance. The wind picked up again as he turned the corner, blowing the rain directly into his face, and his feet squelched in the wide, moat-like pool of water surrounding the hotel.

The double-glazing on the first casement window he came to was intact, and he moved on with a frustrated curse. The second was smaller, set deeply into the stonework. It, too, was double-glazed and secure. He stepped forward again, shivering now in his wet clothing.

A set of French windows came next. Moran paused, cupped his hands around his eyes and peered in. The dining room. One handle was hanging off, the other set in the closed position. He tried it. It moved.

He pulled gently and felt the door give. Encouraged, he pulled harder and it creaked open a few inches. He heaved harder, and felt something snap. Now, however hard he tugged, the door refused to budge, but on redoubling his effort he was eventually able to squeeze through the narrow gap.

He pulled the door to behind him, shutting the rain out, and himself into the dusty stillness of the hotel. He waited until he was satisfied that no-one had registered his arrival, and then began to pick his way carefully between the tables and chairs until he arrived at what had once been the bar. Inverted bottles and dry optics still hung from the wall like bats in a silent cave, while a row of empty bar stools bore testament to long-gone evenings of conviviality.

Now that the sound of the storm had receded, Moran's ears were attuned to any unusual internal noise. He could hear something, the low drumming of some mechanical or electrical device, it was hard to tell, but whatever it was, it was unnatural, distinct from the external pounding of the elements.

He walked to the recess of the internal door next to the bar and found himself looking out into the lobby. He could see the reception desk, two possible routes leading from it into the depths of the hotel and presumably to the labyrinth of corridors where the hotel bedrooms would be located. He didn't want to use his torch, preferring instead to allow his night vision to guide him through the building's various nooks and crannies. As he took a few tentative steps across the lobby, the noise he had discerned from the dining room grew louder. It was more of a low hum now, and in a second he had it.

It's a generator...

Which meant that the hotel was providing shelter from the storm for at least one other person. Moran's heart began to beat faster. Now he had to exercise maximum caution. Now he knew for sure that Chan was here.

Left or right? The sound was definitely off to his left. He followed his ears' instructions. He passed a succession of closed bedroom doors until he arrived at a different configuration. This one had a sign screwed to the wall beside a larger door frame. It read: *Bridal Suite.*

From beneath the door he saw a slim crack of yellow light. Two cables fed from an enlarged gap in the wall along the corridor to a separate door, where they disappeared into a similar customised hole.

Moran followed the cables, the pulsing of the generator gradually growing in volume until he came to a halt outside bedroom number nine. In here, surely? He put his ear to the woodwork.

Let's hope no-one's in…

He opened the door.

The space was set out like a typical hotel bedroom: double bed in the centre, bedside tables next to each pillow. Incongruously, at the foot of the bed was a medium-sized portable petrol generator, the cables feeding into the power outlets in the chassis. There was a control panel on the orange fascia, a series of buttons, one of which read simply: *Off.*

He considered his next move. If he cut the power he'd need to move, and fast. Chan's first port of call would be the room in which he was standing. He calculated he'd have maybe ten seconds of reaction time, just enough to make a dash to the lobby and get out of sight. He was heavily reliant on the element of surprise, but surprise counted for a lot. What he'd do after he'd plunged Chan into darkness was less clear; he'd just have to improvise. There was also Isabel to consider, but, as far as he knew she would pose less of a threat.

It's not much of a plan, Brendan…

But it would have to do. He made sure the door to the corridor was open, bent down and hit the off switch.

Chapter Forty-Four

Had she heard something? Chan tried to recall the layout of the hotel. There was a fire escape at the corridor's half-way point, but the external staircase was broken, the metalwork hanging free from the wall like a rusted iron appendage. Way too risky. She had quickly realised that hiding in a bedroom would be folly; she would be trapped, vulnerable.

Her pride was beginning to reassert itself. Was she not strong? Was she not cunning, able, fit … dangerous? Isabel's story had impressed her – no, it had *unsettled* her. She had forgotten who she was. Even now, it might be possible to turn the tables on this unexpected enemy, despite the fact that her back was throbbing, a dull, pulsing pain she was struggling to ignore.

It's a wound, nothing more … you have lost a skirmish, that is all. The battle's outcome is, as yet, undecided…

Now she knew the way forward. She had made an early error, but that was to be ignored, considered irrelevant. The fight must be taken to the enemy. She had one important advantage over Isabel: she knew the building, its layout, dead ends, hidden storerooms, and Isabel did not. She must select the best terrain, the most advantageous position, and lure Isabel to her.

But there was a serious problem to overcome first; her lack of a suitable weapon. She had left her automatic in her handbag, in her living space. Would Isabel have checked? Was she now armed and stalking her, room by room, corridor by corridor? If so, Chan knew she was in trouble. But she needed to check. She needed the advantage a firearm would confer. She must return to her living space and hope that Isabel was elsewhere.

She clung to the wall, crept back the way she had come, past one anonymous room after another. At the top of the stairs she began a slow descent, eyes straining, ears attuned to the slightest sound. She reached the ground floor; so far, so good. Isabel could be searching a completely different area of the hotel. She would hardly expect Chan to retrace her steps, return to the scene of her injury.

She set off towards the lobby. Had she left her handbag on the chair, or on the desk? It would be a matter of seconds to check.

Something moved in her peripheral vision, a vague blur of motion, followed swiftly by a *swish* of divided air, a sudden stab of pain in her side. She cried out, stumbled forward. Unlike the first wound, this pain was dull, but intense. It felt deep, a searching penetration into her flesh.

She gasped, leaned on the corridor wall for support.

Something wet was running down the peeling wallpaper and with a shock she realised it was her own blood. A voice called softly behind her.

'Run, rabbit, run...'

Chan felt nausea rise in her gullet, but a question came to her lips, overriding the sickness. If she must die, she needed to understand. Had to have a reason...

'Why? Why did you agree to come with me? Why ... this?'

Isabel's reply chilled her to the bone. 'Curiosity, my dear – I wanted to see what all the hype was about. Besides, I needed to get some practice in. Frankly, I'm a little disappointed.'

Chan wanted to shout her down, but her vocal cords were stiff, paralysed, a doomed animal's protesting squeal. A remnant of her survival instinct pitched her forward again ... anything to get away from that mocking voice...

'Shall I give you a thirty second start? Yes, I think I should...'

Chan reached the lobby and collapsed, sprawled on the damp carpet.

Damp? Why is it damp?

Her face was pressed against the worn pile, her eyes swam in and out of focus. Was she imagining the wet footprints leading across the lobby, a second set in parallel, moving in the opposite direction?

She felt hands gripping her shoulders, hauling her to her feet, heard a male voice in her ear. An Irish accent...

'Don't try to speak,' it said in a hoarse whisper. 'I've got you…'

Chapter Forty-Five

Moran didn't have much time to process what had just happened, but to say that it was unexpected would have been an understatement. He half-carried, half dragged Chan across the lobby towards the dining room, in the direction of the French windows and escape.

Chan was moaning softly and leaving a trail of blood on the carpet. He had little time to establish the severity of her wounds; his only thought was to get out before Isabel – and he had to assume it was Isabel – came to finish the job. He was painfully aware of his slow progress, Chan's body weighing him down, her locomotive ability worsening with each passing moment.

He reached the dining room, realised that Chan was muttering something. He put his ear to her mouth.

'The kitchen. The kitchen … steel door. Not outside…'

With a jolt he realised she was right. Even if he succeeded in extricating them both through the French windows, there was still the long haul to the car. And Isabel was fit and able, would easily outstrip them. But would she continue her attack if he simply confronted her, explained that he was a policeman?

Moran elected not to put that to the test. The kitchen, protected by its steel door, seemed a sensible proposition. Charlie was on her way; once she'd arrived and figured out what was going on, she wouldn't lose much time sending a distress signal. *Signal* … With a sinking heart he remembered the lack of network coverage. If Charlie couldn't communicate with the local constabulary, there would be no cavalry to bail them out.

Moran pushed the thought away. Charlie was a good detective. She would approach with due caution. He had to leave it with her, trust her experience. Hell, he didn't even know if she would be able to find the damn place – it was only blind chance that had shown him the way.

Somewhere from the direction of the lobby, he heard a female voice. It carried a playful lilt.

'Ready or not … here I come…'

Chan was a dead weight. Moran bent to his task with renewed effort. He got hold of her arms, but she wriggled and twisted away, struck out. Shocked at a stabbing pain in his thigh, he reeled back, almost lost his balance, managed to steady himself against the interior wall.

Careless, Brendan…

Chan was on her knees, trying to get up. She was holding a thin-bladed knife, her breathing coming in short, ragged gasps.

'Don't be a damn fool,' Moran hissed. 'I'm trying to help you.' He could feel blood running down his leg where the knife had sliced him, but first aid would have to wait. He circled her cautiously, never taking his eye from the wavering knife.

'*You* don't help *me. I* come for *you.*'

Chan launched herself towards him at full stretch, her arm sweeping in a wide semicircle trying to catch Moran's legs, but he had anticipated her and sidestepped the danger. Chan hit the floor spread-eagled, let out a shriek of frustration. She tried to roll and recover, but could only lie prone where she had fallen, panting like an injured dog.

Moran took a cautious step towards her. There was a lot of blood. 'You're hurt. You must let me help you.'

Chan tried to rally, managed to get to her knees a second time, opened her mouth to speak, but her eyes glazed over and she pitched forward. Moran put his foot on her wrist, snatched the knife from her nerveless fingers, threw it into the darkness.

He grabbed her under both armpits and, weaving between the restaurant's tables and chairs, dragged her the last few metres to the kitchen entrance. As Chan had said, the door looked to be reinforced, weighty. With a final heave he got Chan inside and put his shoulder to the door. He could feel its density as it slid shut with a satisfying *clunk*. He drew the top and bottom bolts and leaned against a tall walk-in freezer, his breath catching in his chest.

When his breathing had returned to somewhere close to normal he got down on his haunches to attend to Chan.

He checked her pulse. It was beating, albeit in an irregular rhythm.

'Can you hear me? Connie? *Zubaida*?' He gently slapped her cheek. Blood was running freely from her stomach area, collecting in a pool on the hard kitchen floor. He looked around to see if there was anything he could use to pack her wounds. Finding nothing, he pulled his coat off, unbuttoned his shirt, rolled it into a ball and pressed it against her abdomen.

'Don't let her cut me again…' Chan's voice was barely a whisper. 'My uncle. Is that him? Don't let him hurt me…' Her hand clutched his arm.

He knelt in the darkness, rain battering against the windows, heard himself mouthing meaningless words of reassurance, all the while struggling to suppress a mental image of Alice, Peter and Bernice Swinhoe backing away in shock from a knife-wielding intruder.

He took a few seconds to examine his leg. It didn't look too severe, perhaps a few stitches … a scratch by comparison…

Three sharp raps on the kitchen door broke the silence. 'Are you there, O silent assassin?' Isabel's voice slid through the woodwork like a serpent. 'You don't *really* think you can hide in there forever, do you?'

'Iseul, is that you?' Chan was muttering, semi-conscious. 'Abah? Umi? I'm thirsty … don't leave me … please don't be late … I love you, you know that, don't you…?'

Moran was too busy trying to stem Chan's blood loss to

worry about what Isabel might do next. The door was locked, it was hefty enough and he didn't think it could be broken down. He used his torch to examine the damage. When the weak pool of light exposed the wounds, he drew a sharp breath. Not good; her only hope was to get professional attention – and soon.

He began to look for an exit. The windows were narrow, set high in the walls. Even if he could reach them, he'd never be able to get through the gap. A back door, then, surely, a goods entrance, or…

At the far end, beyond the banks of stainless steel hobs and cabinets, a narrowing of the structure of the room led his eye to the most likely candidate for an exit. He began to drag Chan's body along the floor, ignoring her groans of protest. He was making good progress until the stealthy double-tap of feet slapping against a hard surface made him flinch.

He froze.

'Connie? Are you there?'

Moran was baffled. How had Isabel got in? She could hardly have melted through the walls, and the noise of the door being forced would have given her away immediately.

Isabel's next comment supplied the answer. 'You forgot the serving hatch, lovely girl. Silly you.'

Moran lowered Chan gently to the floor, rifled his coat for the wrench, and waited, crouched in the darkness, for Isabel to find him.

Chapter Forty-Six

Charlie's headlights picked out Moran's car dead ahead. She estimated he'd been roughly an hour ahead of her. She parked directly behind him and doused her lights. Nothing was moving outside that she could see – but then who in their right mind would be out and about in this weather? She got out, wincing as the rain stung her cheeks, and walked to Moran's driver's side window. No guv. She walked a little further to where an open driveway led towards the vague outline of an adjacent outbuilding and, bending her head against the whipping, wet gusts, she began to squelch her way up the driveway towards the hotel.

No joy at the front door. Locked and solid. Charlie moved around the building, peered into a window. No lights. She took out her automatic pistol, felt a twinge of excitement as her fingers closed around the rubberised Hogue grip, moved on to the next. Same story. A few further paces further on she came to a set of French windows, one of which was slightly open.

Following in your footsteps, guv, as usual...

The window wouldn't open fully, so she squeezed herself, not without difficulty, through the narrow gap. Once inside, she paused to take stock of her surroundings. An empty dining area, a musty smell of long disuse. Odd that tables and chairs, fixtures and fittings were still *in situ*. Perhaps bankruptcy had come upon the previous owners overnight, suddenly and catastrophically. Perhaps they'd simply fled, fearing reprisals from debtors, leaving their failed enterprise behind, like a land-locked *Mary Celeste*?

Charlie moved quickly and silently through the dining room towards the hotel interior. She paused by the bar, sensing the open space of the reception area dead ahead. She flicked on her torch and a narrow beam of light picked out the lobby and reception area. She played the beam along the floor. There was a trail, a long stain, leading from the reception desk towards her, where it bore off to the left.

Charlie clicked off the torch, moved quickly into the lobby, and flicked the torch on a second time, this time shielding the beam with her pistol. She bent to the carpet, dabbed her finger. It came away red.

She swallowed hard. The trail of blood led to a closed door. She tried the handle. Locked. She stood back, trying to get her bearings. The door was adjacent to the dining room. It would make sense for the kitchens to be sited nearby. Charlie found her way back to the dining room. There would be a connecting door, surely? She played the beam along the length of the dining room. Nothing.

Wait.

At the far end of the bar, the dark space of a serving hatch. She padded along the bar's length, splayed her fingers and pushed lightly at the hatch. It opened on silent hinges.

She tucked the pistol into her belt and pocketed the torch. It was an awkward height, and she had to use a bar stool for leverage to get the upper half of her body into the gap. Gingerly, she poked her head through the hole, making out the dim shapes of cookers and cabinets, work surfaces and fridges, rows of pots and pans hanging from steel runners like joints of meat from butchers' hooks. Nothing moved.

Charlie wriggled forward onto a cold, metallic surface, swung her legs over and made contact with the floor. She crept forward to the main kitchen door and began to follow the blood trail. She pulled the pistol from her waistband, held the Glock tightly, one hand on the grip, the other keeping it steady.

The trail spread into a wider pool beside a walk-in freezer. She took a breath, felt for the handle. The freezer door creaked open on rusted hinges. She peered into the interior and staggered back, gagging. She slipped the pistol into her belt again and clicked the torch.

The beam picked out the shape of an inverted body, suspended by its feet on two meathooks. Directly below the corpse, an irregular pool of dark blood had spread across the freezer floor. Charlie's heart sank to the pit of her stomach. With shaking hands, she played the torch beam at the corpse's head, which was turned towards her, its matted hair hanging an inch from the freezer floor

She didn't recognise the face. She'd never seen him before.

Charlie almost wept with relief. She quickly played the torch beam around the freezer interior, then lit up the dead man's face a second time. Whoever he was, he was the freezer's only occupant, and he wasn't posing much of a threat.

She shut the door.

My God, guv, just for a moment there...

She took a moment to compose herself, then shone the torch at the floor. A finer trail of blood led away from the freezer towards the back end of the kitchens.

Charlie advanced slowly, the pistol in her right hand, torch in her left. She could see an exit now, the walls narrowing towards what she imagined must be a delivery area or the entrance to a storeroom. Was it her imagination, or was someone sitting on a low table just by the storeroom door, a darker contour against the lighter backdrop of the kitchen wall? As Charlie raised the pistol, she heard a slight movement, followed by the *click* of some instrument or device.

'Police. Put your hands up.' Her voice rang in the metallic echo of the empty kitchens.

Charlie clicked the torch and the beam revealed the source of the noise. It wasn't her imagination; a woman was indeed sitting on the table, holding a chunky cellphone to her ear. She raised a hand in greeting, but casually, apologetically, as though they'd arranged to get together for a coffee, and someone had interrupted the moment of their meeting with the inconvenience of a phone call.

'Stand up and put the phone down.' Charlie shone the torch directly in the woman's eyes.

The woman sighed. 'If you *absolutely* insist.' She placed the phone of the tabletop, slid her legs to the floor and faced Charlie, shielding her eyes from the glare. 'Must you?'

'Give me the mobile.'

'It's a satellite phone, my love. Very expensive, so please look after it.'

'Identify yourself.' Charlie stepped forward, keeping the pistol level, and snatched the phone.

'Isabel Akkerman. Nice to meet you, too.'

'Where is DCI Moran?'

Charlie kept the torch beam directly on Isabel, but the woman's only response was a wide, unreadable smile.

Charlie was puzzled. 'I asked you a question. Where is–'

A sudden crash, followed by the sound of splintering glass from the direction of the lobby made Charlie jump. She turned sideways on, keeping the kitchen entrance in view without moving the torch from Isabel's face.

'That'll just be my minders,' Isabel said, calmly. 'They're a couple of sweeties, really. I think you'll like them.'

Chapter Forty-Seven

Charlie had only taken her eyes off the woman for a split second, but when she refocused the torch beam the only illuminated objects were the cracked plaster and peeling paint of the storeroom door.

She played the beam from right to left. The woman had disappeared. Charlie bit her lip hard, felt her heartbeat accelerate, dropped to her haunches.

The sound of scuffling feet in the lobby. Then, a regular thumping on woodwork, more raised voices...

Charlie crouched low, scanned the torch beam in a slow, three-sixty arc.

Nothing.

She would just have to make a methodical search of the whole kitchen. She rose to her full height, took just a single step before her instincts told her there was someone behind her. She felt the press of cold steel against her neck. A voice whispered in her ear, 'Hand it over, lovely, there's a good girl.'

No choice.

She surrendered the pistol.

'Thank you. *And* the torch. Perfect. Now then, police are we? You *and* my friend's rescuer?'

'Yes.' Charlie heard the tremor in her own voice. 'And there are more on the way.'

'More? Oh *dear*. In which case, I'd better finish up quickly.'

The storeroom door burst open. Isabel adjusted the angle of the shaft of light until it picked out the unmistakeable features of Brendan Moran. He was shirtless, his hair dishevelled, and his torso and trousers were stained dark with blood. He leaned on the doorpost. 'She's gone. It's over, Isabel.'

A crash of splintering wood echoed through the kitchen. Isabel chuckled. 'Over? *What* a shame. I'd hoped she'd have a little more *oomph* than that. How very disappointing.'

Moran took a purposeful step towards them. 'Unless you intend to add two police officers to your tally, Ms Akkerman, I strongly suggest you return the pistol to Detective Inspector Pepper. Any time now this place is going to be overrun by more uniformed officers than you can count.'

'Is that a fact?' Isabel considered the request. Another colossal impact from the direction of the lobby seemed to make her mind up.

'Oh well, as the fun appears to be over and as I'm *dying* for you to meet my friends.' She handed the automatic and torch to Charlie.

'Right,' Moran said, gesturing to the storeroom door. 'In here, *now*.'

Charlie did her best to keep the automatic trained on Isabel's back as she followed Moran into the storeroom but her hands were shaking so badly it was all she could do just to hang on to it.

Get a grip, Charlie...

Moran closed the door behind them and locked it.

The storeroom was a long, low-ceilinged room, with shelving running along each wall on either side. Chan's body was lying prone beside a dry goods cupboard, her head covered by Moran's coat.

'I did what I could.' Moran stood between Isabel and Chan's body.

'Poor thing,' Isabel said. 'And I thought she'd be such a good sport.'

A renewed bark of raised voices floated from the lobby. Male, agitated.

'Friends of yours?' Moran asked Isabel.

'Not *quite* how I'd describe them, but let's not split hairs.' Isabel was leaning on the wall, arms folded. She seemed to be enjoying herself.

'Guv,' Charlie caught Moran's arm, 'I took the liberty of contacting the local station. I know you weren't keen, but–'

'Probably a sensible move under the circumstances,' Moran conceded.

There was a rending noise from outside the store room, followed by a huge crash.

'That'll be the door,' Isabel said. 'Big strong fellows, these two.'

Footsteps moved swiftly through the kitchen until they were directly outside.

A gruff voice said, 'Isabel?'

'What kept you?' Isabel sang sweetly through the door.

'Open up.'

'Police,' Charlie called through the woodwork. 'And we have backup on the way. I'll open the door, but I want you to stand well back, arms up, keep your hands where I can see them.'

They heard a brief, hushed consultation.

'OK,' gruff voice again. 'Deal.'

Charlie glanced at Moran, an unspoken question. Open, or no?

Moran nodded.

Charlie pulled Isabel so that she was directly in front of her, kept the pistol pressed to the woman's neck, moved her hand round to the lock and drew the bolt, unclipped the latch, pushed the door open.

Moran aimed the torch into the darkness. The two men were standing well back as Charlie had requested, their hands reluctantly raised to shoulder height. The one on the left had a thin face and a long Roman nose, the other was shorter, more powerfully built, with large cauliflower ears.

'Identify yourselves,' Moran said.

Roman Nose was the first to reply. 'I'm not obliged to provide a name, but I can tell you that I answer to a gentleman known simply as 'C'.

'Who reports in turn to the Foreign Secretary, and hence to the Prime Minister,' Cauliflower Ears added.

Over the persistent pattering rainfall, the sound of a police siren's ululating wail could now be heard, faintly at first but getting louder by the second. Blue lights flickered through the high windows, exposing traceries of cobwebs high in the corners, beams and wilting plaster of the kitchen ceiling.

Charlie cast Moran a sideways glance, an unspoken question. He nodded.

She lowered the pistol, but kept a firm grip on Isabel's arm. 'OK,' she said. 'Appreciate that. So, you'd better tell us what MI6 have got to do with all this.'

As Charlie went to hand Isabel to the local police for safekeeping, Moran had a quick word with one of the paramedics. The guy nodded, grabbed a colleague, and both moved swiftly into the hotel interior.

Moran took the two new arrivals to the generator room, started the machine up, and followed the cables to the Bridal Suite. He went in, blinking in the brightness of the electric lights and sank wearily into a chair. Chan's belongings were still scattered here and there around the room – a leather handbag, an attaché case, a laptop. Basic provisions, a few personal items and toiletries.

The two men settled themselves on the sofa. Roman Nose kicked off proceedings with a bald statement. 'So, let's be clear. Whatever's been going on here, you can't touch her, I'm afraid.'

Moran had been half-expecting something along those lines, and had determined to oppose it as best he could.

'Is that so? She's a double – possibly treble, now – murderess. And those are the ones we know about.'

Cauliflower Ears put on a sympathetic expression. 'Sure. But, you see, there are much higher stakes in play right now, much higher than you'll hear about – or have to deal with – ever, I'd say.' He glanced at Roman Nose, who nodded emphatically.

'Yep, that's the truth of it, DCI … Moran, was it?'

'Moran, yes.' He leaned forward, propped his elbows on his thighs. He was cold, tired and angry, but expressing that, or allowing his feelings to dictate his words and actions, wasn't going to cut much ice with these two characters. 'So, you'd better tell me all about it.'

'OK. This is how it is.' Cauliflower Ears crossed his legs and curved his spine into the armchair. 'I'll keep it short, because we have things to do.'

'I'm listening,' Moran said.

'You'll be aware that North Korea is a highly militarised state. The regime has a growing – and worrying – nuclear capability, but any all-out muscle flexing involving the use of nuclear weapons would be a suicidal move for the regime, and they know it. Their nuclear programme acts as both deterrent and insurance policy. Unsurprisingly, they want to *survive* any future conflict, not be devastated by retaliatory action from the

West, particularly the USA, who, as you'll also be aware, have a strong association with South Korea.'

Moran nodded. 'With you so far.'

'Good. So, the immediate threat is not by way of their nuclear programme.' Cauliflower Ears paused for a moment. 'Not at all. Their bioweapons programme, on the other hand, is advanced, underestimated, and highly lethal.'

'And that's where you come in.' Moran could see the road ahead and was filled with a profound weariness.

'Yes – or, more to the point, where our mutual friend comes in. Isabel Akkerman is an extraordinary woman, Chief Inspector. Her IQ is off the scale, her mathematical ability … frankly astonishing.'

'And that's even before we mention her physical attributes,' Roman Nose broke in, 'which are at a comparable, or dare I say, even higher level.'

Cauliflower Ears grunted an affirmation. 'This … remarkable woman has contrived to develop close working relationships with North Korea's top scientific community, notably a triumvirate of scientists dedicated to the research, development, and implementation of their country's bioweapons capability. They have not only taken her to their hearts, Chief Inspector, they have *embraced* her, to the extent that they now believe her to be working solely for the purpose of furthering their research into the deployment of bioweapons the nature of which would freeze your very soul, were you to understand the programme's full intentions.'

'But Isabel is actually working for you.' It was a statement, not a question.

'That's correct.' Roman Nose looked pleased. 'And she is about to embark on the most sensitive and critical phase of her mission. If she succeeds – and I have to say that confidence is high – then North Korea's bioweapons programme will be set back by at least fifteen years, if not more. In fact, it's doubtful that it will ever make a full recovery. Which is precisely the result we're looking for.'

'Sabotage? Assassination?' The words came easily, slipped into the damp air as though they were discussing holiday options or picnic sites for a lazy Sunday afternoon, but Moran's anger was now a deep, cancerous weight in his stomach.

Cauliflower Ears appeared to sense that Moran's calm demeanour was masking his true feelings. He furrowed his brow, modified his tone, spoke as though imparting a friendly confidence. 'You are doubtless aware, DCI Moran, that North Korea is the most likely candidate to threaten world peace – and consequently global security.' He went on quickly. '*If* they are allowed to complete the development of these weapons, it's only a matter of time before they decide to deploy them. It may be subtle at first, covert, perhaps, just a few key deaths here and there, but in the end–' He threw his hands up. 'It's a given that there *will* be catastrophic consequences.'

'When will she be back? Moran asked.

'Back?' Roman Nose gave his colleague a perplexed look. 'She may never be back, DCI Moran. For Isabel, this mission is likely to be a one-way ticket.'

'I see.' He took a moment to compose himself. 'I take it that she initially came to your attention at Cambridge?'

'Yes, that's correct. She was recruited as an undergraduate.'

'So, that would be just a few months after she murdered a young woman for no other reason than she felt overlooked on that particular day? And very shortly after that – and you can put this in your case notes – she disposed of another minor irritation in her life, a toddler, her adoptive brother, by smothering him in his cot.'

Cauliflower Ears exchanged another glance with his friend. 'We're aware that Isabel's personality is … volatile. Her presence here is an indication of exactly that. She has a tendency to go AWOL when the fancy takes her. It's curiosity, I think – she has an insatiably curious mind – but then, that's all part of why she's so useful to us.

'I'm sorry to hear about these incidents, but I'm afraid that neither will swing the balance in your favour, Chief Inspector. Isabel is far too important an asset for us to allow her to face trial for any past offences – if indeed she is responsible for the misdemeanours you've just drawn to our attention.'

'Oh, she's responsible. You can file that as fact.'

'But you'll need to prove it, DCI Moran. And by the time you've gathered the evidence, made your case to the CPS, Isabel will be long gone.'

'Not if I get in touch with the Home Secretary.'

Roman Nose shook his head. 'I wouldn't advise that. It really would be an unwise move on your part, Chief Inspector. You should consider your career, before coming to any decisions.'

'My career is coming to an end. It has much less value now than it did twenty years ago.'

'In which case, you ought to look to your health in order to enjoy a long and rewarding retirement.' Cauliflower Ears said with a disarming smile.

'And your pension, of course,' Roman Nose chipped in. 'Shame if anything were to prevent that from coming through. A man with your service record deserves a little comfort in his twilight years.'

Moran looked at them both in turn. 'I was always taught that the love of money is the root of all evil.'

'I think we're done,' Cauliflower Ears concluded. 'We'll look after Isabel. Seems you have quite a mess to clear up, Chief Inspector. I'd say you have plenty to keep you occupied without concerning yourself too much about us.'

Moran stood next to Charlie just outside the entrance to the Borderlands Hotel as the Welsh uniforms – albeit reluctantly – released Isabel into the custody of the two spooks. He'd found some moth-eaten blankets and wrapped one around his torso in an effort to keep warm and cover the bloodstains.

'I wonder if I might have my satellite phone?' Isabel extended her hand to Charlie.

'You'd better let her have it,' Moran advised. 'I'd hate to think that she might miss any important calls.'

Charlie placed the phone in Isabel's outstretched hand.

'Much obliged. It's been nice meeting you both.' Isabel flicked a wind-blown lock of hair from her eyes. The rain had reduced to a slow trickle, and dawn was on its way; an as yet teasingly faint line of brightness had appeared on the horizon.

'It was self-defence, of course,' she said. 'I was taken against my will from my lodgings at Simplicity, but thank *God* I eventually managed to get the upper hand. Goodness knows what might have happened. It's been a terrifying experience – the poor woman must have been crazy.' Her expression assumed a studied sadness. 'Still, I'm sorry she didn't make it. Crazy or not, a life is a life, isn't it, DCI Moran?'

'If you do return to the UK, I'll be waiting,' Moran said. 'You can be sure of that.'

'Oh, I may, I may not. Life is so unpredictable, isn't it? Anyways, I think I'm trying their patience, so I'd better get off.' She inclined her head towards her minders, waiting by their car.

They watched the car crawl along the pot-holed drive until it turned left by Moran's and Charlie's parked vehicles and disappeared from view.

'I can't believe I'm saying this, but I feel sorry for Chan,' Charlie confided, as they went back inside. 'How weird is that?'

'It's not weird at all,' Moran replied. 'She's a troubled

soul. There's a vulnerability about her and, in spite of the terrible crimes she committed, even she doesn't deserve this. And Collier has my sympathy, too. Unpleasant character or not, this isn't the kind of justice I had in mind for him.'

They moved to one side as Collier was brought out in a body bag. 'How could he have known?' Charlie chewed her lip. 'Talk about walking right into it.'

'Well, I suppose one of my problems has gone away as a result of his demise,' Moran found a seat in the lobby and sat down. His leg was throbbing, but at least the bleeding had stopped. The blanket wasn't doing much to warm him, though, and he'd refused a paramedic's offer of a foil blanket on the grounds that it made him feel like a victim. Which, in a way, he did, but he wasn't going to admit that to anyone any time soon.

'The thinnest silver lining, guv, is better than no silver lining at all.'

'You don't have to call me *guv*, you know,' Moran smiled. 'You have your own team, now.'

'I *did*, you mean. Now this is over, God knows what they'll do with me.'

'You're always welcome, you know that. I can put in a word.'

Charlie was about to reply when Moran added, 'As long as you don't try to foist any more profilers on me, that is.'

'That wasn't entirely my doing. In fact–' she stopped and frowned. 'I'll be speaking to DS Luscombe about that. He was the one who came up with the name.'

'Well, as long as you don't fall out over it,' Moran said, a twinkle in his eye. 'But look, I think it's well past time to find somewhere that can rustle us up some coffee.'

'Good plan,' Charlie agreed. 'Wait, though.' She frowned. 'They haven't brought Chan out, yet. I only counted one body bag.' She gave Moran a quizzical look. 'Hang on – you were talking about her in the *present* tense just now…'

'Here she is.' Moran pointed to a gaggle of paramedics who had just emerged from the entrance doors. The medics were moving at a smart pace, saline drips held aloft along with all the usual paraphernalia of severe trauma. They slid the stretcher into the waiting ambulance with practised ease.

Charlie looked at Moran, mouth agape. 'Guv?'

Moran shrugged. 'I lied. She has a chance, a slim one, granted, but a chance at least.'

Charlie shook her head slowly from side to side. 'I thought she was–'

'I know. But I needed Isabel to think that, too.'

Charlie nodded, looked at the ground. 'That woman. She took the pistol off me like … like I was a child.'

Moran took her arm. 'Don't beat yourself up. We know what Isabel is now. She'd run rings around all of us.' He worked up a smile. 'Come on, you're a wee bit shaken up. Time for that coffee.'

'We have a pretty good canteen.' A young uniform had overheard the exchange. 'Only twenty minutes away, look. Follow me, why don't you, and I'll sign you in.'

'That sounds like an offer I can't refuse, Constable Wiltshire,' Moran said. 'I don't suppose you could throw in the loan of a shirt while you're about it?'

'No problem, sir.' Wiltshire grinned. He was a tall fellow, but a tad overweight in Moran's estimation, judging by the swell of his stomach beneath his jacket. 'I'll fetch you one of my own. I always keep a spare at the station, just in case. I'd say we're about the same size.'

'Hm. Perhaps I should take that as a compliment,' Moran said. 'Lead on, Constable. We're right behind you.'

Chapter Forty-Eight

'Too young.' Alice took Moran's hand and squeezed it. 'Why is life so unfair to some people?'

Moran was finding the visit harder than he'd imagined. Laura Witney's grave was nestled in a far corner of a large cemetery five miles outside Brockford. The gold lettering on the headstone had peeled away in some areas, whether picked off by a malicious hand or by a combination of time and the elements, it was hard to say. He allowed Alice's rhetorical question to drift and disperse in the warm air. No one would ever be able to provide a satisfactory answer.

'Friday, the thirteenth of February, 1981,' Alice read. 'Our darling Laura, taken from us so unexpectedly.'

This quarter of the cemetery backed onto allotments, and the sound of muted conversation drifted across the hedgerow as two gardeners met and compared notes, discussed the merits of various seeds and fertilisers, and who was likely to achieve the year's most promising crop of runner beans.

Moran bent and ran his finger along the inscription. 'Her parents – they both died within a year of each other, the mother almost ten years to the day after Laura died, the father just a few weeks shy of the next anniversary.'

'It must have broken their hearts,' Alice said. 'I can't imagine it. Their only child.'

'I dream about her, you know,' Moran said quietly. 'We chat about her job, the catering, her hopes and dreams. A few nights ago we were onboard an aeroplane together; the pilot was one of her admirers, a nice chap – I met him last week, briefly, in his garden.' He turned to face Alice. 'She always wanted to fly. That was why she was sticking it out in the kitchens. And she would have, I'm sure, in time. Who knows? She might even have become a pilot herself.'

Alice took his arm. 'You did everything you could, Brendan. You found out what happened. You've named the culprit.'

'Only in confidence, to my seniors.' Moran sighed. 'The name is buried deep. Any attempt on my part to exhume it would represent a serious breach of the Official Secrets Act. I'd be shut away in some forgotten dungeon in Whitehall, never to be seen again.'

Alice gave him a tight, possessive smile. 'Well, we can't have that, can we?'

'I suppose not. But–' he squared his shoulders, 'if I ever get wind of said person's return, I'll be on said person's case faster than you can say *official secret*.'

'You never know what's ahead, Brendan. I'm sure that

justice will be served, perhaps in an unexpected way, but it will come to pass, in time.'

'I wish I had your optimism,' Moran said. 'I'm afraid my outlook is rather more cynical these days.'

'And I'm going to make it my task to mellow that cynicism. It's the job that's made you like it.'

'Oh, I know that full well. After all this time, it's inevitable. I've seen too much of the world's darker side.'

Alice tapped him lightly on the shoulder. 'In which case, perhaps it's about time you stepped back into the light.'

Moran knew where this was going, and truth be told, as time passed, he was becoming more open to her suggestion than he was prepared to let on.

They stood quietly, the afternoon sun on their backs, enjoying the peaceful trill of birdsong, the lack of traffic noise, the low, soporific murmur of the allotment tenants beyond the hedge. His thoughts circled and looped from here to there, mimicking the flight of swallows swooping and diving in the clear June air directly above them. However, he knew that they would alight here from time to time, perhaps less frequently as the years went by, but regularly, nonetheless, so that he might spend a short while in silent reflection, even murmur a short prayer, just to let Laura know she was not forgotten, and that for as long as he was spared, she had a friend who was prepared to watch and wait for weeks, months – years, if necessary – for the smallest opportunity to bring her murderer to justice.

'We should go,' Alice said presently. 'Peter will be wondering where we are.'

'Yes.' Moran felt Alice tuck her arm in his as they walked between the gravestones. He glanced up at the sound of an aircraft, watched its contrail blossom, leave a fluffy white trail in the blue as it crossed a similar white band left by an earlier flight. Together they formed a wide cross in the sky, the age-old symbol of sacrifice and forgiveness.

Moran's eyes were moist as they left the cemetery and walked the short distance to his car.

Goodbye, Laura. We'll talk again, very soon, I promise.

Epilogue

'So, it's a collar, but not a collar?' Chris Collingworth took a sip of lager and cocked his head. 'How does that work?'

Charlie opted for the honest and direct approach to the question she knew would be at the forefront of everyone's minds. The debriefing had been frustratingly skeletal, the long and short of it being that, due to the Official Secrets restrictions, there was very little the guv had been able to disclose.

'I can only repeat what the guv said, Chris – he's been ordered to discontinue the investigation into the circumstances of both Laura Witney's and Christopher Akkerman's deaths.'

'We have DNA samples from Rita Dempster's car, so all we need is a sample of Laura's and the Akkerman woman's DNA to check against the rest of the forensics. Simples.' Collingworth shrugged.

'If only it *was* that simple, Chris.'

'You know something, don't you, DI Pepper?' Bola had

been silent up to this point, but now his expression was one of deep suspicion. 'What happened last night? What went down at the hotel?'

'Probably best just to move on,' Bernice broke in. 'We're obviously not going to get an answer, but–' she smiled, 'we can always draw conclusions from what we *did* manage to find. The passports might be a good place to start.'

'Yeah,' Bola agreed. 'And they might just have been the find that saved me from the chop. Even if I did have to hand 'em over.' Bola made an expression of regret. 'But the guv seemed pleased enough that we'd found them.' He brightened at the thought. 'All he said to me was, "I won't be taking the matter of your indiscretion with the Air Commodore any further, Bola".'

'Well, lucky old you,' Collingworth said. 'So you live to fight another dead-end cold case. Just don't forget to take your best buddy with you next time.'

'Don't be so negative, Chris,' Charlie said. 'They don't all turn out like this. What about the Emma Hardy case? That ended well.'

'I suppose,' Collingworth conceded. 'Leastways, for our esteemed leader, it did.'

'Speaking of whom,' Bola frowned, 'where is the guv? I thought he said he was joining us.'

'Three guesses,' Collingworth raised an eyebrow.

'Ah.' Bola smiled. 'Priorities, eh?'

'He's all loved up, the guv.' Collingworth's smile was close to a smirk.

'Speaking of which…' Bola was looking at the bar where one of Brian Carroll's new staff members was serving a recently arrived group of office workers.

Collingworth followed his gaze. 'Aha. Nice. Planning to ask her out?'

'Already in the diary,' Bola said, lifting his glass to his lips.

'Ahem, women present,' Charlie's eyes narrowed. 'Don't you two ever think about *anything* else?'

'On occasion.' Collingworth downed his lager. 'But never in the evenings.'

'You need to get in touch with your inner self, Chris,' Bernice said. 'It's all physical with you. There's more to life, you know. There's your soul to consider, for a start.'

'Didn't you know?' Bola said, wide-eyed, 'Chris ain't *got* no soul.'

'True,' Collingworth agreed, 'but what I *do* have is a raging thirst. Anyone for another?'

'Count me in,' Bola held out his glass. 'DCB?'

Bernice shook her head. 'No thanks. Got to pack. I'm off for the rest of the week.'

'Anywhere nice?' Charlie asked.

'I hope so. It's just a break, you know. I need to chill for a bit.'

A thought occurred to Bola. 'Oh, by the way, anyone seen Val?'

'Yes,' Bernice said. 'He was clearing his desk last time I saw him. That was late this morning.'

'Waste of time he turned out to be.' Bola shook his

head ruefully.

'Let's not go there,' Charlie said brightly. 'Sore point. I'll have a Dubonnet and lemonade, Chris, if you're buying?'

'Who said anything about buying?' Collingworth looked affronted. 'On my meagre salary?'

'Go on, then,' Charlie handed over a ten pound note. 'Stick this in the pot.'

Bola took out his phone, began to scroll through his texts.

Charlie nudged him. 'Come on, Bola. And you. We're supposed to be celebrating.'

'Some celebration.' Collingworth made a face. 'One in ICU, one question mark.'

'Maybe not a celebration, then.' Charlie shrugged. 'But you all did a great job, from what the guv told me. It's not your fault the way things turned out. Let's just call it the closing of a chapter.'

'And the beginning of a new one?' Bernice suggested.

'I'll drink to that.' Bola lifted his glass, taking care to keep the new barmaid in his line of sight. 'Here's to us.'

Bernice paused at the gates, engine idling. She still wasn't sure what had surprised her the most – Catton's invitation, or the alacrity with which she had accepted. Still, the offer of reduced rate accommodation for a few days in such a beautiful setting had been impossible to resist.

Is that the whole truth, Bernice?

Of course it was. What else? She needed to recharge her batteries, get back in touch with herself. Perhaps time spent at Simplicity would inspire her to deepen her spiritual connections, rediscover the real Bernice, the person she sometimes forgot about when work took her over, body and soul, for the duration of a case.

As for Catton, well, he was an interesting guy, for sure, but she definitely hadn't based her decision to spend a few days here solely on his attractiveness, charm, or good looks.

Had she?

You can work that one out later, Bernice…

She slipped into first gear and the car moved forward.

Character Outlines

DCI Brendan Moran

Moran is a loner, but not a natural one. Born and raised initially near Cork and later in Co. Kerry after his parents moved away during his teens, he was left in the care of the Hannigan family where he met and fell in love with Janice, the Hannigans' eldest daughter. They were engaged to be married, but Janice was tragically killed in a car bomb incident in the late 1970's. The bomb had been meant for Moran, but a change of work routine that day prompted Moran to suggest that Janice borrow his car. He has never forgiven himself for Janice's death, nor has he been able to settle into a relationship since.

Moving to England in the early nineteen-eighties, he joined the Thames Valley Police and rose through the ranks on merit. Moran has experienced various setbacks in his career since Janice's death: he was almost killed in a car accident in bad weather conditions near Reading, and after his recovery was also injured during the course of an investigation into a suspicious death at Charnford Abbey ('Black December'). Despite this, he has a warm sense of humour, a great sense of loyalty to his friends and colleagues and an acute knack of being able to figure people out. He has a taste for Italian wine, preferably Sangiovese, and any quality scotch whisky. He is an appalling gardener and owns a hyperactive cocker spaniel named Archie. He has lately formed an attachment to Alice Roper, the sister of one of the main characters in 'The Cold Light of Death.' He is approachable, reliable, a little old-fashioned, intuitive, optimistic, and something of a romantic at heart.

DI Charlie Pepper

Originally from the Midlands, Charlie Pepper is a career police officer. She has been on the receiving end of violent crime more than once, but has been able to overcome her fear and continue in a senior role. In a relationship with DS Ian Luscombe, whom she met while working on the mysterious care-home murders in 'When Stars Grow Dark'.

DC George McConnell

George is an irascible Scot. Short in stature but in possession of a big heart, he has struggled in the past with alcohol addiction, but is now teetotal and intends to stay that way so as not to affect his blossoming relationship with DC Tess Martin. Excellent detective, but can be distracted by personal matters.

DC Bola Odunsi

Bola is a well-built, athletic black guy with an eye for the ladies – a trait that has caused him problems in the past. His enthusiasm is offset by a tendency to rush in and ask questions later, a pattern that has often drawn unwanted attention from his seniors. Despite this impetuous streak, Bola always has his fellow officers' backs, and is a popular and sociable member of the team.

DC Chris Collingworth

A good detective, but his character tends towards the self-serving, a trait that often lands him in trouble. Following an embarrassing and dangerous error of judgement ('When Stars Grow Dark'), Chris has made some effort to reform himself, but still has a way to go. He passed his sergeant's exam with excellent marks, and is looking forward to a future role in the new grade. The rest of the team are also looking forward to his departure. Although married he has a roving eye, and female team members tend to avoid social contact with him for this reason.

DC Tess Martin

Tess is a tough, determined police officer but suffers from bouts of self-doubt and depression. She hit a low trough during the investigation into the death of the singer, Michelle LaCroix and fell foul of the assassin, Ilhir Erjon, in 'Gone Too Soon', succumbing to a potent cocktail of drugs and lapsing into a near catatonic state. It was feared that she would not recover, but thanks to a combination of excellent care and George McConnell's encouragement, she is now making good progress.

DC Bernice Swinhoe

One of the newer members of the team, Bernice is naturally shy, but has a well-ordered and disciplined mind. Her casework is both methodical and logical, and she shows great empathy for victims of crime. Her mother died when she was young and this is a matter of great sadness for her. She is a serious thinker, in touch with her inner self and her spirituality. Hates her Christian name. Prefers to be known as DC Swinhoe, or DCB, as her colleagues often call her. DI Charlie Pepper is a role model, and Bernice aspires to ascend the ranks as she gains experience in Moran's team.

DS Ian Luscombe

Scottish detective sergeant seconded to Moran's team from Police Scotland, Aviemore who were running a parallel investigation re the care home murders in 'When Stars Grow Dark'. Has formed a relationship with DI Pepper. A reserved but capable officer, he keeps himself in peak physical condition and is no stranger to the tougher side of police work.

John Herbinson

The new Crime Investigations Manager. Canadian by birth. Direct, determined, sometimes confrontational. A self-confessed results man, he doesn't suffer fools gladly.

Duncan Brodie

Serial entrepreneur. First appeared in 'When Stars Grow Dark'. Owns a number of private residential care homes across the UK. Became a target for Connie Chan and narrowly escaped with his life in the aforementioned book in the series.

Connie Chan

Real name Zubaida Binti Ungu, native of Malaysia. Wanted by Malaysian authorities. Suspected of killing her uncle and absconding with his worldly goods. Arrived in the UK 1990 or thereabouts. Escaped from hospital following attempted murder of Duncan Brodie. Also wanted in connection with several care-home-related murders. Ruthless, driven, yet emotionally flawed.

Alice Roper

Sister of Emma Hardy, the police officer who went missing in 'The Cold Light of Death'

Peter Hardy

Alice and Emma Hardy's autistic brother. Lived originally with Emma, but now lives with Alice. A sports fanatic, his favourite pastime is watching reruns of the best Olympic moments through the history of the games.

Glossary

ARU
Armed Response Unit

ASNT
Area search, no trace

Code 11
Off duty

ICU
Intensive Care Unit

IR
Incident Room

IDR
Inner Distribution Road

MCIRT
Major Crime Investigation Review Team

MIT
Murder Investigation Team

Misper
Missing person

NPASS
National Police Air Support Service

The DCI Brendan Moran Series – have you read them all?

Black December

DCI Brendan Moran, world-weary veteran of 1970s Ireland, is recuperating from a near fatal car crash when a murder is reported at Charnford Abbey.

The abbot and his monks are strangely uncooperative, but when a visitor from the Vatican arrives and an ancient relic goes missing the truth behind Charnford's pact of silence threatens to expose not only the abbey's haunted secrets but also the spirits of Moran's own troubled past . . .

Black December is an atmospheric crime thriller that will keep you on the edge of your seat until the stunning climax. This is the first in the DCI Brendan Moran crime series, one of the new breed of top UK Detectives.

'...gripping, with a really intriguing plot.'

Creatures of Dust

An undercover detective goes missing and the body

of a young man is found mutilated in a shop doorway. Is there a connection? Returning to work after a short convalescence, DCI Brendan Moran's suspicions are aroused when a senior officer insists on freezing Moran out and handling the investigation himself.

A second murder convinces Moran that a serial killer is on the loose but with only a few days to prove his point the disgruntled DCI can't afford to waste time. As temperatures hit the high twenties, tempers fray, and the investigation founders Moran finds himself coming back to the same question again and again: can he still trust his own judgement, or is he leading his team up a blind alley?

'...non-stop action and convoluted twists. Another brilliant read in the Brendan Moran series...'

Death Walks Behind You

DCI Brendan Moran's last minute break in the West Country proves anything but restful as he becomes embroiled in the mysterious disappearance of an American tourist. Does the village harbour some dark and dreadful secret? The brooding presence of the old manor house and the dysfunctional de Courcy family may hold the answer but Moran soon finds that the residents of Cernham have a rather unorthodox approach to the problem of dealing with outsiders...

'...a pleasure to read – gripped from start to finish...'

The Irish Detective - digital box set

The first omnibus edition of the popular DCI Brendan Moran crime series. Contents includes the first, second and third in series, plus an exclusive CWA shortlisted short story 'Safe As Houses'...

Silent As The Dead

A call from an old friend whose wife has vanished from their home in Co.Kerry prompts DCI Brendan Moran to return to his Irish roots. The Gardai have drawn a blank; can Moran succeed where they have failed?

Moran's investigation leads him to a loner known locally as the Islander, who reveals that the woman's disappearance is connected to a diehard paramilitary with plans to hit a high profile target in the UK. Time is running out. Can Moran enlist the Islander's help, or does he have to face his deadliest foe alone?

'Superb storyline with plenty of twists and turns...'

Gone Too Soon

Moran is called to a burial in a local cemetery. But this is no ordinary interment; the body of a young woman, Michelle LaCroix, a rising star in the music world, is still warm, the grave unmarked. A recording reveals the reason for her suicide. Or does it?

Why would a young, successful singer take her own life? To unlock the answer, Moran must steer a course through his darkest investigation yet, as the clues lead to one shocking discovery after another...

'...endlessly twisty – an explosive finish...'

The Enemy Inside

DCI Brendan Moran's morning is interrupted when a suicidal ex-soldier threatens to jump from a multi-storey car park ...

Moran soon regrets getting involved when an unexpected visitor turns up on his doorstep to confront him with what appears to be damning evidence of past misconduct. Can the Irish Detective clear his name, or must he come clean and face the consequences? One thing seems certain: by the time the night is over, his reputation may not be the only casualty...

'…a cracking, fast-paced thriller.'

When Stars Grow Dark

A fatal road traffic collision uncovers a bizarre murder when it transpires that an elderly passenger in one of the vehicles was dead before the accident. All indications point to the work of a serial killer – but with little forensic evidence, how can DCI Brendan Moran and his team run the killer to ground?

To add to Moran's problems, an unexpected discovery prompts the Irish Detective to undertake a dangerous and unscheduled journey to Rotterdam where he believes his former friend and MI5 agent, Samantha Grant, is being held.

Can Moran succeed in his rescue mission whilst juggling the heavy demands of his most perplexing murder investigation to date? *When Stars Grow Dark* is number seven in the popular DCI Brendan Moran crime series

'…another brilliant outing for the DCI. No red herrings, page fillers or unnecessary characters, just gripping story leading to an unexpected ending…'

The Cold Light of Death

July, 1976 – Thames Valley, UK. Long, scorching days of blue skies, water shortages, and record temperatures. A newly promoted Detective-Sergeant is tasked with investigating the murder of a local shop owner – an investigation that goes tragically wrong...

Fast-forward forty-five years to 2021, when a chance discovery exposes a grim secret that forces a reexamination of the circumstances surrounding the ill-fated murder inquiry.

DCI Brendan Moran is assigned this coldest of cases, and it soon becomes apparent that he is dealing with a cold and calculating criminal mind. Can Moran and his team piece together the events of that long forgotten summer and unmask the killer before history repeats itself?

'A most satisfying read, with a plot zooming back to the mid 70s. As usual, wonderfully evocative. The entire series is a must for any crime fiction fan'

The Irish Detective 2 digital box set

The second omnibus edition of the popular DCI Brendan Moran crime series by CWA shortlisted author, Scott Hunter. Contents includes the fourth, fifth and sixth in series, plus an exclusive short story 'Inside Job'…

A Crime For All Seasons (short stories) - FREE via website

From the midwinter snowdrifts of an ancient Roman villa to a summer stakeout at an exclusive art gallery, join DCI Brendan Moran and his team for the first volume of criminally cunning short stories in which the world-weary yet engaging Irish detective reaffirms that there is indeed a crime for all seasons…

'…great characters, plot lines and dialogue. More please!'

For more information – www.scott-hunter.net